Evergreen Conservatory

BY

HEATHER SCHNEIDER

Evergreen Conservatory

This is a work of fiction. All names, characters, and events are the work of the author's imagination. Any resemblance to real people or events is entirely coincidental.

Summary: A teenager returns to an academy for magical botanists in the woods of her hometown.

Editor: Red Adept Editing Services

Cover Design: Krafigs Design

Paperback ISBN: 979-8-9850507-9-0

Evergreen Conservatory

BY

HEATHER SCHNEIDER

Property of
Evergreen Academy Library

For those who dream of seeing the other side of the waterfall.

Chapter One

"*Folium volare*," I said, straining as I concentrated all my energy on the bright-green palmate leaves of the Big Leaf Maple tree just off the trail. The leaves didn't so much as quake.

Huffing out a breath, I began to volley off some nonsensical, nonexistent Floracantus. "Leaves levitate. Foliage flight. Le—" I cut myself off quickly at the sound of shoes crunching along the trail. One of the many downsides of only being able to practice my botanical magic outside of Evergreen Academy grounds was that—unless I went somewhere very remote—I was constantly on guard for nonmagical people, also known as residents of the city of Weed, California.

I began to walk away from the sound so that if anyone saw me, they'd assume I was just another person out for a summer stroll on the Wildflower Trail. It had been about time to give up for the day anyway.

"Darn you, Callan," I murmured. At the end of the school year in May, Callan—my tutor and a very powerful magical botanist with a tree affinity—had made me an enticing promise. If I could figure out how to tap into my advanced tree affinity powers to send him a message across country via the leaves, he would text me.

So far, I'd had no luck in figuring out that tricky bit of magic, and the result was radio silence from Callan. The man knew how to hold out and keep his word, I'd give him that.

I had my copy of *Compendium Floracantus*, the reference book for all magical botanical spells, but there was some trick to the leaf communication method beyond simply reciting a Floracantus that the book didn't explain.

I was learning that while the established Floracantus had been fairly well documented in the ancient book, there were many nuances that hadn't been recorded. Apparently, a lot of this was passed down through oral tradition, and since I'd learned I was a magical botanist barely a year ago, I hadn't grown up with any of that insight.

I reached the parking lot without encountering anyone else and headed straight for Vera's Café, the bakery my aunt owned where I'd been pulling a few shifts over the summer.

"Check out the display," my aunt Vera said as soon as I entered the café, a hint of excitement in her voice. I scanned the pastry counter, where my eyes were instantly drawn to vibrant cookies and cupcakes decorated with flowers for midsummer.

My aunt, whose pale olive skin and long dark curls were looking stunning as always, was wearing a vibrant red flower crown made with real flowers. The sunlight caught on the diamond ring that had been on her left hand for a few weeks, and the gem sparkled, casting rainbows around the room. She had never looked happier or healthier, and I was counting down the months until she and her fiancé Bryce officially tied the knot. It had been a long time coming for those two.

Aunt Vera placed a purple flower crown on my head, and I noticed that the other employees were wearing them as well.

"We're celebrating midsummer all week!"

Right, midsummer. While I couldn't tell my aunt much about

Evergreen Academy, she did know that we'd had an event on the last winter solstice as well as activities on the fall and spring equinoxes. And I'd brought up midsummer to her last year before I had known what was really going on at Evergreen Academy.

Her imagination had run with the rest.

"This looks amazing. Everyone is going to love it." I situated the purple flower crown—composed of violets, gladiolus, and bell-flowers—more securely on my head then went to wash up.

I had been trying to distract myself about this week's upcoming midsummer—the longest day of the year and an impor-tant one for magical botanists, especially those at Evergreen Academy.

The summer solstice was one of four nights of the year where the campus's verdant shield was recharged. This could only be done by founders' descendants, of which Callan was one.

I still didn't know if Callan would be coming into town to charge the shield this week, which would keep the academy hidden from the community and strengthen the other magical protections the shield provided.

I shivered at the memory of the shield's most recent recharging on the spring equinox as I pulled an apron over my head. The magic of the founders who had created the shield had fought back when I had dared to try helping charge the shield, which had been failing due to poisoned soil.

At that time, Professor East thought there was a chance I was a founder's descendant and could use my magic to strengthen the shield. As I had painfully found out, I was *not* a founder's descen-dant, and now the founders' curse made it so that I could no longer use my powers on campus.

Callan had saved the day by investing too much of himself and been seriously injured for nearly a month. After that incident, neither of us were sure if Professor East would let Callan continue to charge the shield or if our professor would find alternative solu-tions, like inviting alumni founders' descendants to assist.

"Can you deliver a wedding cake order later today? They want it there before the ceremony starts at four," Aunt Vera said.

I peeked in the fridge to see a three-tier cake, beautifully adorned with floral baubles made of fondant and buttercream, carefully wrapped and ready to go.

"Sure, where to?"

"It's a riverbank wedding. I'll send you the GPS coordinates. Oh, I think it's not too far from the Evergreen Academy grounds."

I straightened at that bit of information. Since I wasn't a founder's descendant, I wasn't invited to the midsummer events at the school, which was closed for the summer. But the idea of getting close to it again was irresistible, especially today.

"I'm on it," I said a little too eagerly.

Aunt Vera raised her eyebrows but didn't ask any follow-up questions. She was far too busy at the peak of tourist and wedding season to wonder why I might be eager to go by my school's campus in the summer.

The shift flew by, and soon, I was on the way to the riverbank wedding, the back of my car filled with securely packed cupcakes and the multilayered cake. The car rambled along the bumpy road as I followed an old road map. Cell service was spotty in this part of the forest. There were scattered colorful fabric streamers tied to the trees, letting me know I was on the right track.

I parked near the other cars and then took both loads of sweets to the ceremony site, leaving them with the bride's mom at the picnic tables. There were colorful wildflower bouquets on each table, and I hurried away when I noticed them bending their blooms in my direction.

As I navigated out of the ceremony site, I considered how close Evergreen Academy might be. I was still feeling a strong pull to at least cruise by. The academy was slightly due west of here, and I didn't want to have to go all the way back out to the freeway.

Seeing a dirt road to my left, I decided to take it.

Twenty minutes later, I smiled in satisfaction as I glimpsed the massive brick wall that surrounded Evergreen Academy's grounds. I pulled over near a tree, deciding to hop out and get my bearings. I wasn't sure which direction to take to get to the front gate.

As I scanned the brick wall, an anomaly in the weathered, moss-covered brick caught my attention. There, built into the brick, was a tiny arch that met the ground. It looked like what I imagined a fairy door would, compact and well-blended with its surroundings.

I remembered the previous summer when Maci had jokingly claimed that the ring of stones outside the Evergreen Academy gate was a fairy ring.

Curious, I walked closer and crouched to examine it. In the center of the arch, there was a carved symbol of roots and swirling vines. The symbol looked familiar, but I couldn't recall where I might have seen it before. Most likely, I had come across it in one of the many textbooks I'd been absorbing like an oversaturated piece of moss throughout the past year. I ran my fingers across the engraving on the rough brick.

Just then, I heard a rustling overhead and looked up automatically. My heart rate accelerated as I scanned the canopy. I knew that sound. Someone was tree walking above.

I peered into the canopy, trying to make out a figure. Unless someone was randomly climbing trees out here in the woods, it had to be one of the tree affinities from the academy.

"Hey!" I called out.

The rustling stopped.

A moment later, a girl with straight, fading dyed-black hair and a heart-shaped fair face dropped down from the nearest oak.

I didn't recognize her from school. "Who are you?"

She cocked a hip. "I could ask the same of you."

"I've never seen you on campus before." As I studied her more closely, I noticed a few thin purple streaks sprinkled throughout her hair. She was wearing black skate shoes and a spaghetti-strapped black romper.

"So, you're a student." She broke into a coy smile. "You can never be too sure. There are always random people poking around out here in the woods."

Out of nowhere, a slithering vine came rushing my way, and I lifted a hand.

"*Discedite.*" The word was out of my mouth instinctively, and the vine came to an abrupt halt.

The girl smiled broadly, and there was a hint of mischief in it. "Nicely done. I'm Meadow."

"What was that for?"

"Just making sure."

I let out a breath as my heart rate slowed, grateful that I was a few feet back from the academy walls and that my powers worked here. "Thanks for the warm welcome. I'm Briar. Are you here for the solstice, or..."

Her mouth formed a small o before she smoothed her expression. "Briar Whelan? I've heard of you. You made quite a splash on the spring equinox."

I felt myself tense. "How do you know about that?"

"They tell all of us founders' descendants relevant information when we enroll."

"You're a founder's descendant?" Things began to click into place then. That would explain why she was here on the solstice. Then I remembered the tree walking. "A tree founder's descendant?"

"No, mosses. I have a trailing tree affinity, though. Makes tree walking a little risky, but that's why I like it. And to answer your question, yeah, I'm here for the solstice with my parents."

"Are any other founders' descendants here?" I didn't want to ask about Callan directly, so I resorted to fishing.

"It's just me, Rhodes, and Hollis at the academy this year. Hollis has been here since Tuesday. I heard Rhodes and his parents arrived late last night, but I haven't seen him yet." Her eyes sparkled, and she asked, "Want to have a bit of fun?"

I narrowed my eyes, still not fully trusting her after the surprise vine attack. "What do you have in mind?"

"The festivities are kind of taking a turn. I'm used to the solstice being an all-out party, but the vibes are off this year."

"Off, how?"

"It's mostly because of talk of some new things being implemented. Let's just say the environment between the teachers and the board is a little... tense."

Concern had my stomach clenching. What was going on with the board that would upset the instructors?

"What do you mean by 'have a bit of fun'?"

"Let's sneak you onto campus. We can go hang out in a treehouse or spike the punch or something."

I shifted my weight as I took her in. Was she being serious? I was already on a short string with the campus now that I had no access to my powers there. I didn't want to give Professor East any reason to kick me out or add to his stress during a tense time. But still, if Callan were here, maybe I'd have a chance to talk to him about whatever these developments were that Meadow was hinting at. And outside of those concerns, being so near the academy now made it almost irresistible. It was a miracle I had been able to stay away for a few months as it was. It was like the invisible verdant shield that surrounded the place was inviting me in. I made up my mind.

"No to the punch spiking. But I'd be lying if I said I didn't miss the food here. Maybe we can raid the leftovers in the kitchen."

Meadow grinned. "Follow me." She scaled the tree she'd come down from, and I frowned, knowing I wouldn't be able to tree walk once we reached the brick wall.

"Don't we have to scan our gems at the gate?"

"Nah, there's a pass-through point right here. You'll need one of these, though." She pulled a glass pendant from her pocket and handed it to me. "I only have one, so we'll have to take turns."

"What's this?" Even as I asked, I was already studying it. There was a preserved white flower inside.

"Petal of a Shasta lily," Meadow said.

"And I need this... why?"

"If you have one of those"—she pointed at the pendant—"you can get through right here."

I frowned again. This seemed like a security weakness.

"Where'd you get this?" I asked, wondering if it were a special founder's descendant perk.

"Now that," Meadow said, taking the pendant back, "I can't tell you. Are you coming or not?"

I was tempted to back out, but this was a founder's descendant. If she was anything like Callan, this was all at least mildly aboveboard. "Okay, but I'm going to have to climb down once we get over the fence."

"Riiight," Meadow said once I joined her in the canopy. "I was told about your little incident on the spring equinox. That was pretty badass. But cut off from your powers on campus? Brutal."

"It has made school more challenging," I admitted.

"All right, let's go over. Nobody's around this part of the academy. They're all in the teahouse and courtyard."

When I stood next to Meadow on the thickest part of the tree branch, the branches ahead pulled together in a tight, clear path in stark contrast to the loose overlapping they had been doing a moment before.

Meadow sighed. "And there goes all the danger. They weren't kidding. Your tree affinity is strong."

"Thanks?" I murmured, still unable to get a read on Meadow. We walked through the canopy until we hovered just above the brick wall, and I took a moment to mourn the impending loss of my tree walking abilities.

"Okay, I'll cross then toss the pendant back to you," Meadow said before dashing along the branches above the brick.

I waited until she was settled into a tree on the other side then opened my hands. When Meadow tossed the pendant, I caught it with a tight clasp of my right hand and held it firmly as I crossed the brick wall. My breath caught in my chest as I passed through where the verdant shield would be, firmly expecting something bad to happen.

But nothing did, and I joined Meadow on the tree branch inside the campus grounds.

We both dropped to the forest floor, Meadow with much more grace than me.

"Told ya," Meadow said before taking the pendant and returning it to her pocket.

"How does that pendant work?" I asked as we began to walk on the forest floor.

Meadow shrugged. "I'm not sure of the details. I didn't create it, if that's what you're asking. I'm not even *technically* supposed to have it."

Well, *that* was cryptic.

We crept through the forest until the glass academy building came into view. My heart expanded a little at the sight of it covered in flowers and vines, glorious in the summer sun.

"I'll walk to the side door and make sure the coast is clear then signal when it's safe to join me."

Before I could respond, Meadow began walking overly casually across the open field and to a door that I knew led into one end of the central vein.

As I waited, tufts of purple, bell-shaped flower blooms floated toward me on the summer breeze. I reached my hand toward one of them, catching a hint of grape fragrance. At the sound of a door opening, I dropped the blossom and looked at Meadow.

She peeked inside then turned back and waved me forward.

I jogged to the door, and we slipped inside. Upbeat but classical-sounding music was coming from the teahouse, and the voices of the various founders' descendants, board members, and other important people that I presumed were invited to the summer solstice event trickled into the central vein.

"Meadow?" a woman's voice called.

Meadow straightened, and I jumped behind a group of potted trees.

Peering through a small gap in the branches, I saw a woman

with Meadow's same heart-shaped face step out toward Meadow. "Where have you been? You were supposed to chat with Regent Yarrow after dinner."

"Sorry, Mom. I got distracted in the woods."

"Really, Meadow, I can't keep you focused for a few hours?" The woman sighed, but she didn't sound angry. "Come on, let's go find her."

I heard the click of heels walking away and poked my head out from behind the tree. Meadow turned and cast me a mildly apologetic look then followed her mother.

Once they were gone, I sighed and stayed hidden behind the fluffy, bright-green leaves, debating whether I should go back through the door and return to my car. But how would I pass over the wall without the Shasta lily pendant? Could I manage to sneak out the front gate? Following Meadow hadn't been my wisest decision ever, and now I was a sitting duck.

Before I could form a plan, I heard voices coming from the white stone staircase that led to levels two and three of the academy.

"I'll let you charge, but you must swear you won't overdo it." I recognized Professor East's voice immediately.

"I won't," the other voice said, and I sucked in a breath when I realized who it was.

Callan.

"Good. And," Professor East lowered his voice, and I leaned forward, "there is a full box from the latest collection at the Wildflower Trail. Please sort and dispose of it for Professor Bowellia."

"Will do," Callan said.

"Now, I must get back to the donors. Can you handle organizing the auction winnings?" Professor East's voice grew louder. "Ms. Whelan, you might as well help him."

Chapter Three

I startled, in complete shock at hearing my name. I didn't move.

"I know you're behind the potted elms, Ms. Whelan."

Exhaling, I stepped out from my obviously ineffective hiding place. "Hello, professor."

Callan's eyes were on me like a hawk.

I returned his gaze, taking in the fancy tuxedo and deep-green bow tie he was wearing. He always looked put together, but this was a whole other level. If possible, he'd gotten even *more* handsome since I had last seen him, his usually tousled brown hair lightly styled for the occasion.

I tried not to fixate on the fact that I was wearing jean shorts and a Vera's Café T-shirt as his eyes combed over me in return. At least I had taken to using the fancy magical botanist skin care and makeup I acquired last year. I was pretty sure my eyelashes had grown a few millimeters over the summer. Did Callan notice things like that?

Professor East cleared his throat, and I forced my attention to him. Like Callan, he was dressed in a dashing tuxedo. Knowing a little about the magical botanist community now, I guessed both of their suits were made of plant-based fabrics. "Well, then I'll leave you two to it." He departed through the doors to the teahouse.

I let out a breath as I realized Professor East wasn't punishing me for sneaking into the academy. Not yet, at least.

"What are you doing here, local?" Callan said it slowly, and there was a tinge of exasperation in his voice but not surprise.

"It's a long story."

"And you have time to tell it now that you're helping me package the silent-auction prizes." He turned on a heel, and I hurried to follow him down the central vein. I could hear a smile in his voice as he asked, "What's with the flower crown?"

I reached to touch the crown on my head, having completely forgotten it was there. "My aunt's celebrating midsummer at the café now. She gave these to all the employees."

Callan led me into an office that I had never been in before. The tables were crammed full of items with delicately labeled tags. My eyes roved over books, vases, plant cuttings in jars, hand-thrown mugs, and magnifying glasses.

"What is all this?"

"Items that sold at the silent auction today, raising funds for the academy. Some have been magically enhanced. Others hold historical and sentimental value for botanists."

I looked closer at a framed letter on thick, cream-colored paper. The label read, *Letter penned by George Washington Carver. Describes his first experience using a Floracantus.*

I let out a sharp breath as I read the figures on the paper beside it. "Callan, this letter sold for eighteen thousand dollars."

"It's our biggest fundraiser of the year, outside of the research grants we get. The instructors collect items to sell, and it's part of the field work for some of the second-years who are interested in history and curation. It was, at least."

"So what do we need to do?"

"Package them up so they're ready to be sent home with their purchasers tomorrow." Callan set a large pile of flattened white boxes on one of the tables but didn't make a move to assemble them. "Now, are you going to tell me what you're doing here?"

I brushed past him and picked up one of the boxes, easily folding it in three dimensions. They were similar to the pastry boxes we used at Vera's Café.

"Meadow invited me."

Callan raised an eyebrow, his face carefully neutral otherwise. "*Meadow* invited you? How do you know Meadow?"

"I don't. Well, we just met. She was tree walking outside the wall."

Something flickered across his face at that, but he stayed focused on me. "And you were outside the wall because..."

"I was delivering a cake to a riverbank wedding and thought I'd pop by."

"You thought you'd pop by?" Callan's words were even, and I couldn't sense if he was mad, amused, confused, or something else that he was perfectly masking. It made me want to spill my guts.

"I knew it was the summer solstice, so I figured there would be people here charging the shield. Possibly you. And others." Why was I blathering? I grabbed a nearby leather-bound book and nestled it carefully into a box.

"Briar, you have to be more careful. There are people here who —" He cut himself off and balled his hands into fists before relaxing them and turning to package one of the auction items. He whirled his hands and muttered something, the box perfectly folding together on all sides.

Of course. The paper boxes had come from wood materials. Even dead, the cells in wood could respond to botanist's magic.

"There are people here who *what*? Meadow said things were tense between the board and the teachers."

Callan exhaled. "They are. Things have... kicked up over the summer. I'm hoping that it will get sorted out today. But as far as you're concerned, being around when members of the Board of Regents are here is asking for trouble."

"You mean your parents?"

"They're included, yes."

We worked in silence for a few moments, me stewing about what he wasn't saying and him, presumably, stewing that I was here when he certainly hadn't expected me to be.

"So, how's your summer been?" I asked once the room had been unbearably quiet for too long.

Callan choked out a laugh. "You're unbelievable, local."

"Why?" Of all the questions I'd asked, I hadn't expected *how's your summer been* to be the one that sent him over the edge.

"Just making small talk after casually breaking into the academy grounds. How'd you get in anyway? Professor East would have responded if the gates had opened."

"Meadow showed me a pass-through point on the south side of the academy. She shared a special pendant that let us cross over without setting off the shield."

Callan stilled. "*What?*"

"I'm guessing she wasn't supposed to share that with me?"

"She's not supposed to *have* that," Callan said. "I'm not sure how she even knows about it."

I whistled. Meadow was even more mischievous than I'd realized. "I thought it was a founder's descendant privilege or something."

Callan shook his head. "What, exactly, did she say?"

I squinted, trying to remember her words. "Pretty much what I just said. That you could pass over in that spot if you have one of those pendants. Wait..." My stomach clenched. "Does this have something to do with the shield being weakened last year? But shouldn't it have sealed back up once the shield's functions were restored?"

"No, it's not related. The shield is fully functioning."

My breathing relaxed a little at that even though Callan wasn't being forthcoming about the pass-through point and the pendant. But now that we were on the topic of the shield, I wanted to know more. "Has Professor East learned anything about who was poisoning it?"

Callan shook his head. "He's working on some innovative tests, but no, he hasn't."

The door swung open, and a handsome man around our age burst in, practically sliding on his shoes as if he were completing a dance move. His close-cropped black hair was stylishly cut with a fade, and his white dress shirt was unbuttoned a few buttons down.

"They're getting ready to break out the—" He cut himself off as his eyes focused on me. "Who's this?"

Callan spoke up. "Hollis, meet Briar. Briar, this is my best friend, Hollis."

Hollis's eyebrows rose, and a movie-star smile slid across his face. "*The* Briar?"

Callan shot him a look.

Hollis took a step toward me and extended a hand. "We finally meet. Callan has told me so mu—"

Callan cleared his throat, and I reached out to shake Hollis's hand, returning his smile with a bright one of my own.

"Hollis is a fern founder's descendant," Callan said, seeming to not want Hollis to keep sharing his thoughts aloud. "He'll be starting here in the fall."

"Ferns? My three best friends have lead fern affinities," I said, wondering if any of them knew of him.

"You'll have to introduce me," Hollis said, and there was a flirty note to his voice.

Callan rolled his eyes.

The sound of laughter drifted through the cracks of the door as people passed by the office.

Callan glanced toward the door and straightened, as if remembering where we were. "Glad we got the introductions out of the way." He turned to me. "We need to get you out of here before anyone else sees you."

"Gee, you founders' descendants are full of warm welcomes and farewells tonight. Excluding you of course, Hollis."

He gave a half bow. "Always willing to welcome a lovely lady, especially one who—" This time, he cut himself off, glancing at Callan.

"One who?" I asked.

"One who asks so many questions," Callan answered for him.

"It was nice meeting you, Briar, but duty calls me elsewhere. You coming back soon?" Hollis's question was directed at Callan.

"Be out in a while," Callan said, noncommittal.

Hollis gave me a nod and a smile then left the room.

I finished packaging my artifacts with a flourish then reluctantly moved from the table.

Callan's tone softened as he opened the door for me. "Let me drive you to your car."

I didn't protest, eager for a few more minutes with him. We hurried across the central vein and out the front door. I heard two people talking in the rose garden, but if they saw us, they didn't pay us any attention.

The thick purple blossoms I'd noticed on the way in were filling the air now, streaming toward us from the south and catching in my hair and on my flower crown. I reached up and pulled one from my dark-auburn strands.

"What are these?" I asked.

"A rare species of jacaranda. The tree is blooming right now."

My lips parted, something tugging at my memory. "I think Yasmin mentioned it last year. The big tree out by the pond? Didn't she say it only blooms once a year?"

"Yes, on midsummer."

My eyes widened. "Can we swing by and see it?"

At the immediate shaking of Callan's head, I added, "Please? It might be my only chance to witness it bloom."

"Sorry, local. This little soiree has moved out there for the next part of the festivities. You'd be noticed."

I sighed. It had been worth a shot. "Well, enjoy it for me, will you?" I inhaled, soaking in the rich grape fragrance that must have been coming from the brilliant violet-blue trumpet-shaped flowers.

"Who says you'll never enjoy it yourself?"

I perked up, wondering if he'd had a change of heart.

"*Not* this year," he clarified, dampening that little glimmer of hope. But if not this year... Did he think I would get to be here on midsummer at some point in the future? That thought made me feel warm all over, and I snagged a few of the jacaranda flowers from the air and tucked them into my pocket.

We climbed in Callan's truck, and the subtle cologne smell I'd caught a few hints of in the academy hit me more strongly.

I tried to place the notes. It smelled like sandalwood and was that... peaches? I felt the telltale signs of the cologne taking effect on my limbic system, and I cracked the passenger-side window, letting the fresh air cool me off. Given that it was summer, it didn't help much.

I looked at him again, his svelte tux in stark contrast to the pickup truck, which was dusty from driving across the dirt roads that led to campus. I was finding it hard to keep my eyes from darting to him, taking in all the subtle ways he had changed since I had last seen him.

The tousles of hair on top of his head were a little longer, and it stirred in the gentle wind that came through the open window. His olive skin was clear and smooth except for the stubble that lined his jaw.

"Which way are you parked?" he asked, and I quickly refocused out the windshield and pointed to the right. "How are your summer classes going?"

"Brutal, since they're condensed. But I'm surviving. I even got an A on my most recent Calculus test." I suppressed a smile, waiting for his reaction.

"You're taking calc?" The note of surprise with a tinge of admiration in his voice sent a little thrill through me.

"You kept saying I should continue my math studies." I shrugged.

"Yeah, but I didn't realize you were listening."

"Hey!" I said in mock offense. "I'm powerless on campus, not incapable of hearing." I was delighted by the amused expression that formed on Callan's face, though a shadow crossed it again at the mention of my loss of powers.

"Still no progress with figuring out the leaf messages, or are you just ghosting me?"

My jaw nearly fell open at his playfulness as well as the message. *Me* ghosting *him*? More like the other way around.

"The magic has eluded me. But it's not for a lack of trying. Maybe I'll surprise you when you least expect it."

The corner of his mouth twitched. "I have no doubt."

He swung the truck around a corner, and my car came into view, abandoned and looking like the forest was going to overtake it at any moment. A cloud had settled in front of the low sun, and I was extra grateful I hadn't had to walk out here alone.

"Thanks for the ride. Hope I didn't take you away from the midsummer celebrations for too long."

"You did me a favor in that regard."

I hesitated before broaching the next topic. "Is everything okay here? When you said things were 'kicking off,' what did you mean?"

Callan spoke slowly. "The Board of Regents is trying to exercise their control even more this year. They say the faltering of the shield last year is proof they need to have greater influence. Professor East is pushing back. As you can imagine, that is not going over too well."

I swallowed. None of that sounded good. "Is there anything I can do to help?"

"Just promise me you'll stay out of trouble until school starts? No more unsanctioned trips onto campus?"

"I'll do my best." I saluted him, and he rolled his eyes, but a slight smile played on his lips, and I decided that this entire trip had been worth it.

He reached over and felt the ribboned strands hanging in my hair from the flower crown.

I shivered at the feeling of his hand so close to my face.

He met my eyes once before turning back to the front window. "Happy midsummer, local."

Chapter Four

The following day, I took up my friend Maci on an invite for a lake day, deciding it might help me unwind from the previous day's events.

I lay on my stomach on a flower-print towel, flipping through a biography on Renaissance painters. The discovery that I was related to Leonardo da Vinci at the end of last school year was a bombshell that I hadn't fully processed.

But my eyes glossed over the words on the page as I thought about the encounter with Callan the night before. I had never been more desperate to figure out the secret of the leaf messages, if only to prove to him I could do it. I'd taken Calculus to impress him, and now this. He brought out an ambitious side of me I hadn't leaned into before I met him.

Beside me on a purple polka-dot towel, Maci was toned and svelte in her yellow swimsuit, her Laotian skin always a lovely tan. Meanwhile, I was rubbing sunscreen on my arms and legs every few hours, wishing that the fern students at Evergreen Academy had already finished developing the plant-based sunscreen pill they'd been working on last year.

"You've been on the same page for ten minutes," Maci said

casually. "Why are you reading a biography anyway? Is it for one of your summer classes?"

I snapped the book shut. "Yep, and my brain is not processing it right now. Want to swim?"

She nodded, and we stood and raced each other into the water. Lake Siskiyou was beautiful on clear days like this. Mount Shasta, the fourteen-thousand-foot mountain, loomed nearby like a steadfast friend, its brilliant reflection cast across the deep blue water.

As we swam farther into the lake, my awareness of the aquatic plants below my feet grew. I could feel them performing gas exchange and swaying as their roots clung to the soil. But I pushed the allure of them away, trying to focus on my nonmagical friend.

The intrusion of plant sensations had increased over the summer, as if urging me to notice them and get more practice in. I'd been reluctant to do so outside of my visits to the Wildflower Trail, nervous about causing something irreversible.

Last winter, I cast a Floracantus on my aunt's poinsettia to make it bloom longer, and it had worked so well that I'd had to secretly whisk it away in May and tell my aunt that it had finally died. Now, I didn't dare experiment on the flowers on Aunt Vera's balcony.

"How are things going with Alex?" I asked, flipping onto my back and gently kicking my feet.

"I'm not really sure." Maci's voice was hesitant, and I instantly tensed.

"Did something happen?"

"Not really. He's just kind of gone MIA. We've texted a few times, but part of me wonders if he has a summer fling going on back home or something."

"Hmm." I wasn't sure what to say. It sounded like red flag behavior, but Alex had been a little hard to pin down from the start. He was extremely friendly and likeable, but then he would do something that signaled things weren't what you thought they were. Is that what he was doing to Maci?

"Yeah, I'm really not sure what to think. We'll see what happens when he gets back for the school year."

My friendship with Alex had fizzled out after an awkward kind-of date at a Halloween party. It had been a surprise when he and Maci had begun to pick up a relationship, but my feelings for him—whatever they'd been—were long over.

"Well, you're smart. Trust your intuition, and go from there. And if you need me to play detective, I'm in." I let my hand glaze along the surface of the water as we floated along a buoy line, trying to push the strange feeling about Alex out of my mind to examine later.

"How about you? Any word from your handsome tutor?"

I rolled my eyes but laughed. "We're just friends, Maci."

I was unable to explain the dynamics that seemed to be plaguing us to my nonmagical friend. Things had been so strange between me and Callan's mom when she had shown up for my art gala at the end of the spring semester. It was clear that, if his parents had their way, he was destined to end up with another founder's descendant as a romantic partner. But despite all that, he was in my head more often than not. And how had he seriously gotten *more* handsome these past few weeks?

"If you say so," Maci said knowingly, flipping onto her back to float. "Is he going to tutor you again this year?"

I thought about it with a sinking sensation that felt like there was a stone in my stomach trying to drag me down to the bottom of the lake. Without the ability to do magic on campus, it seemed unlikely that our tutoring relationship could go on like it had last year.

But the thought of a school year without studies with Callan in the treehouses felt wrong. "I'm not sure. I hope so," I said, deciding to be completely truthful.

"You could always tutor him with kissing lessons," Maci said, throwing me a devilish smile.

I coughed out a laugh and splashed water at her. "Maci!"

"What? I'm sure you'd both enjoy it."

No. *Nope.* I could not let thoughts of kissing Callan get into my head right now. I had enough things on my plate without letting that take over all my thoughts.

If I was going to be successful at Evergreen Academy this year, I would need a clear head to balance my courses and the field studies we'd be assigned as second-year students. Plus, Professor East wanted me to dig more into my heritage and the unusual way in which my magic had been passed to me.

Kissing anyone, let alone Callan, was a distraction I most definitely did not need. Still, there was a little bubble of warmth in my stomach at the idea, and instead of confronting *that* revelation, I plugged my nose and ducked underneath the water, letting the awareness of the aquatic plants below draw my attention from a certain dark-haired boy with a tree affinity.

Chapter Five

As the weeks of summer rolled on, my aunt and I got deep into wedding planning. Today, we were stuffing wedding invitations into cream-colored envelopes. I was using it as a mental break from studying for my upcoming Calculus final.

"I wanted to keep the ceremony small," Aunt Vera said, eyeing the large stack of filled envelopes.

"Too bad. A Belrose getting married? Everyone in town wants to be there," I teased.

I was so happy for my aunt and Bryce, but I had begun to realize over the weeks since her announcement that my life was about to change. The wedding was set for this October, which would be here before I knew it.

We hadn't discussed it yet, but their marriage meant that either my aunt was moving in with Bryce or Bryce was moving in with us. I didn't want their first year as newlyweds to be spent awkwardly tiptoeing around my aunt's college-aged niece.

As I put a floral postage stamp on the millionth envelope, an idea came to me. It was so obvious that I wondered why I hadn't thought of it sooner. But proceeding with it would mean further dipping my toes into the world of Evergreen Academy—and out of the world of the rest of my life.

As if reading my thoughts, my aunt asked, "When is Yasmin coming back?"

"Next week. I'm so excited to see her."

"Tell her she's welcome to come over any time."

"Thanks, I will. Which reminds me... I want to try to catch Professor East before he heads out for the day. Are you okay finishing this up on your own?"

Aunt Vera eyed the mound again and the much smaller pile of envelopes that still needed to be stuffed. "We're almost done. Thanks for your help licking envelopes. Hope your tongue's not too raw."

I stuck my tongue out at her jokingly but dashed to the kitchen for a big drink of iced sun tea before leaving the apartment.

When I got to Professor East's office on the SCC campus, the door was cracked. The campus was much quieter during the summer semester, with hardly anyone milling around. I knocked and poked my head inside.

"Ms. Whelan, come in, come in," Professor East gestured to the seat across from his desk. "How has your summer been?"

"Pretty good, thank you. How about yours?"

"Busier than ever," he said, and I noticed a few sprinkles of gray at his hairline that I didn't remember being there that spring. "What brings you here today? Are your classes going well?"

"They are." I hesitated. "I came to talk about the residence rooms on campus at Evergreen. Is there any space available for a second-year, if I wanted to move in?"

He leaned back in his chair and studied me. "Have your circumstances changed?"

"Kind of. My aunt—who I live with—is getting married in October."

"Aw. Well, let me look into it. No promises, but I believe there is still a space available with your friend Ms. Ortega."

I tried to suppress a wide smile. This was even better than I'd imagined. "Oh, that would be great. I'd love to room with her."

"Then let me check on a few things. I'll be in touch by the end of the week."

"Can I ask you something else?"

"Go ahead." Professor East nodded, and I had a feeling he anticipated the next question.

"Have there been any developments in figuring out who was poisoning the soil last year?" I whispered this question even though the door to his office was closed.

"Unfortunately not. But we've set up sensors all around the grounds, and there have been no further changes to the soil. Whoever was doing it seems to have been scared off by our efforts."

"That's good," I said, though I wasn't completely satisfied with the answer, and I was sure he wasn't either. If we didn't know who was poisoning the soil and, therefore, putting the school's verdant shield at risk last year, we would never know why they had done it.

"Anything else?"

I shook my head. "Thanks, Professor East. Enjoy the rest of your summer."

When I left the science building on SCC's campus, I texted Yasmin.

> It's not official yet, but I think you and I might be roomies this year!

Her response was immediate.

> You can't see me right now, but I'm squealing.

I was grinning as I drove home.

Chapter Six

I walked out of my Calculus final, relief melting from my shoulders from one course being fully off my plate. I had given my all to my full load of summer classes, and I couldn't believe they were ending. My Calculus work had been the most intensive, but my other courses required a ton of writing, and I constantly had to open my laptop on work breaks and evenings to squeeze in an assignment or two.

After saying a jovial goodbye to a few Calculus classmates, I took a seat at a picnic table on the campus grounds, ready to put the final details on one of my essays and officially be done for the summer. I was settling in to my work when the tree above me began to drop its leaves as if it were being shaken. I felt a soft rustle against my arm as one of the leaves slid down it.

"What on earth?" I jumped up as soft wisps of green began to cover the table, the bench, and the ground all around. Then, as suddenly as it started, it stopped. A rustling breeze blew a note, mixed with a few leaves, into my hand.

> Still haven't figured it out yet? Didn't think
> I'd have to wait all summer. -C

I laughed, so relieved to have heard from Callan that it soothed some of the taunting in his words.

He wasn't wrong. I had tried all summer to figure out how to send him a leaf message but had failed miserably. And without access to the library at Evergreen Academy over the summer, I couldn't go digging in the books beyond those I'd brought home.

Plus, something told me that finding the answer in a book would go against some unspoken rule anyway. Callan wanted me to figure this one out on my own.

I tore a scrap of paper from my notebook and scrawled a message.

> Don't have to rub it in. Not everyone can be the
> best in the class.

After I sent the note off with the leaves that were waiting to bring Callan my return message, I submitted my final essay then packed up my books and laptop. I decided to do a quick walk on Wildflower Trail, which snaked through the forest around the campus's grounds, to celebrate the end of my finals.

Weed had received a summer rain the previous night, and the fragrance coming from the forest was fresh and earthy. I inhaled deeply as I walked, trying to identify the different smells.

I stopped at one of the named trees, Isabella. It had been months since I had written a tree letter or a drawing, which was usually my preference. In fact, I hadn't sent one since I'd learned that students with tree affinities at Evergreen Academy were the ones who collected the letters.

I angled myself toward Isabella and really studied her. She was a large black oak tree, bigger than most of her species in the forest. Her leaves were bright green and healthy, and I opened my magical botanical senses, noticing the gas exchange that was happening in the leaves, the water uptake in the roots, the microscopic growth in the stems.

"You really are magnificent," I said aloud.

And then I felt it.

It was as if Isabella were beckoning me to take a few of her leaves. They detached from her branches and swirled around my head. The leaves pointed themselves into an arrow formation like a flock of birds, ready for a message. I let out a startled laugh. "That's what it takes? A compliment?"

But I didn't dwell on it in case I was missing an opportunity and tore a piece of paper from my notebook.

Ignore my last message. Your favorite pupil figured it out.

The leaves and note continued to hover around me, and I realized I didn't know how to send it on its way.

"Um, deliver to Callan Rhodes, magical botanist, please?"

The leaves hovered there, my message mixed between them.

I thought about how trees communicated through a complex system in their roots that involved fungi threads, all happening underground. Maybe I was missing a link, like the role the fungi played.

"What else do you need?" I murmured. "Something to connect you to Callan?"

I searched my bag, and a shiver of adrenaline shot through me when I remembered Callan had left me a pencil during our last tutoring session. Was this why he had insisted I keep it?

I brought the pencil to the leaves, and they swirled around it, as if picking up its woody scent.

Then, to my immense surprise, my note was swept along in the black oak leaves as they disappeared into the wind.

I'd done it.

Take that, Callan Rhodes.

Chapter Seven

As I climbed into bed later that night, my phone dinged with a text. Thinking it would be Maci or Yasmin, I opened the notification lazily.

The message was from an unknown number.

> I knew you just needed a little motivation to figure it out.

I sat bolt upright. Callan. It had to be.

> Ha ha. How did the solstice recharge go?

> Shield is fully charged. No issues.

> That's a relief. Did you stick around in Weed for long?

> No, we left the day after the solstice. What have you been up to? Snuck onto any academy grounds lately?

I bit down on a smile and decided not to take the bait.

Very funny. I've been helping my Aunt Vera with wedding planning. She's getting married in October.

Please tell me you'll wear your plant-lady costume to the wedding.

I snorted in disbelief that he still remembered my quirky costume from last Halloween.

No promises. When will you be back?

First day of school. Hopefully.

Hopefully? What did that mean? Most magical botanists were returning to campus over the next week.

Callan kept things close to the chest in person, and it appeared that the trait carried over into his texting habits as well.

I debated telling him I was moving on campus but decided to hold back. If Callan could be mysterious, I could surprise him with a thing or two.

Got to go. Big fancy social event. Right up my alley.

Sounds dazzling. I'm sure you'll survive.

It'd be better if you were there. Later, local.

Thoroughly awake now, I got out of bed and found my aunt on the couch, watching TV with a wedding-planning book sprawled out on the coffee table.

It'd be better if you were there.

I would be saving that text message to analyze later.

"How's everything going with the wedding plans?"

"Most of the details are falling into place. Catering is all lined up. I'll be making the cake. I just need to pick a florist."

I stood up straighter as an idea came to me. "I just thought of something. I'd love to do the flower arrangements for you."

Aunt Vera's eyes widened. "That's a nice offer, Briar Rose, but do you know how?"

"We work with flowers at Evergreen Academy. I have access to every variety you could imagine. Just give me an idea of what you're looking for on the tables and how many bouquets and boutonnieres you need, and I'll take care of the rest."

"Well, that would be amazing. It makes me a little less resentful of the fact that you can hardly breathe a word about that place." Her tone was light, and she flipped a page in the wedding-planning book. "Speaking of bouquets, I'm planning to have Adriana and Brit be my bridesmaids."

I nodded approvingly. Both had been friends with Aunt Vera for as long as I could remember. "Which one is going to be the maid of honor?"

"I was hoping to give that role to my niece." Her voice was quiet, a tinge of anticipation under it, as if she'd been sitting on this announcement for a while. "If she's interested, of course."

"Really?" I gasped, sinking onto the couch to give her a hug and practically squashing her in the process. "This might be the best thing I've ever been asked."

A mixture of warmth and excitement swelled in my chest. My aunt, who had been so much more to me my whole life but especially these past seven years, was giving me the honor that I knew would have been my mom's if she were still alive. Tears pricked my eyes, and I wiped them away then noticed that my aunt was doing the same.

"Now that that's settled"—she squeezed my hand—"let's talk about those flowers."

Chapter Eight

"Good Lord, I never thought we'd be able to fit all of that in your car." My aunt was staring at my compact sedan, which was stuffed to the brim with clothes, room essentials, and art supplies.

"Maybe we have a shot at being on one of those extreme packing shows," I said.

We both eyed the hodgepodge piles smooshed against the windows.

"Or maybe not." I said, and we laughed.

"Are you sure I can't help you move in?" Aunt Vera asked, offering one more time despite the fact I had already told her that only academy attendees and instructors were allowed on campus. Aside from the fact that Aunt Vera didn't know magical botanists existed, she didn't have a charged ring and wouldn't be able to enter the campus grounds and see it for what it really was.

"I've got it under control, but thanks for offering," I said.

"Well, then let's not get sappy. I'll see you for your work shift Saturday, and you stop by for dinner any night you'd like. You've got all those maid-of-honor duties to attend to, you know. And don't forget to pop off campus every now and then to check your phone notifications."

"Of course. To all of the above." We hugged, and then I was on my way.

A tug of nerves pulled at my stomach as I drove toward campus. Not only was I returning as a second-year, but I would also be experiencing life as a live-in student, my first time living away from home.

When I rounded the corner of the forest road that led to the academy gates, I pulled into a line of vehicles that I hadn't been expecting. Last year, I had missed the start of the school season. All the action of moving in had been over.

With a zip of excitement, I took my place in line, easing my tiny car behind a biodiesel Mercedes Benz that looked entirely out of place on the overrun dirt road.

When it was my turn to reach the gate, I held my emerald ring to the scanner, feeling the old familiar buzz as it recognized my gemstone and signaled the gates to remain open. Professor East was standing inside the gate, greeting each passenger car as they came through. Farther ahead, Professor Bowellia was directing parking.

"Good morning, Ms. Whelan. Ms. Ortega arrived last night, so you can go straight up to your room."

"Thanks, Professor East." I rolled my window back up and parked. I watched in amazement as students and their magical botanist parents created nets out of vines, large rolling baskets out of straw, or—in the case of some of the stronger tree affinities—floated their belongings inside on a wave of breezy leaves.

I opened my trunk and began to pile my things into a laundry basket, trying not to let my elation at being back on campus deflate as I prepared to make at least twenty trips.

But then a rolling cart made of ferns tapped my bumper, and I looked up and smiled as Yasmin and Aurielle greeted me.

"Coral's not here yet. She should be arriving in a few hours,"

Aurielle informed me as my two friends helped me load my belongings into the fern cart.

"I cannot believe we're going to be roommates. And Coral and Aurielle are right next door. This year is going to be epic," Yasmin said, taking the handle of the cart and tugging it forward, the ferns rustling slightly to help her along.

Yasmin wheeled the fern cart to the glass elevator behind one of the white stone staircases. Professor Sage was emerging in his wheelchair as we arrived.

"Welcome back, botanists. Briar, are you living on campus this year?"

I nodded. "I am. I'm excited to eat your delicious food three times a day now."

Professor Sage grinned and pointed a finger at me. "I knew there was a reason I liked you." He rolled off toward the kitchens, and we took the elevator up to the dorm level.

The white stone of the interior walls was covered by creeping plants, with light streaming from the panel of glass windows that went from the top floor down to the central vein. The sight was like a balm to my artistic soul. Everything about the place still took my breath away.

Yasmin and I spent the next few hours unpacking, Aurielle flitting between her room and ours. Yasmin's rounded bed had been replaced by two thinner rectangular ones, each with a half-moon curve at the top to accommodate the rounded window.

We squeezed our clothes into the closet together, and I took over the recently installed second desk to set up my art supplies. I had stockpiles of colorful notebooks, pens, and paints at my aunt's house, and I'd brought them all along. If I couldn't complete my course studies like a normal student this year, at least I would have something to fill my time.

The ferns around the room shimmied as Yasmin turned on the fairy lights that were strewn all over the walls, intermixed with the snaking strands of pothos. "This place looks pretty cozy, if I do say so myself."

We high-fived.

"Now, all we need is Coral," Yasmin said, settling onto her luscious green bedspread. "Oh, B, you get to experience the autumn equinox celebrations this year! I'm already dreaming about the food."

I heard a voice I recognized in the hallway and stuck my head out to survey the landing. There was a swish of freshly dyed black hair and the familiar shape of Meadow, moving into the room that I assumed was designated for moss descendants.

"Looks like Meadow's moving in," I said, slipping back into our room.

"Meadow?" Aurielle asked, and I remembered that my friends likely hadn't met the new first-year student yet.

"She's the new moss founder's descendant."

"You've met? I thought you just arrived?" Yasmin asked.

"It's a long story—" I began then was cut off as the door swung open.

"I have arrived!" a familiar voice called. Brown curls and a flowy white summer dress enveloped Coral as she sashayed into the room.

"Coral!" we cried in unison.

We each took turns hugging our friend then paused our conversation to help her bring her luggage from the parking lot, putting the fern cart to use once more.

"B's got intel on the new founder's descendant," Aurielle said as Coral unpacked.

"There are actually two new founders' descendants. And not intel," I said. "But we met over the summer."

"Spill." Coral pinned me with a look.

I filled them in on my experience sneaking onto campus with Meadow then being caught by Professor East and Callan. When I got to the part about meeting Callan's best friend, Hollis, Coral gasped.

"*Fronds*. I'd forgotten he'd be enrolling this year," she said.

"You know him?" Aurielle asked.

"Kind of. We were in a competition together a few years ago that was open to fourteen- to sixteen-year-old fern affinities in our region. The winner got a trip to the fern conservatory. Like he even needed to enter. Don't founders' descendants visit the conservatory all the time?"

"Depends on the family, I think," Yasmin said. "So, I take it he won?"

"Yes, and my project was much more innovative. His was flashier, though. If you couldn't tell by how he carries himself, B, that showmanship comes through when he presents."

"I may have noticed a bit of... charisma," I admitted.

"Thinks he's a young British royal or something." Coral snorted.

"Sounds like you two really hit it off," Aurielle said, and we both clenched our lips together to hide our smiles when our eyes met.

"Ha! He wishes," Coral said.

Yasmin turned her attention back to me. "Sounds like someone had an eventful midsummer. And here we thought you'd be missing out on all our magical botanist traditions."

"I can't believe Meadow convinced you to sneak onto campus." Aurielle arched her eyebrows.

"She sounds like trouble. Which, of course, I have nothing against a little of," Coral observed. The ferns in the room shimmied.

"And you and Callan doing some extracurriculars together... What a treat," Yasmin said, expression coy.

"More like luck that Professor East didn't give me detention or expel me or something."

"Evergreen Academy doesn't have detention," Aurielle said as if that was obvious. "But he could have given you an extra kitchen botany rotation."

"Normally, that wouldn't even be punishment. But without powers, I wonder if the herbs and harvester students would run me right out of there."

"It's going to be a great year, B." Coral flung her arm around my shoulder. "As long as Hollis doesn't ruin it."

Chapter Nine

"We have five new fern recruits joining our ranks," Yasmin said as the four of us sat down for breakfast in the teahouse a week later.

Whoever was on kitchen botany rotation was outdoing themselves. They had created a fresh food buffet fit for royalty, complete with multi-tiered displays of pastries and fruit, an omelet bar that had every ingredient imaginable, and a crepe stand with options both savory and sweet. I opted for a sweet crepe with a spread created from hazelnuts and cocoa powder grown at the academy. The coconut whipped topping melted in my mouth, and I had to force my brain away from the food and to the conversation.

"I can already tell that one is going to get on my last nerve." Coral pointed her spoon toward where Hollis was surrounded by a group of students.

"How's it going having a founder's descendant with the ferns now?" I asked. As usual, I had been pulled in multiple directions all week, trying to touch base with each of the different affinity groups.

"You tell me. Look at him. He's like an attention magnet." Coral eyed him and shook her head.

"Well, he *is* a founder's descendant," Aurielle said.

"Yeah, but that's not exactly beneficial when you're trying to do real work," Coral said. "Look how he holds himself. He knows all the power the founders' descendants have here. With Rhodes, he has a calm sort of confidence that exudes power."

"How has the first-year affinity testing been going?" I asked, sensing a change of subject was needed. "I've caught a little bit of some of them, but I don't have a sense of the overall results."

Yasmin spoke up to fill me in. "Based on what I've heard, the quantities of affinity powers fell under fairly typical distribution, with florals being the most common and defensives being the least."

"I heard no one tested positive for defensives this year," Aurielle said. "With Nevah gone, it's just you, B."

"Perilous Grove is going to be perilously empty this year without my ability to practice," I said, trying not to feel the loss acutely again.

"I wonder how the mosses are doing with *her*." Coral nodded behind me, and I looked over my shoulder, spotting Meadow taking a seat with a few fellow first-years.

The new female founder's descendant was making a bit of a splash. Between her antics and Hollis's magnetism, speculation was buzzing through the school like wildfire. If my initial encounter with her on the summer solstice had been any indication, she'd earned her reputation as a rabble-rouser.

"I wonder if they'll do more crossover work with the trees this year than usual," Yasmin mused.

"She and Callan could do some interesting things. Trees and mosses are the closest pairing of any of the affinity powers," Aurielle said.

Interesting things. The hair on my arms stood up. *Not romantic things, Briar. She didn't say that.*

I tried to refocus on the conversation and not make false associations between Meadow and Callan as I had with Nevah last year. I wasn't even under the influence of *Scopolia*-spiked cupcakes this time.

"Honestly, I'm just glad she and Hollis are here," Yasmin said. "After everything that happened with the shield last year and two of our founders' descendants moving on from the school, I'm glad Callan isn't the sole descendant this year."

My chest squeezed at that, and I was reminded how painfully aware I was of the fact that he still hadn't arrived at school. "Yeah, that's true. It'd be nice to have more than three for charging, but Professor East seems to think the shield is stable and those three will be plenty." I hesitated. "Speaking of Callan, has anyone seen him yet?"

"What, like he wouldn't seek you out as soon as he got here?" Coral teased.

I bit my lip and suppressed a smile.

A shout of laughter came from across the room, and we all turned our heads to see Meadow growing moss across the table.

"I'd give anything to grow some moss right now," I sighed, wistful at the little evidences of the other botanists using their magic around the teahouse.

"You know you're always welcome to study with the ferns. You do have a lead affinity for them, lest you ever forget among all your other affinities."

"The coolest affinity around," I said, grateful for the welcomeness Yasmin had shown me since the first day I'd arrived at Evergreen Academy. "But I have no idea where they're going to put me for field studies."

"Let's not dwell on that yet. It's the autumn equinox tomorrow. No talk of school until after that," Coral advised.

"Now *that* I can get behind," Yasmin raised her tea mug, and we mirrored her, clinking our assorted mugs together in a hearty breakfast toast.

Chapter Ten

"That's the last box," Aurielle said, stacking a wooden crate full of seasonal fruits and vegetables onto a flatbed trailer. The boxes were headed for the local food bank, a tradition of the autumn equinox celebrations at Evergreen Academy.

My friends and I high-fived with some nearby botanists who had been part of our packaging and loading group, then Yasmin and I returned to our room to change and get ready for the evening's festivities.

"One of the best perks of living here so far is having access to your closet twenty-four seven." I said, flicking through Yasmin's dresses.

Yasmin grabbed a deep-crimson, thigh-length summer dress with a modest slit and held it out to me. "Wear this one."

"You're always so much better at dressing me than I am. I wish I could keep you as my personal stylist forever."

"Maybe my calling is in fashion. I could debut a dress made of ferns at Paris Fashion Week." The ferns in the room shimmied at her words.

After applying botanically enhanced makeup on our faces and

dotting our ears and fingers with Yasmin's endless supply of jewelry, we met Coral and Aurielle outside our room and made our way down the staircase to the central vein.

I tried not to be disappointed every time I scanned the vicinity and didn't spot the deep-chestnut hair and assured posture that was Callan. *Where was he?*

I had considered reaching out via leaf communication—or sending a text when off campus—but I didn't want him to feel like I was bombarding him. I rolled my shoulders back, trying to ground myself in the present. If Callan wasn't here, surely he was busy doing something important.

When we arrived at the field by the pond, I took a moment to take in the scene. The place was decorated like other harvest festivals I'd been to, with leaves and pumpkins and all things orange, yellow, and rich red like the color of my dress.

But I had never been to a harvest festival where magical botanists were actively growing food in front of my eyes then rapidly preparing finger foods for us to eat, fresh off the vine. And the pumpkins ranged from the size of my thumb to ones that could have been turned into Cinderella's carriage.

"The harvesters have been working hard," Coral said, snagging an appetizer plate of vegetables and hummus from braided-leaf trays that were being floated throughout the field by the tree affinity students.

Wind chimes began to sound a melodic note, and we turned our attention to Professor East. "Hello, everyone. To announce today's signature activity, I am joined by a member of the Board of Regents, Kale Brightmoor."

There was soft clapping as a man slightly younger than Professor East joined him. "Thank you all for the warm welcome. As a harvester affinity, it gives me great pleasure to be here today at one of the most bountiful times of year. In the past, we have hosted a combined activity at this time. Today, though, we would like each affinity group to have their own activity. These have been designed by your associated representatives on the Board of Regents."

"What the spores?" Coral murmured from my left.

"Please gather with your lead affinity groups, and follow the instructions of your designated instructor. Harvesters, I look forward to joining you all."

There were a series of murmurs as the crowd began to divide into affinity groups.

"Does this mean there aren't going to be any pumpkin rides?" someone asked as they walked by us, sounding entirely dejected.

"Since you have all the affinities as leads, where do you go?" Yasmin asked, turning to me.

"I think I'll just join you all for the fern activity," I said.

Before I could take one step, a voice came from behind us. "Which one of you is Briar Whelan?"

Chapter Eleven

At the sound of my name, I turned to see Kale Brightmoor standing there, smiling pleasantly. He appeared to be of Korean descent and had a neatly groomed beard and was wearing khaki pants and a flannel shirt. The casual outfit belied his status as a member of the prestigious Board of Regents.

"That's me," I said, swallowing.

"Why don't you join the harvesters today?"

"Oh," I said, taken by surprise. "Sure, okay." My friends waved goodbye and began to walk toward the fern gathering, casting looks over their shoulders to check on me.

"The harvesters will be meeting by the gate for a foraging competition," Kale Brightmoor said. "Let's walk together."

I fell into step alongside him.

"So, Briar, have you expressed an interest in any particular affinity more than the others?"

"Oh," I said again, stalling. I wasn't sure how to frame my answer here. Callan had warned me time and again to be careful with the board members, and I wasn't going to forget that advice now. "I don't think so. They all have things that are special about them."

"They do indeed. And how about the harvesters? Have you spent much time among them?"

"I rotate during my affinity studies, and I did some work with them this morning when we prepared the harvest donations."

"Good. Well, I hope you haven't selected which field you'll be working in without giving each of them a full and fair exploration. I heard you were partial to trees, but that could simply be a rumor."

Alarm bells began to flare, and again I heard Callan's warnings in my head. Still, my curiosity kept me from holding my tongue. "Interesting. Where did you hear that?"

"Wendy Rhodes seemed to think you were friendly with her son last year. Was that incorrect?"

"We are... acquainted, yes. I'm friends with a lot of people here at Evergreen Academy." Something in me chilled at the revelation that members of the Board of Regents had discussed me and my... friendships.

"Well, I'm excited to see how you do working with the harvesters today." He nodded toward the gate to Evergreen Academy, where Professor Variegata was surrounded by harvesters. "Healthy food production is one of the most critical issues of our time. Just a friendly reminder."

As Kale Brightmoor peeled away, I tried to calm the nervous twist in my stomach. Was he buttering me up for the harvesters? Had I said the right things? More than ever, I wished Callan were here. He always seemed to know what to do. I took a deep breath and joined the other harvesters.

Professor Variegata was standing by a stack of small baskets, and the vine that was often snaking around her wrists was in full motion today, moving across her forearm and palm like a calming massage.

"We'll be doing a foraging task today. Here's your objective," she began. "You have thirty minutes to return here with a basketful of edible foods. At least two different types of foods are required. You must prepare whatever you forage for consumption, so don't get too creative. Nothing poisonous, of course, unless you know how to counter them." Her eyes shot to me. "Please pair up. Any questions?"

When we all shook our heads, she took a seat on a large stump and gently waved a hand at us in the universal signal of *well, get going*.

I looked around as harvesters who were well acquainted began to group up in twos. When my eyes landed on Kaito, a second-year I knew, I caught his eye. "Want to be partners?" I asked.

"Sure." Kaito reached down and picked up a basket. "I wasn't expecting this to happen outside of the campus walls. You're local, right? What's best for foraging around here?"

I thought about it for a moment. "I admit I've never foraged before beyond picking blackberries. Those are in season, so we should keep an eye out. Mushrooms are common here too. Do mushrooms count even though they're fungi and not plants?"

Kaito contemplated it. "The only rule was that it had to be edible."

"Okay, I think mushrooms and berries are our best bet. Maybe some nuts."

Kaito began to walk, the basket swinging from his hand. "I'll reach out with my senses to see if I feel any, but with the quantity of trees out here, I don't know how loud those signatures will be."

I nodded. "I'll do the same." I was grateful that the task was happening outside the gates, which meant my powers were alive and well. I didn't have much experience using my powers to locate something, but I tried to tap into what I did know. Last year, during a game of Capture the Roses, we'd used our tree affinity powers to have the trees communicate and guide us to the other team's rose. Maybe the same could apply here.

I searched my brain for what I knew about the *Rubus* genus, which contained brambles like blackberries and raspberries. Nothing very helpful came to mind, so I tried envisioning the roots and rhizomes, the green leaves, thorns, and dark, juicy fruits. I pictured the blackberry bushes I had seen growing up, clinging to the edges of roadways.

"Let's get out of the forest," I suggested. We were walking near a river that ran parallel to a road when I sensed a change in the soil nearby. My attention was drawn to a massive oak tree whose roots were creeping out toward the river. Without a word to Kaito, I shot toward the tree and began to scan the ground below it. "Kaito, over here!"

"What is it?"

I pointed to the pale-brown shapes in the ground. "It's a mushroom gold mine."

"And they are edible?" Kaito crouched down next to me and began to examine a mushroom. One look at the distinctive pits and ridges that formed the mushroom's cap was answer enough, and Kaito seemed to know his mushroom anatomy too. "Good. These are morels. We can eat them."

Kaito was already tugging the mushrooms from the earth and adding them to his basket. "How'd you sense them?"

"It wasn't them. It was something about the soil. I think the pH is a little higher here."

"You could sense the soil?" Kaito paused the mushroom collection to look up, a piece of straight black hair falling across his forehead. "That's not a common power."

I knelt and helped him collect the mushrooms. "I'm not very precise about it, but yeah."

"No wonder Kale Brightmoor is trying to schmooze you."

"Noticed that, did you?"

"He personally tasked you to join the harvesters today, right?"

I nodded.

"My mom says all this affinity separation has been brewing for a while. All it takes is for one affinity to start a power grab, and the others will follow. Each board member wants their affinity group to have the most influence in society."

"Wouldn't it be better for all the affinities to work together? We're all magical botanists, right?"

"That's the idyllic scenario and one Evergreen Academy was established on. Times are changing, though. As the environment becomes more under threat, magical botanists get more... desperate, I guess. Ready to find our second edible item?"

I nodded in agreement and looked around, trying to process everything Kaito had said. Changes had obviously been happening within the society over the summer, and Callan wasn't the only one to notice. My eyes snagged on something farther along the road.

"I think those are blackberry bushes." We hurried toward the bushes and began to pick the plump berries. With my harvester affinity active here outside the gate, I didn't have to be careful as I plucked the berries from the vines. The thorns that would normally poke me had no effect. I smiled and quickened my pace until we topped off the basket.

"I'll work on cooking the morels by pulling water from the air and steaming them as we walk," Kaito offered as we began to hurry back toward the grounds.

"Brilliant," I said.

Occasionally, I heard a subtle whistling sound and a murmured Floracantus as Kaito worked miracles with steam, but otherwise, we walked in companionable silence.

When we got back to campus, two other pairs were gathered near Professor Variegata just inside the gate. One pair was finishing eating, and when they got a nod of approval from Professor Variegata, they walked back toward the academy.

Kale Brightmoor was standing back and slightly off to the side from Professor Variegata, watching each student carefully.

"All right, Nori and Graham, go ahead," Professor Variegata said to the second pair.

The first-year student Nori held a basket that was brimming with acorns and nuts. She began murmuring a Floracantus that I vaguely recognized from my time working with the harvesters last year. Graham rotated the basket slightly in a rocking motion as Nori spoke.

Nori ran the acorns through her hands, and they ground down into flour then congealed and formed two small muffins. A moment later, Nori and Graham presented the muffins with a side of nuts.

"Impressive," Professor Variegata said. She turned to us. "Kaito and Briar, what did you forage?"

"Mushrooms and blackberries," Kaito said. "Cooked and ready."

He held out the basket for Professor Variegata to examine, and when she nodded, each of us reached for a mushroom to taste. Even without any butter or seasonings, Kaito's on-the-fly preparation was mouth-watering.

"Who prepared the mushrooms?" Kale Brightmoor asked.

"Kaito did," I said.

"Briar found them," Kaito said kindly.

"How so? Mushrooms are fungi, and we don't usually sense them," Kale Brightmoor said.

Between the sharp curiosity in his voice and what Kaito had said a few minutes earlier, I had the instinct to bite my tongue. I cast a glance at Kaito. "It was a lucky find. I spotted one near the base of a tree, and there were a dozen more nearby."

Kale's brow furrowed slightly, but he let it go and turned to watch the next group of students who had returned with their basket.

"Wise choice," Kaito said as we walked away. "Don't give them more fuel than they already have to fight over you."

"Thanks for not saying anything," I said.

"It's always best not to show all your cards." There was something in his voice that indicated he wasn't only referring to not telling Kale Brightmoor about me being able to sense the pH in the soil.

"Enjoy your autumn equinox, Briar. I have a feeling we'll be working together again soon."

Chapter Twelve

"How did your task with the harvesters go?" Yasmin asked as we settled at the long table in the forest. Leaves were floating by overhead, ferrying tiny gleaming candles.

The grand jacaranda tree was lit by the sunset, its leaves a brilliant yellow. I was still a little bummed that I had missed out on the fantastical bloom on midsummer, but I had to appreciate that it was stunning today too.

"It was fine. I paired up with Kaito. Our conversation was interesting, though. He mentioned that a separation of affinities has been brewing outside of the school. Have you heard anything about that?"

"There have been some stirrings among the ferns, from what I've heard. I didn't think it would trickle into the academy. With the board getting involved with this autumn equinox activity, though... something feels off," Yasmin said.

"My parents were talking about potential changes within the society of magical botanists this summer, and I wonder if this is related to that," Aurielle said.

"Callan was hinting at this even last year," I said. "He was hoping it would get resolved at the midsummer gathering, but I don't think it did."

"Historically, the board being too involved in the school hasn't boded well. We can't be innovative with too many competing interests trying to have a say, you know?" Yasmin said.

"Kaito didn't seem too happy about it," I said.

"Well, I can't say any of us would be happy to have drastic changes made to the school while we're here. Not only would it impact our personal experiences, but societal norms and cross-affinity connections are developed here. Only those already in positions of power would benefit from any kind of splintering," Coral said.

"Is there some way we can make our voices heard? Are Board of Regents meetings open to the public?"

Coral let out a soft laugh. "Yeah, right. They have always been closed door, and attempts to change that have never gone anywhere."

"There must be something we can do." I buttered a croissant more intensely than I'd planned, and delicate pieces of the pastry disintegrated into flakes that landed softly on my plate.

"As long as founders' descendants sit on the board and the founders' descendants have the keys to charging the verdant shield here and at the conservatories, the rest of us will never have an equal say," Yasmin said.

I contemplated Yasmin's words as we continued to dig into the equinox feast, and gradually conversation shifted in other directions.

"So, I'm thinking of starting a cartography club this year," Aurielle said as we moved on to the second course.

"Cartography club? To do what?" Coral asked.

"I did some work with maps over the summer, and I got kind of into it," Aurielle explained. "We don't focus on that type of work much here at the academy, but I think others might be interested."

"The club would be for learning how to use maps?" I asked.

"To start. But what I'd really like is for us to develop ecological maps of the campus. Things are always changing with the plants, and we could document some of the microenvironments throughout the seasons," Aurielle explained.

Yasmin swirled a spoon in her bowl of harvest soup. "Sounds interesting. Do you think you'll have time to host it with field studies?"

"I'll figure something out," Aurielle said. "I'm going to run it by Professor Sato this week."

By the time we finished the harvest meal, the sun had fully set, and the clearing was lit by the candles that were being floated above us on the leaves as well as the tall, tapered ones that lined the table.

Coral rubbed her hands together as she rose. "Time for Orchard Lantern Tag. I've been looking forward to this since last year. Waylon tagged me out then, and I'm planning to get him back."

"Orchard Lantern Tag?" I asked, rising from my seat as well.

"It's my favorite autumn equinox tradition, after the meal," Aurielle said. We streamed along with the other students, who were moving in the direction of the orchards.

"Remember when we played Capture the Roses last year? For tag, we split into two teams like that, but instead of finding the other teams' rose, we illuminate as many of our opponents as possible. The lanterns have bioluminescent powder in them, genetically modified into the plant powder from algae. If you hold up your lantern and say *Lux dispere*, it will cling to your target and their clothes will glow. It's one point for every person who is eliminated but one hundred points for whichever team eliminates the other team's captain first. Sort of like a queen bee situation," Yasmin explained.

"So you're pretty much guaranteed to win if you take out the other team's captain as long as the strengths of the two teams aren't totally lopsided. Everyone has to stay within the confines of the orchard," Aurielle added. "But we are allowed to use our powers, so we can get creative in deterring others from getting close enough to light us up."

My stomach sank a little at the realization that I would be the only defenseless one in the group, but I had to admit the game sounded fun.

When we reached the orchard, Professor Bowellia was there, and he began shepherding us into two groups. Since we arrived in a quartet, he immediately split us in half. "Yasmin and Coral, Team Summer. Briar and Aurielle, Team Autumn."

"Yes! Looks like Waylon's already been assigned to Team Autumn. I'll have my chance for vengeance. Wish me luck." Coral pumped a fist before dashing off to join the others on Team Summer.

"Team Summer, your captain is Hollis. Team Autumn, your captain is Meadow. Circle up, make your plans, and get your lanterns. We start in three minutes," Professor Bowellia announced.

Aurielle and I joined the group of students gathering around Meadow.

"As far as I'm concerned, the only objective is for you all to not get lit up and to take out a handful of others, and I'm not going to dictate how you do those things. Leave Hollis to me, but feel free to take a few shots at him in the meantime. It can't hurt to keep him busy and let him think we're trying for him. Everybody good?" Meadow asked, and I internally chuckled at her vastly different founder's descendant leadership style compared to how Callan had operated during Capture the Roses last spring.

At the thought of Callan, I glanced around. With the charging of the verdant shield happening in a few hours, shouldn't he be here by now?

"Team Autumn!" Our group called in a joint cheer, then each person picked up an orange-ember lantern and began to scatter. I looked toward the other side of the orchard and saw green lights beginning to stretch across the orchard like fireflies. Those were our targets.

"Stick together?" I asked Aurielle, and she nodded.

"Of course. Ferns are notoriously good at hiding things. If you're willing to get low with me, we can hide out until things slow down and then try to take out a couple of targets?" Aurielle suggested.

"Sounds good to me." I followed Aurielle as we dashed through the trees. This wasn't a typical orchard, where trees were planted in neat rows and clear of underbrush. Instead, a mixed variety of fruit trees were scattered in among the towering trees of the forest, and the floor was littered with grasses, ferns, moss, and fall flowers.

About twenty feet to my left, I saw an orange burst of light as someone from Team Summer was presumably splattered with bioluminescent plant dust. The receiver let out a squeal and a disgruntled, "Well, *hollyhocks.*"

"*Lux dispere,*" I heard from above and jutted my gaze into the trees, where a tree affinity with a green lantern was aiming their light in my and Aurielle's direction.

"Aurielle, run!" I shouted. We picked up the pace and veered to the right, away from the large tree above us that was raining down green dust.

After about thirty seconds of sprinting, Aurielle called, "Follow me!" She dove into a thicket of ferns feetfirst and promptly disappeared. I didn't have time to do anything but pray for luck and follow her.

To my shock, we slid into a smooth, slender hollow in the earth. When my heart rate slowed enough for me to take in our surroundings, I saw that we were covered from above by a perfectly convex ceiling of ferns.

"We made it!" Aurielle gasped. "I was just looking for the right spot to create a thick covering for us. This should protect us from the tree walkers, and most people on the ground will run right past us."

"Good thinking," I said, still breathing a little too fast. "I think the ferns are shimmying, though. Won't that give us away?"

"Oh, *fronds*. Relax, everyone," Aurielle said, and the ferns stilled.

We lay on our bellies in the hollow for a few minutes, listening to the commotion outside. There were periods of quiet followed by shouts of "*Lux dispere*" and then usually some level of magical botanist profanity.

We both froze as a quiet but sharp rustle came from overhead, and the ferns began to frantically shake.

"Gahhh!" I shouted as a pair of booted feet came flying into the hollow.

Aurielle screeched, and the ferns rustled closer to us, creeping toward the intruder.

I turned and spotted a swoosh of chestnut-brown hair and a flash of familiar tattoos.

The body wasn't just anybody.

"Callan!" I gasped.

The tree founder's descendant had finally made his arrival.

Chapter Thirteen

"Y ou're here!" I blurted, all chance of vocal eloquence dissolving with my excitement at seeing him.

"Couldn't have picked a larger hollow, could you?" Callan crouched on his forearms the same way Aurielle and I were and brushed away the ferns that were trying to overtake him.

Aurielle waved them off, and they returned to shielding us.

I smiled so broadly that I could feel it in my cheeks. Callan was here. Finally. "How did you find us?" I asked.

"I was tree walking, hoping to catch sight of you. I had a feeling you'd be with a fern, so I headed for this dense grove. Sure enough, I saw you two dive in here a few minutes ago. I had to wait for an opening, and then I joined you. Nice job on the cover." He aimed this comment at Aurielle. "I couldn't see your lantern light from the outside."

It was then that I noticed the orange lantern that had slid in with him. "You're on Team Autumn?"

"What? Did you think I'd come in here to ambush you from Team Summer?" Callan's mouth quirked. "So, what's the game plan?"

"We were going to hide in here until it thins out then try to sneak up on an opponent or two," I said.

Callan raised his eyebrows, and the motion was illuminated by his lantern. "Oh, I think we can do better than that."

"What do you have in mind?" I asked.

"Hollis is captain of the other team, and in the spirit of friendly competition, I'd like to take him out. We can't have a first-year founder's descendant thinking he runs the place this year, can we?"

I couldn't help smiling. Hollis had both Meadow and Callan gunning for him. "Why didn't you just go straight after him?" I asked. "What do you need us for?"

"Taking down Hollis will be more fun with witnesses." He winked.

I glanced at Aurielle. "What do you think? Stick with our original plan or follow this madman?"

"Taking down a founder's descendant sounds like fun to me," Aurielle said. "But I have a feeling Callan's plan involves tree walking."

"Oh, Aurielle, ye of little faith," Callan said. "I can tree walk all three of us. And you might be our secret weapon. Hollis has a fern affinity, so you can counter some of his moves."

"He's quite a bit stronger than me, from what I've heard, but I'll help if I can," Aurielle said.

"And what should I do?" I asked.

"You are going to serve as the distraction." Callan grinned.

"Oh, joy," I said, voice dripping with sarcasm. But I knew it was a good plan. Without access to my powers, distracting Hollis was one of the only ways I could actively contribute. "Do you have any idea where he is?"

"I can confidently guess he is *not* hiding in a fern hollow. Hollis's style is flashier. I'm sure he's in the center of the orchard, lighting up as many people from Team Autumn as he can. Let's tree walk in that direction and see if we can find him."

We climbed out of our hiding spot, and Callan used wind to help Aurielle and me climb the tree. Aurielle's legs were shaking as she stood on the tree branch twenty feet off the ground. "Maybe I should wait in the hollow, and you two can go and take down Hollis," she said, looking at the forest floor far below as if she was going to be sick.

"You can walk between Briar and me," Callan directed, glancing to me to make sure that was okay. I nodded. "I'll create wind binds around both of you so that even if you slip, the wind will grab you. But you *won't* slip. Just stay right on my heels, and you'll catch the trail I'm making."

The gentle confidence in Callan's voice must have buoyed Aurielle because she nodded. "Let's do it."

We began to walk, and I felt Callan's binds snap into place around my lower back as the three of us walked. If I hadn't successfully tree walked in the past using my powers, I probably would have been way too nervous to risk such a maneuver, but instead, I was... exhilarated. It was good to be tree walking with Callan again, even if there was someone between us.

I scoured the ground as we walked, occasionally seeing students tagging each other out with their lights. The crowd seemed to have thinned substantially in the fifteen or so minutes since the game had started. A grasses affinity was sending a ripple through the grasses along the ground and grazing the heels of anyone it passed, making them screech. One girl was lying in a field of flowers, the chrysanthemums and goldenrods having stretched over her so that she was invisible except for a small hole for her nose and mouth.

Finally, the commotion increased, and I spotted ferns rustling all along the forest floor.

"I think we found him," Aurielle said, confirming my guess.

Several of our fellow Team Autumn students were walking away from the area covered in glowing green dust.

"What now?" I asked. My gaze darted through the woods, and

I caught sight of a few other flecks of orange and green lights at our level. There were other tree affinities here, and not all of them were on our team.

"Aurielle, do you think you can draw the attention of some of those ferns? You can do anything that would break Hollis's concentration," Callan said.

Aurielle nodded. "I'll think of something."

"Good. Let's stop here." Callan paused as we approached a large Douglas fir. Callan coaxed the branches into forming a small platform for us to stand on.

"Aurielle, start messing with the ferns once Briar is on the ground. Briar, walk with your lantern around the perimeter of where the ferns are most concentrated. Do you see?"

I studied the forest floor and nodded.

"I'll get as close as I can from above then drop down and surprise him. Everybody ready?"

When Aurielle and I nodded, a breeze tucked under me and floated me to the ground. I lifted my lantern and began to walk. As I made my way around the ferns, they began to slow and reversed direction.

"What are you doing?" I heard a voice call. I froze and held my breath but then realized the sound had come from a ways off. It continued, "Why are you spinning that way?"

It must have been Hollis, picking up on Aurielle's interference.

Every step felt like I was about to engage a mousetrap. If Hollis —or any other Team Summer student—saw me, I was done for.

After an excruciating minute of waiting for Hollis to notice me, a twig snapped behind me, and I jumped. I spun around, and my eyes widened as I made out the figure of Meadow, completely covered in moss, emerging from where she had been pressed against the front of a tree. She had been completely camouflaged by it.

Meadow lifted a finger to her lips. Even the light of her lantern was mostly dimmed, moss having grown over its glass panes.

I could do nothing but watch, transfixed as Meadow passed me like an earthen goddess. Meadow moved in silence until she was ten feet from where Hollis was holding court, taking down any would-be challengers.

I glanced overhead and saw Callan perched there, ready to attack.

But Meadow made her move first. She darted forward and lifted her lantern, which was rapidly clearing of moss. The area began to illuminate with her orange light as—voice calm and clear —she said, "*Lux dispere.*"

Hollis turned at the sound of her voice, and his mouth fell open as orange dust painted him like sparkling, fairy-made confetti.

Chapter Fourteen

"Can I talk to you for a second?" Callan took my elbow as Team Autumn began to chant in victory, lifting their orange lanterns into the air.

"Sure," I said, still breathing hard and grinning from the exhilaration of the last half hour.

Meadow was being lifted onto a stretcher of vines that was serving as a throne. Where our team intended to parade her to, I had no idea.

"Sorry Meadow stole your thunder," I said.

Callan shook his head. "As long as someone took Hollis down a peg, we're all good. Though now Meadow may be the one with the overinflated ego."

"You all have to go charge the verdant shield soon, right?" I asked, glancing toward the star-littered sky. It had to be nearing midnight.

Callan nodded. "Yes, but I'll be leaving after that."

"Leaving?"

"I'm working on a few projects before school starts, and unfortunately, they're going to keep me away from the academy for a little while longer."

My stomach twisted as my heart sank. "But you only just arrived."

"I had to come back for the charging. I should only be out for another week or so."

"Is everything... okay?"

He broke eye contact for a moment to fist-bump with another tree affinity who walked by and shouted, "Ayyye, Rhodes!"

"That's what I wanted to ask you. I heard someone from the board was here today."

"Oh, yes. Kale Brightmoor from the harvesters."

"He spoke with you?"

"Yeah, it was weird. It seemed like he was almost... selling the harvesters to me. Seems pretty silly for a girl who doesn't even have access to her powers."

Callan frowned. "I think you can probably expect more of that throughout the year."

"I feel like I should be flattered, but I can't help wondering what they want."

"Power is beginning to... shift hands," Callan said slowly. "The affinity groups are surveying their assets. Some may see you as one."

"As an asset? That sounds like some spy business." I tried to joke, but Callan's face was entirely serious.

"I'm sure you handled yourself like a champ just don't... Don't make commitments to anyone, okay?"

"What kind of commitments could I even make?"

"Promises to visit their conservatories. Concessions to focus your research in their affinity area. That sort of thing."

I swallowed and nodded. "Okay, I won't. But nothing like that has technically been asked of me."

"Good. Let's hope we can keep it that way." He glanced toward the academy building. "I have to get to the shield and rescue Meadow from the celebrations, but I'll see you in a week or so, okay?"

"Good luck, Callan."

My friends pounced on me as soon as Callan left, as if they'd been waiting for their opening. My eyes tracked the head of chestnut hair disappearing in the dark even after Coral started jumping up and down.

"I lit Waylon! I lit Waylon! He's *covered* in green dust."

Coral's enthusiasm finally wrenched my attention from Callan, and I smiled and gave her a high five. "Nice work. And not a spot on you."

"I managed to hold out until the end. An aquatic affinity from your team tagged Yasmin, though."

I looked at my roommate and confirmed that she was covered in orange dust.

"Honestly, I don't even care that we lost. I'm just celebrating accomplishing my mission." Coral looped her arm through mine, and we began to walk back to the academy.

"So, tell us how Meadow took out Hollis," Yasmin said.

Aurielle rushed to fill her in on the thrilling tale, including her role in it. But I tuned it out as I wondered what Callan was doing and why he wasn't attending classes on Monday like the rest of us.

Chapter Fifteen

Yasmin slid into the seat next to mine in our prop creation class at SCC. Because I'd taken winter intersession courses and then a full load over the summer, I only had to take one class each semester to be on track to graduate with my associate's degree in the spring. I was broadening my horizons with my art electives and had chosen prop creation, a new class designed in collaboration with the theater department.

"Let's hope today's class goes better than last week's," Yasmin murmured. She had surprised me when she enrolled in the class. As she put it, "Our art class last year really pushed me out of my comfort zone. And I saw you pushing yourself into taking Calculus. You inspired me to not always take the easy route."

I hadn't let on how much the words had touched me.

"Hello, class. Exciting news. I've just learned that the theater department has selected the play they'll be putting on this spring. They've gone with *A Midsummer Night's Dream*, and we are tasked with creating much of the set design and costuming. I'd like each of you to sign up for your first design of interest, and you'll work in small groups to draft these and determine your needed materials."

Our instructor pointed to colorful papers that were scattered throughout the drafting tables in the room. "Walk around and see the group options that are available, then sign up for the ones you want to be on."

I reached for the nearest paper and read it aloud to Yasmin. "Trees for the forest. They need to incorporate lights and fireflies. Sounds interesting," I said.

"Put that in the *maybe* category," Yasmin agreed, and we proceeded to make our way around the classroom, exploring our different options. By the end, there were two more set pieces that appealed to us.

"So, we're down to the forest—which they need a large team for—the fairy faces and crowns, or the flower that gets struck by cupid's bow," Yasmin said.

"I'm really interested in the flower." I lowered my voice. "It needs to look enchanted, and I wonder if we could use a real flower from the academy and make modifications to it."

"So long as it looks plausible that we could have created it with materials here."

I scribbled my name onto that paper. "I think we can make it work. I'm going to sign up for the forest, too, since they need a lot of hands for that one."

"Same." Yasmin followed my lead in writing her names on those two groups. We were the only ones who signed up for the flower, and we made plans to start working with the tree group during the next class period.

"Still no sign of Callan?" Yasmin asked as we cleaned up our workspaces.

"He's missed almost the first two weeks of class. What could he be doing that's that important?" I was glad Yasmin asked since I had been itching to talk about him.

"Maybe it has something to do with his field study? Could he be starting earlier than the rest of us? Who knows when it comes to founders' descendants. Speaking of descendants"—she lowered her voice—"have you learned anything more about your history? I know you were doing some reading this summer."

"Nothing groundbreaking." I matched her hushed tone. "I don't know what I was expecting. Obviously, I wasn't going to find anything about his... botanical heritage in regularly published books. I wish the collection at Evergreen Academy was bigger, but there is hardly anything about botanists of the Renaissance period there."

Yasmin frowned. "That's kind of strange. Why were records so poorly kept of that era? I wonder..." She pushed open the door of the classroom, and we emerged into the crisp autumn air. "Most of the magical botanical conservatories have their own libraries, from what I've heard. Perhaps the information you need is stored at one of those?"

I perked up, eager for a new lead. "Really? Can anyone request books from them?" I could almost feel the warm, tingly feeling in my hands that had occurred when I first picked up one of da Vinci's journals.

She shrugged. "They all have different rules. I know that with the fern conservatory in Alaska, you can only access the books there in person. They don't let people remove them from the library unless they're a VIP academic researcher."

"Well, it's something to think about. But which conservatory would be most likely to have books on the Renaissance-era botanists? If what Professor Tenella said last year is true, many botanists back then had all of the affinity powers. So could books about them be in any of the conservatories?"

"It's possible. I wish there was some kind of directory that listed all the books in each of the conservatories, but as you've probably gleaned by now, information sharing across affinity groups isn't always a top priority in the magical botanist community. That's part of what makes Evergreen Academy so special. Things are less siloed among the affinities there. At least, that's how it's been." Yasmin worried her lip.

"We'll make sure it stays that way. As students, we should have a say in the goings-on of our school, shouldn't we? If all the affinities want to continue collaborating with each other, we should be able to."

"Tell that to the founders' descendants who think they and their affinities rule the world."

"Good point. Want to swing by my aunt's apartment with me before we head back to the academy? I need to pick up a few more art supplies. I might have some things we can use to start working on these props."

When Yasmin agreed, we drove from SCC to my aunt's apartment. "Looks like she's working down in the café. We'll say hello on our way out." I headed straight for my room and let Yasmin give herself a tour of the apartment.

"Is your aunt planning to rent this place out after she gets married?" Yasmin called from the hallway.

"That's the plan. She's already started moving a bunch of things to Bryce's house, but I have a feeling she'll go slowly on getting this place completely cleared out."

I heard the door to the balcony open.

"Wow, your aunt has a green thumb," Yasmin said once I found my art supplies and joined her on the balcony.

"She's always kept a nice little garden out here." Since the first frost of the year hadn't come yet, many of my aunt's flowers were still in bloom. And Rosie—our trailing rose plant—was putting on a dazzling pink display as it scaled the building on a large trellis. "I have no idea how my aunt is going to move this plant to Bryce's house. It's been on this trellis for years. I'm not sure how she moved it before."

Yasmin stepped closer to look at Rosie. "That's an interesting variety of rose. I don't think I've ever seen one like it before." She peered at the petals.

"It's been in our family for generations."

"I don't even see any thorns on it." Yasmin was leaning in, examining the plant with a practiced botanist's eye.

"Really?" I studied Rosie more closely. I had never looked beyond the green leaves and the ultra-vibrant flowers she gave off most of the year.

"Are you sure it's a rose?"

"That's what I've always been told. Hold on." I took out my phone and scanned Rosie with a plant identification app.

"It's bringing up a similar rose, but I don't think it's the exact variety."

"Roses can be hard to pin down, with all the selection and crossbreeding that's been done over the years," Yasmin said.

"And the app's ability is only as good as the data it includes. Maybe I'll bring one of the roses to the academy at some point and use one of their advanced taxonomy books to place it. Should we go grab some of Aunt Vera's famous lavender scones on the way back to the academy?"

"You don't have to ask me twice."

Chapter Sixteen

The next week at Evergreen Academy, Professor East called all the second-year students into the tearoom.

"Do you know what this is about?" I whispered to Yasmin.

"My guess is field studies."

We filed into the tearoom, where sunlight was streaming from the glass panels along the wall. My breath caught in my chest as my eyes immediately gravitated to dark-chestnut hair and an olive complexion across the room, tattooed arms crossed as he leaned casually against a wall.

Callan.

My pulse sped up infinitesimally. So he was back.

His eyes met mine, and he nodded then seemed to turn pointedly to the front of the room.

I followed his gaze and saw Professor East, then swallowed as I recognized who was standing beside him. Wendy Rhodes, Callan's mother, was at our instructor's side, her own olive skin smooth and silky, her dark hair swept into an elegant chignon.

My heart rate kicked up—this time unpleasantly—as I remembered the words she'd spoken to me at the end of the spring semester: "We look forward to seeing you again soon, Briar."

Innocent words, but there had been a bite behind them that had felt like a threat in the moment. I hadn't had a chance to bring it up with Callan since and wasn't sure if I even should. That was his *mom* we were talking about.

Wendy Rhodes's eyes found mine, gaze assessing, and after a few moments of scrutiny, she turned her attention to Professor East.

Professor East cleared his throat and began without preamble. "As you all know, your second year of education at Evergreen Academy involves a field studies component. Traditionally, these opportunities have been carefully curated for you based on local ecological issues." He angled his body slightly toward Callan's mom, and I noticed that his movements were stiff.

I straightened in response.

"This year," he continued, "the assignments will be a little different. We have a prestigious member of the Magical Botanical Board of Regents here today. Regent Rhodes, would you like to tell us more?"

Wendy Rhodes stepped forward, a demure smile gracing her lips as she looked over the group of students gathered before her.

"Thank you, Professor East. As you all know, each second-year will participate in a field studies assignment. This year, the field studies opportunities have been hand selected by the Board of Regents. These studies will open many doors for you and, if you do well, should lead you directly into work or to opportunities for more advanced training."

The room was completely quiet, and students were casting glances at each other. Yasmin's posture was straighter than I had ever seen. My eyes shot to Callan. I wanted to know what he thought of all this. Is that what he had been helping to put into place these past few weeks? His eyes were firmly locked on his mother, his expression a stony mask of nonchalance.

"Keep in mind that your field studies this year will have an impact on future opportunities in our society. The field studies are your chance to present yourself in your best light. Highest performers will be fast-tracked to top careers. Treat this as a competition because it is."

And there it was. The added stress that would come with this new twist on the field studies. I noticed Yasmin tense beside me.

Professor East spoke again. "Now, I'm sure you will all have questions. Those can be brought directly to me. As always, the field study assignments for this year will be stashed in envelopes scattered throughout the campus. When you find one, read the assignment and determine if it is a good fit for you. If it is, please bring the envelope to Professor Tenella. If it is not, leave the envelope where you found it. That's it for now. Have a good evening."

There were murmurs all around as students filed out of the tearoom. "Shall we all get some tea and discuss this in our room?" Yasmin asked, voice too calm. I could tell that her type A brain was rapidly trying to determine what all of this meant for her future.

Everyone nodded, and I said, "I'll join you in a minute."

She noticed Callan across the room and smiled knowingly. "Take your time."

I paused at the beverage table and prepared two mugs of lavender tea, with a sprig of honeysuckle for Callan, then went to greet him.

"Hey, stranger." I handed him one of the mugs.

There was a distance in his eyes that seemed to clear when he focused on me, and he ran his gaze all over my face, as if checking for something. "Hey, local."

"So, that was interesting." I nodded toward where his mom and Professor East were still standing, locked in formal-looking conversation. All around us, the din of the room began to increase.

"My mom never misses a grand dramatic moment."

"Did you know it was coming? Field studies picked by the board?"

"Yes, it's been in the works all summer."

Things clicked into place then. "Is that why you were away?"

His jaw clenched slightly then relaxed as he took a sip of the tea. "I was recruited to help set them up. I served as a student ambassador." I could tell by the flat tone of his voice that doing so had not been his choice.

"This isn't the worst, right? Professor East made it sound like there are options. I'm sure you'll get a medical study, like you've always wanted."

"I'm afraid the choice has already been made for me."

My chest constricted, concern tugging at me. But before I could ask him to elaborate, Callan stepped away from me and rearranged his face into a neutral expression.

I startled, wondering why he had moved away, until I noticed who was joining us.

"Hello again, Briar," Wendy Rhodes said, nodding at me. "Am I interrupting?"

"Not at all," Callan said coolly.

Wendy turned to me. "What do you think of this exciting news?"

"Oh, it's quite the surprise," I said, keeping my tone pleasant. Everything in my body warned me to be tactful with this woman.

"Callan here will be using his field studies time to hone his political alliances. It's about time our family had another senator."

My gaze flicked to Callan as I internally blanched at the news. His face was still impressively blank. That couldn't be right. Medical research was what he'd wanted to do since he was a child. If the Board of Regents had set up the field studies, surely they would have made plenty of opportunities in medical research for him and others like him. Wouldn't they?

"A senator? I didn't realize that was something that could be arranged," I said, trying to keep my voice calm and professional despite wanting to drag Callan to safety and ask how he really felt about all of this.

Wendy gave a soft smile at that. "Well, not exactly. He will have to work at it like anyone else, but the right connections will certainly position him correctly. And if not a senator, there are always ambassadorships and appointments within the magical botanical congress. Do you have any political ambitions, Briar?" There was something in her tone that made me suspect she was fishing.

"Me? No, not at all. I've always planned to go to art school."

Wendy's brows rose slightly, though the movement was subtle, and her forehead remained smooth. "Art school? That's an... interesting choice. You're a magical botanist. Why art school?"

"I've always loved art. It comes naturally to me. And my mom went to art school. It's just something I have always envisioned myself doing."

Wendy pursed her deep-crimson lips. "How quaint. Well, we'll see how the year goes."

I tried not to prickle at the implication in her words and forced levity into my tone as I shifted the conversation away from my personal choices. "What brought on this change? Was the school having trouble sourcing field studies assignments?"

"We have found that, of late, the research opportunities the school has sponsored are a bit too... broad. Being a magical botanist affords you opportunities that others can never imagine, Briar. These curated studies will help facilitate that while ensuring they are approved by botanists in each affinity field. Don't you think your classmates deserve a clear path to top opportunities?"

"If there are options that fit everyone's goals and passions, yes."

Wendy's eyes slid to her son for a moment before returning to me. "Passions are... romantic. But this world needs focus, commitment. Botanists can't make change without power."

"And power can't have meaning without passion," I said lightly before taking a sip of my tea. Part of me wondered if I was playing with fire, sparring with her like this. But I didn't regret my words. Whether the boldness was inherent to me or fueled by the injustice of forcing Callan into a political career and ignoring his obvious talent for medicine, I couldn't be sure.

Wendy sighed. "You're young. And you've been raised in this tiny town. Your world is small, but it doesn't have to be. These updated studies are what our students need. You'll see." She turned to Callan. "Walk me out to the car?"

He followed her without turning to look at me, and I tried not to stiffen. The way his body language toward me had completely shifted at the arrival of his mom had thrown me. I tried not to feel stung by the distance he put between us. Was he trying to signal to her that he and I weren't friends?

But then I felt the touch of a warm breeze against the back of my neck, tenderly reassuring. I inhaled sharply, knowing exactly where it had come from. So it had been an act—and a convincing one.

I watched as they left the teahouse together, Callan's body language still tight, and he never cracked a smile.

For the next few minutes, I lingered near the beverages, sipping on my tea, until I realized that I was waiting for Callan to return. Finally, reason told me I had no idea if he'd be back in the teahouse that evening, and my friends were waiting for a debrief up in our rooms.

I went up the stairs to the second floor and found my three friends in Coral and Aurielle's room. Yasmin had a green knit scarf twisted up between her hands and was squeezing it like a stress ball.

Oh boy.

"What did I miss?" I asked, taking a seat in the fluffy papasan chair near Aurielle's bed.

"We're discussing whether our futures are doomed or hopeful based on the new field studies developments," Aurielle said.

"Got it. What's the verdict so far?" I wanted to remain neutral until I heard them out, afraid that Wendy's words had already swayed me.

"I'm not sure yet, but this puts pressure on field studies even more than before," Yasmin said.

The dorm's window rustled as something whisked through the crack between the window and sill.

"What is happening?" Coral asked as the leaves spun straight into my lap.

I plucked the note out of the pile, trying not to grin like a fool in front of my friends.

"I have a feeling B's about to ditch us," Yasmin said.

Coral gasped. "Is that from Rhodes? Sneaking out at midnight to meet your lover, Juliet?"

I glanced at the clock on the nightstand, which read nine p.m. "It's hardly midnight, Coral."

"So you admit he's your lover?" She raised her eyebrows, and I threw a fern-shaped pillow at her.

"No! But maybe I can get some intel on these new developments," I said.

They all made expressions that said they didn't believe me.

"Waylon never sends me leaf messages," I heard Coral say as I made to leave the room.

"He doesn't have a tree affinity," Yasmin said. "What do you expect?"

"He could come up with *something*. Those two aren't even dating, and he shows more interest th..."

It was the last I heard before I closed the door softly behind me and headed for the forest.

Chapter Seventeen

When I climbed into the treehouse, Callan was already there, leaves rustling through his fingers like a game of cat's cradle as he leaned against the inside hollow of the tree.

"You called?" I asked, finding a stool and planting myself on it firmly.

"Thanks, I wanted to see you after..."

I studied him. His posture was relaxed, but there was that underlying tension that I so often noticed. He was good at hiding it, but once you knew him, you could spot it. The way I had learned to notice it was because of the times it *hadn't* been there. Times when we'd been having fun.

"Yeah, what was that back there?" I tried to keep my voice gentle rather than accusatory.

Callan let out a breath. "It's better if my mom doesn't know how close... friends we are."

My stomach flipped. What had that little pause meant?

"Bad news. I think she already does. When I met Kale Brightmoor at the autumn equinox, he made it sound like it was common knowledge that I was *friendly* with the trees."

His jaw ticked. "Did he?"

"I tried to brush it off and explain I'm friends with a lot of students of different affinities, but I don't know if he bought it."

"I was worried about this. I wonder if someone saw me escorting you out on midsummer."

"So do we just act like we're strangers when anyone from the board is around?" I asked, thinking that seemed like a simple-enough idea.

Callan sighed and shook his head then ran a hand through his hair. "I'm afraid there's a little more to it than that. The board has extra eyes and ears at the school this year."

"What do you mean? Will your mom be sticking around?"

"Not human eyes and ears."

When I must have looked terribly confused, Callan explained. "I doubt they have permission from Professor East, but I've sensed scouting plants since returning to campus. I don't know who is keeping an eye on who, but it's safest to assume we're being reported on."

"Scouting plants?" That particular bit of botanical magic was new to me.

"They're unsanctioned without approval. But, again, I think we're beyond that now. We just have to be... cautious. I want you to fly under the radar as much as possible through all this."

"Okay. And speaking of all this... how are you feeling about the whole senator thing?" I said the last part softly, leaving an opening for him to share how he felt.

Callan released the leaves he was flipping through his fingers, and they flew out of the tree on a silent breeze. "Please don't tell anyone about that. If I have anything to do with it, it will never happen. But for now, I have to go along with it..." His voice trailed off, and he sighed.

"But why? I mean, you're an adult. You can choose your path, right? Professor East wouldn't force you into a field studies assignment you didn't want."

Callan sighed and scrubbed a hand through his hair. "I'm afraid the decision has already been made." He glanced out the hole that formed a window in the treehouse.

"I see," I said, though I didn't see at all. I had to cool my temper on his behalf and not judge his reactions. I couldn't imagine what it would be like to have such an adversarial relationship with your family. My aunt was my greatest cheerleader in the world. She would never try to control me like Callan's parents did him.

I decided to shift gears. "Since you seem to have some inside intel, any idea what my field studies assignment will be?"

"I think yours is going to come as a surprise to everyone."

"Wonderful nonanswer," I teased. An idea occurred to me then, and my face fell once more. "Wait. Since my powers are blocked on campus, will that impact my ability to find an envelope?"

Callan shook his head. "I don't think so. The envelopes are set up with the professor's plant powers, not yours."

I let out a breath. "I hope you're right. If I can't get a field studies assignment, I'm officially screwed this year."

"You'll get one."

I was taken aback by the sureness in his voice.

Callan's face relaxed, and he gave my shoe a gentle nudge with his. "It's really good to see you again, local."

I couldn't help but smile. "I thought you might be a college dropout with how long it took you to come back."

"What? And leave you here to have all the fun without me?" He spun on his stool so that he was facing me directly. We were sitting so close that our knees brushed and that scarily attractive cologne he was wearing momentarily distracted me.

"Well, you already know Meadow and I can get ourselves into some good trouble. We need you here to bail us out."

Callan let out a breath. "I don't know. Keeping an eye on both of you would be a full-time job. I might need some scouting plants of my own. So, fill me in on what I've missed. How many new tree affinity first-years are there?"

"A bunch," I said and embarked on filling him in on the first few weeks of class. I soaked in the time with him like this, where he was lighthearted and his passion for science and plant life broke through all his other burdens. For this one evening, at least, life felt just as it should.

Before I knew it, I checked my watch and was shocked to see how late it was. Coral's words rang in my mind. *Sneaking out at midnight to meet your lover, Juliet?*

I was loath to end the time with him, but I needed to get back to my dorm before even Yasmin was tempted to speculate. We began to clean up the notes and sketches we'd made all over the table, and our hands briefly touched. I felt a spark of warmth shoot all the way through me.

I pooled my courage and broke the silence in a quiet voice. "So, there are no scouting plants here in the treehouse, correct?"

Callan paused what he was doing and leaned a hip against the table, crossing his arms. "Why? Have some secrets to spill?"

"Just wondering if we always have to watch our backs or if we can be... friends when no one is watching."

Callan was so silent and still for a moment that I worried he'd turned into a tree.

"Callan?"

"You're trouble, local."

I made an innocent face. "What? It was just a question."

Callan stepped closer, so close that the sandalwood and peach fragrance felt like it nestled into my hair. "No, there are no scouting plants in here. But if we become... better friends *here*, I'll have a very difficult time faking it out *there*." He nodded his head toward the window.

From the way his intense expression was turning me into a puddle, I had to admit he had a point. But I wanted a little more. After an entire summer and the first weeks of school spent eagerly waiting to see him, I needed to know where we stood. "Fair. But hypothetically speaking, what if we were both the world's greatest actors?"

Callan's mouth twitched at the corner. "We aren't. And with the way things are going this year, I don't want there to be a whiff of something for the board to pick up on between us."

"*Is* there something to pick up on between us?" I pressed, putting all my chips on the table.

Callan looked me straight in the eyes. "You know there is."

I sucked in a breath but tried to play it cool.

"But as far as anyone else is concerned... we have been and still are tutor and tutee?" I suggested, relieved that his words confirmed how I thought we both felt but wanting to confirm how things had to be.

Callan took a step back and leaned his head back against the wall, a little smile touching his lips. "Still think you need tutoring?"

"I can't tap into my powers on campus. So, yeah, I think I could still benefit from a little extra support."

"Then yes. I'm still your tutor, hypothetically speaking." His voice was low and playful.

I didn't know what to do with myself after all the revelations and partial commitments in this conversation. It felt like all the air had been sucked out of the treehouse. So I did what seemed easiest and bought myself some time.

"Well, I better go before my roommate wonders if I got lost in the woods."

"Your roommate?" Callan raised an eyebrow.

"Right." I'd forgotten that he didn't know yet. "I moved onto campus."

"Why?"

"My aunt's wedding is next month. I wanted her and her fiancé to be able to start their life together without feeling like they're waiting for me to move out."

Callan pushed off the wall, and my eyes were briefly drawn to the tattoos on his arms as he tucked his hands into his pockets. He leaned in and whispered, "Then I guess I'll be seeing you around much more, local. Try to stay out of trouble."

I smiled, suppressing a shiver at his proximity. The cologne that I had been savoring all night lingered in the air, and I didn't want him to step away.

"Worried I'll sleepwalk into your room at night?" *Whoa.* That had slipped out, and I had *not* meant it the way it sounded.

Callan's eyes flashed, and he gave me a delighted little smile that set my heart thundering.

"My treehouse is your treehouse. If you can get past the protective Floracantus, that is." He turned and hopped down to the ground then, leaving my cheeks flushed and the delicious sandalwood and peach scent lingering in the air.

Chapter Eighteen

When I entered the teahouse a few days later, there was fevered conversation happening among the second-years. I made myself a coffee then joined my friends at our usual table.

"What's all the excitement about?" I asked.

"The first field studies envelope was found this morning by an aquatic affinity. Conway went out for an early morning swim and found an envelope made of seaweed waiting on the shore when he surfaced," Aurielle explained.

"His assignment is something to do with developing aquatic plant-based antibiotics," Coral added.

"Well, that assignment doesn't sound too different from before, right?" I asked.

"A sample size of one isn't very big, but you're right, that isn't a major departure from previous years," Yasmin said.

"Am I the only one who's a bit nervous? What if I get an assignment I don't want?" Aurielle asked.

"Professor East said you can turn it down. Just leave the envelope where it is," I said.

"But what if I don't find another one?" Aurielle frowned.

"Is that possible? Don't all second-years do field studies?" I asked.

"I can only speak for how it's been done in previous years. If you passed on too many, they might stick you on a weed removal project or something," Yasmin said.

We all groaned at that idea, and I vowed not to pass on the first decent assignment I found. I was up for a lot of things, but an academic year of weed removal was not one of them.

After breakfast, we split to get ready for class in our rooms then met up outside. Aside from the fact that I couldn't tap into my magic, I loved our Advanced Ecological Studies class. We were learning research techniques that would likely be useful once we started our field studies, and I enjoyed spending the time outside while it wasn't too cold yet.

Today, we were conducting population studies with Professor Sato. I made detailed sketches and notes in my Anno Duo notebook as we examined a bed of seaside succulents on a makeshift coastline by the pond.

My eyes flicked to Callan a couple of times during class. He was working a few yards away in the forest with the other tree affinities, studying a different population. Every time I looked over, he was working at full speed, barely glancing away from his notebook.

I couldn't help replaying what he had said in the treehouse. There was something between us even if we couldn't act on it right now. I wasn't sure how long the warring emotions of elation and disappointment those confirmations brought on could exist in me, but I was going to do my best to act natural in front of our classmates.

Still, I couldn't help it if an inquiring question or two slipped out. "Is it just me, or is Callan extra focused this morning?"

"Extra sexy, maybe," Coral said with a smirk. I rolled my eyes.

"I'd be throwing myself into my work, too, if my mom was interfering at my college," Yasmin said sympathetically. "I get that she's on the Board of Regents, but still."

I didn't say what I was thinking, which was that Callan was facing more than interference with the school. His mom was pressuring him to go into politics when anyone who even slightly knew Callan could see that that path wouldn't make him happy.

At the end of the class period, I strolled over to him.

"Have a second?" I asked.

He shrugged his book bag across his body. "I always have time for my tutee." There was a playful edge in his voice, and I grinned as I fell into step alongside him.

"Want a quick tree walk? I need to collect some cellulose fibers from the silk-cotton tree for Plant Adaptations, and you can get to it more easily than me." It was a blatant excuse to spend a few more minutes with him, but it wasn't false.

A lazy smile pulled at the corner of his mouth. "Always tempting me with a good time. Let's do it."

We scaled a nearby tree, and Callan led the way while I stayed close on his heels. The trees dipped their branches together to form a solid path for him as we approached, and I matched his pace to catch the tail end of it.

"I heard one of the aquatic affinities found an assignment today," I began.

"Right. That was Conway."

"And it seems to be a medicine-related project," I prompted.

"Yeah, I'm happy for him. I think it will be a good fit."

"Maybe you can join him sometimes?"

He shook his head. "It doesn't work like that. But I'll make do with what I have."

"Wait a minute. Do you know your assignment already?"

He gave a little shrug, still putting one foot in front of the other. "I found the envelope last night when I left the treehouse."

Memory of that conversation had my cheeks burning, but

thankfully, Callan was walking in front and couldn't see me. Given that his assignment had arrived last night, he'd likely been the first one to receive an assignment, not Conway. But it fit. He wasn't one to tell tales about himself. The news would spread like wildfire on its own, eventually, since he was a founder's descendant.

"Do you want to tell me about it?" I didn't want to press too hard, given what his mom had said about the plans for his future, but I was dying to know.

"It came in a pine-needle envelope when I was walking back to campus, right at the edge of the forest. It was floating past me in a rush of leaves."

My heart rate sped up, but I kept quiet and let him continue.

"I'll be working at one of the local field offices."

"That doesn't sound so bad," I offered tentatively. The local field offices weren't known to be overly political.

When Callan spoke again, his tone was calm, almost disassociated. "It comes with a requirement that I report our findings directly to our connections in Sacramento."

Aw. Now, I understood, and my heart sank. Was that why he'd been quiet during class? I tried to put a positive spin on it. "Maybe you'll have an opportunity to share some of your medical findings with the botanists in Sacramento. I'm sure once they see how much you excel at it, your advisor will have no choice but to support you in that goal."

"I don't know if that opportunity will arise. But maybe... Maybe you're right," he said after a moment.

I didn't say the rest of what I was thinking. That life was short. Sometimes cruelly short. I closed my eyes momentarily, thinking of my mother, gone at age thirty-two. A woman so full of hopes and dreams that she could have conquered the entire world if she'd never been in that car accident. But I had never shared any of that with Callan.

I cleared my throat and stumbled forward as I missed a step.

Immediately, I felt a gust of wind press along my back. Once I was stable, I noted Callan hadn't even looked back at the disturbance.

Of course. He had made a wind cocoon for me like he had done for Aurielle and me during Orchard Lantern Tag. I hadn't felt it this time, which meant he'd been intentionally subtle.

"All I'm saying is don't hold yourself back because of other's intentions. Take your opportunities—or challenges—and make them your own. That's what you've taught me to do."

Callan turned around then, and I almost ran into him. He touched my arms gently, steadying me. "That's good advice. Thank you. I'll try."

I startled, not expecting him to agree with me that easily. Maybe the emotion behind my words had come through despite my efforts to hide it.

Callan removed his hands from my arms and turned back around. "The silk-cotton tree is coming up on our left. Do you want me to grab the fibers for you? How much do you need?"

I walked him through my instructions but couldn't stop noticing the ghost of the feeling of his hands on my arms. I was a candle, and Callan was the wick whose light lingered on me with the briefest touch of flame.

When I got back to the academy, I went straight for the library, hoping to read, sketch and clear my head. I settled onto a cushioned seat in the window and opened one of the da Vinci journals. There was a lot to distract me from learning more about my ancestry, but I wanted to at least skim through the journal that was available to me every few weeks. I noticed new details to da Vinci's sketches with each subsequent viewing of a page.

After about thirty minutes of copying some of da Vinci's sketches into my own notebook, a soft tapping sounded on the window behind my seat in the library, and I turned. Leaves were swirling outside. With a glance in either direction to make sure that I was alone, I opened the lower window, let the leaves in, then sealed it closed again. I found the note mixed in with the leaves.

As my eyes scanned the paper, my excitement morphed to a sharp curiosity. The only person who had sent me notes this way was Callan, and this was not his handwriting. The note wasn't handwritten at all but instead contained raised typeface text, as if created by a typewriter.

Follow the lights at midnight. Come alone.

Chapter Nineteen

The din of the library faded away as I flipped the note over, scouring for anything I might have missed. The back of the paper contained a stamped logo consisting of roots and swirling vines. A feeling of déjà vu came over me as recognition dawned. The same logo had been carved into the tiny fairy-sized arch I had seen embedded on the brick wall on the summer solstice. I read the note again.

Follow the lights at midnight. Come alone.

That didn't sound daunting at all.

What on earth was this? Some kind of invitation, clearly, but to what? And who had it come from? Was I really going to wherever these so-called lights led in the middle of the night—by myself?

And who uses typewriters these days?

I cleaned up the workspace where I had been studying, stuffed the note in my pocket, and headed to my room. When I entered, Yasmin was there, everything seeming perfectly normal. She was writing in her notebook at her desk, the moonlight shining through our window like an iridescent beacon.

My first instinct was to tell her about the note, but the *come alone* part was a clear warning to keep this secret. Could the message have been from Professor East? But why wouldn't he just invite me to his office if he needed to meet?

Yasmin stretched her arms over her head and yawned. "I'm beat. Affinity studies were hard core today. Professor Sato is really pushing us second-years."

"I'm sure you crushed it," I assured her.

We got ready for bed, but I didn't try to fall asleep. Instead, I kept an eye on my watch and snuck out of bed just before midnight once I heard the soft breathing that indicated Yasmin was sleeping. I dressed in dark colors, made sure the note was in my pocket, then snuck out of the room.

I tiptoed down the stairs and through the central atrium, not spotting another soul. "Follow the lights," I whispered, scanning each area as I passed through it.

Once outside, directly beyond the front entrance to the main atrium, I spotted a moonflower, altered for bioluminescence, glowing with a soft white light.

As I scanned the area, I saw another incandescent white flower in the distance, near the line of trees where the forest began. From there, the flowers appeared in roughly twenty-to-fifty-foot intervals, leading deeper into the forest. The white petals were like solar lights, guiding me forward.

"Hopefully, this isn't some kind of strange prank," I murmured. Tension was coiling through my body, my instincts debating whether this was a good idea.

But despite the tension, the feeling of inquisitiveness I was experiencing was even stronger. Despite the novelty of the mission, I was encouraged to keep going. I eyed the flowers suspiciously. Were they emitting some kind of calming fragrance?

At a flash of light above, I craned my neck and saw that one of the flowers was growing in the canopy of the trees.

I realized I was expected to tree walk and wished I had access to my powers. But then I looked ahead and saw the dark imposing figure of the brick wall. It appeared the flowers were leading me over the wall, where I would be able to use my affinity powers on the other side if they were needed.

A jolt of excitement hit me as I spotted wooden foot panels on the tree closest to the wall. Taking that as a sign, I used the panels to climb the tree more easily. At the top, a pendant exactly like the one Meadow had leant me on midsummer was hanging from a branch beside a moonflower lamp. The words Carry Me were printed on a delicate paper tag.

Was this whole thing some scheme of Meadow's?

I palmed the Shasta lily pendant then carefully stepped across to a large branch of a tree on the other side of the wall where another flower was glowing.

My affinity powers kicked in immediately, the tree branches rearranging themselves to make a path for me. There was another flower beacon in the distance.

Enjoying the freeing feeling of tree walking, I made my way through the trees for what felt like ten to fifteen minutes.

Finally, I noticed a few moonflowers on the ground and took that as my cue to climb down. As I descended, I heard a soft whooshing noise that hadn't been audible from the canopy.

I turned toward the sound and then walked until the forest opened to a small clearing. I sucked in a breath as the moonlight glimmered off the water. The view before me was enchanting.

There were a few thin waterfalls, at least twenty feet tall, cascading into a large, glimmering pool. Water lilies floated along the surface, and water bubbled over smooth rocks in the shallow portions of the water.

My heart rate ratcheted up as I gazed into the natural pool.

The moonflowers were glowing from the bottom of the lake. Were the flowers directing me to swim *under* the waterfalls?

"Okay, aquatic affinity, don't fail me now." I assessed the area one more time but couldn't make out much beyond what the moonflowers and stars above were illuminating.

Taking a deep breath of determination, I removed my shoes and sweatshirt and stepped into the water. I expected a shock of cold but was pleasantly surprised that it was the temperature of a soothing bath.

With one last look up at the rushing waterfalls and the moon above it, I inhaled a deep breath and dove down, kicking my legs to propel me forward. My eyes stayed open as I swam, the moonflowers lighting the way.

There was a ripple along my skin as I sensed the aquatic plants calling to me, as if curious about my visit. I counted as I pulled my arms through the water, trying to stay focused on my path instead of the plants as I swam through the near dark, the moonflowers providing a continuous shimmer of light as I streamed through the water.

Twenty-one... twenty-two... twenty-three... and before I could count to twenty-four, the pool ended, and I shot upward. My head emerged from the water, and I breathed deeply then looked around. I climbed out of the shallow pool to step into a damp, moss-covered cave. A few crystals were sparkling, lit by some scattered moonflowers, but otherwise, the area was dimly lit.

The entrance to the cave was overflowing with plant life, various shades of green sprouting from the sides and top of the cave as if by magic. There was an odd assortment of plants—ones that shouldn't be growing out of rock in that fashion. I saw the expected plants for a cave, like moss, but also ferns, trailing flowers, grasses. A tuft of strawberries hung from the ceiling, practically asking to be eaten.

I hesitated by the edge of the pool, not seeing the moonflowers leading anywhere else.

"Nicely done," came a voice from behind me. I jumped and spun around but relaxed slightly when I recognized a fellow second-year. It was Kaito, my harvester affinity partner from the autumn equinox. He held a fluffy pink plant in his hands.

"Before we go further, I must ask you a few questions."

I thought this situation was utterly strange, but the high from connecting with the aquatic plants and the magic glimmering of the cave had me wanting to know why I had been called here.

I nodded. "Ask away."

"Everything about tonight is secret and meant only for a privileged few. Do you swear never to tell anyone else about what you have seen or heard tonight or to reveal this location?"

I debated it for a moment, finding it difficult to commit to a promise like that when I still didn't know what was going on. But my intuition was telling me it was okay, and I decided to trust it. "I swear," I agreed.

Well, I guess you're going all in now, Briar.

The fluffy blooms of the pink plants were positioned perfectly upright, not extended toward me like a floral should be doing.

Kaito glanced at it. "Okay, you're clear. Follow me."

We proceeded deeper into the cave, the air smelling like moss and something sweet. I looked up to see trailing honeysuckle and abundant wisteria lining the ceiling. I began to reach out with my floral affinities to examine their cells but was interrupted by Kaito coming to a pause.

"Our last recruit is here." He stepped to the side, and I took in the view in front of me. We were in a large cavern, the limestone interior lit completely with lanterns and moonflowers lining the ground beside the circular walls. And were those... yes, lightning bugs were flitting around the cave. I had never seen one before since they weren't fit for the climate here. Or so I had thought. As usual, Evergreen Academy was proving to me that nothing was impossible, even outside of its official grounds.

I recognized some of the others who were gathered in the

center of the room and placed each of their affinity powers as a pattern emerged. There was Laurus—a top herbs affinity second-year I had once done a project with, Hollis—the fern founder's descendant—and other excelling students with floral, grasses, and aquatic affinities.

Lastly, my eyes fell on Meadow, founder's descendant for mosses. With Kaito having a harvester affinity, every lead affinity was represented except for trees and defensive plants.

"Congratulations to each of you for making it here along your individual paths," Kaito said. "Remember how you came as that's how you will return if you are called here again."

"And where is here?" Nalin, the aquatics affinity student, asked.

"The falls are known as Moonlit Falls. The rest of this area"—he waved a hand around the nonsensically plant-covered cave—"is colloquially known as the Evergreen Conservatory. Knowledge of its existence is by invitation only."

There were murmurs as my classmates sorted through that nugget of news. Evergreen Conservatory? I knew there were nine plant conservatories in the United States, one for each of the plant affinities. But Kaito was right—this regional one was obviously a well-kept secret.

"Let's get this party started," a wonderfully familiar voice said, and Callan stepped out from a dark area of the cave.

Callan. *Of course* he was part of this.

"And what is *this party*?" I asked.

Meadow was grinning broadly, as if she already knew.

Callan's eyes snapped to mine with a twinkle of amusement before roving over the rest of the group. "We're called the Root and Vine Society. And you are our newest recruits."

Chapter Twenty

"The what and what society?" Laurus asked, clearly skeptical about what was going on.

I couldn't blame him. We were in a cave, after midnight, under circumstances cloaked in mystery. It was captivating, and I was brimming with excitement.

I waited for an answer with bated breath, glad someone else had asked.

"The Root and Vine Society. A tradition of Evergreen Academy that has been dormant for some time. We decided it was time to revive it," Kaito said.

"What does this society do?" Laurus pressed. I could see the wheels in his brain spinning, trying to process a new facet of the academy he hadn't been aware of.

"We hope that you all will be able to help us determine that. Our primary motivation is to protect the integrity and beauty of Evergreen Academy," Kaito said.

"Is this about the changes happening with the school and the board?" This time, it was Meadow who spoke. Her face was bored, but there was a sharpness to her posture that betrayed her. She was interested.

Kaito nodded. "We know there are students here that feel... less than satisfied with the changes that are occurring. We would like to help give the original purpose of the school the upper hand."

"How will we do that?" Laurus asked.

Callan stepped forward. "By acquiring something that the board has long sought but so far has been unsuccessful in getting."

"Such as?" Meadow asked. I noticed that Hollis was watching quietly and I wondered if, as Callan's best friend and a founder's descendant, he already knew where this was headed.

Callan spoke again. "The Root and Vine Society was originally founded to track down an object of great value. They were unsuccessful, and eventually the group disbanded. The object we seek is a book. We do not believe that the *Compendium Floracantus* we study here is the only book of Floracantus in existence. In fact, we believe another was penned at nearly the same time."

Beside me, one of the other students gasped, though I didn't fully grasp the significance of his words.

"You're not talking about"—Laurus's eyes widened—"the *Vanished Compendium*?"

"I am," Callan said.

"That's just a fairy tale," Ravenna, the grasses affinity student, said.

"Or maybe the fairy tale was invented to keep the truth alive," Callan countered.

"But how long has the society been looking for this... *Vanished Compendium*?" I asked. "The *Compendium Floracantus* is hundreds of years old, right? If this other book exists, why hasn't anyone found it by now?"

Kaito spoke first. "There is reason to believe the book *has* been found a few times throughout history, but information about it was tightly controlled. Historical documents, and lore"—he nodded toward Ravenna—"indicate it disappeared again for good about one hundred years ago. Various groups have been searching for it nearly ever since."

"What historical documents?" Ravenna asked.

"There's a top-secret letter, copies of which are stored in the vaulted areas of some of the libraries at the magical botanical conservatories, which reference the book. Scholars of the Root and Vine Society have authenticated the document," Kaito explained.

"Can we see a copy of this letter?" Laurus asked.

"Perhaps in time. There are no copies here," Kaito said.

"So, you invited us here to... what? You think we can help find the *Vanished Compendium*?" Laurus asked.

"The school is at a crossroads. We can accept the new changes that are already being implemented, or we can fight for what the school was and what we want it to be. With a tool like the *Vanished Compendium*, we would have leverage. At a minimum, our goal is to keep it out of the hands of those who would use it to consolidate their power even further. Intel says they have increased their search efforts," Kaito said.

"How were we selected?" Heath, the floral affinity botanist, asked. "I know they're founders' descendants"—he nodded toward Meadow and Hollis—"and she's got all the affinities"—he waved toward me—"but how were the rest of us chosen?"

"You've all been carefully observed and found to be the strongest in your affinity groups, under various criteria that we will not disclose here. Suffice it to say that we believe each of you would not only be a benefit to this cause but would be a trustworthy member of the society," Kaito explained.

"Can we invite others?" Laurus asked.

"We have deliberately chosen to keep our group to one person per affinity now, like it was with the original Root and Vine Society. Each of you has influence within your affinities. Plant the seeds, and we'll grow our group if and when the time is right," Kaito said.

The grasses affinity botanist, Ravenna, held up her Shasta lily pendant. "Are you going to explain how these work? How were we able to climb over the wall without setting off any alarms?"

I cast a look at Meadow, remembering when we'd used the pendants together months before.

"We won't be explaining their mechanism," Kaito said. "It's enough to know that as long as you have it in your possession, you may safely cross through the petal portal and enter the Evergreen Conservatory. This should only be done on official Root and Vine society business."

Petal portal. I absorbed the term. Callan hadn't given me much detail about it on midsummer, but for some reason hearing its official name made it even more intriguing. No wonder he and Meadow hadn't answered my questions about the pendants before. They were members-only privileges for a secret society. One Meadow apparently knew about before she was even invited.

"There are only nine of these pendants in existence," Callan said. "One for each affinity group." He, too, cast an eye at Meadow, and I wondered if he had already figured out how she had gotten her hands on the moss pendant early. "Lose yours, and... don't lose yours."

The cave was silent, and I felt for the pendant in my pocket. I would have to place it on a necklace or something more secure than the small clasp it was currently attached to.

"What happens now?" Meadow asked, seemingly over the small details that she was obviously already privy to.

"Now"—Callan stepped forward—"you decide if you want in."

"But we've already seen and heard all this," Ravenna said. "What if we say no?"

"We have ways of helping you forget this, but we don't think that will be necessary," Kaito said, and I raised my eyebrows as the cave became eerily quiet once more. I would have to press Callan on what that meant later. "Now, if you do not wish to proceed with initiation tasks for the Root and Vine Society, you are free to leave."

No one moved. Including me. My curiosity was working overtime, and I had been hoping for a way to get involved with protecting the school for weeks. There was no way I was turning back now.

"Excellent. Now, for your next steps, initiation requires each of you to complete a series of tasks. These have been revived from when the society was previously active. There are four pillars to our work: stealth navigation, distractions, communication, and detection. When you get a message with our insignia, you'll know your tests are about to start. But first..." Kaito nodded to Callan, who waved a hand. A floating tray of leaves brought a small metal cup to each of us. "A toast. To celebrate our newest recruits."

"Do you think it's spiked?" Hollis leaned toward me to whisper, a merry expression on his face. It seemed like he was excited about the prospect of a little extra something in this mystery drink.

I sniffed the tiny cup, which contained no more than one swallow worth of a citrusy liquid. I began to prod it with my affinity powers to determine its origins.

Callan caught my eye and gave me a quick nod.

Around us, the other students began to drink, so I tilted my head and tossed the liquid back. It was sweet with an aftertaste of something spicy, and it went down smoothly.

"Spike free. What a shame." Hollis winked, and I rolled my eyes, though I was secretly appreciative of his humor taking the edge off the situation. Everyone else in the room was stock-still, except for Meadow.

Callan's leaf tray collected the empty cups, and Kaito grinned. "Okay, that's it for tonight. Thank you for coming, and we hope to officially welcome you all into the Root and Vine Society soon."

My fellow botanists began to leave, but I examined the cave, wondering if any more surprises were lurking within its damp interior. *Evergreen Conservatory.*

My eyes sought Callan, but he was having a whispered conversation with Kaito. I decided it was better not to try to talk to him now. For now, I was just another recruit. I'd grill him later.

I swam the reverse direction under the waterfall and tree walked back to the campus wall then surreptitiously made my way through the forest and back to the academy. I was tiptoeing through the silent central atrium when I spotted Hollis about to head up the stairs.

"Well, this was an interesting turn of events." He was whispering, but the volume was still much too loud for my comfort level. I was intent on sneaking back into my room completely unnoticed by others at the academy.

"Did you know about it?" I asked.

"I had a suspicion this might be coming. We grew up hearing lore of the Root and Vine Society but heard it was defunct. It's not surprising that Rhodes revived it. Okay, I'm off to get my beauty sleep."

"We'll be lucky to get three hours shut-eye tonight," I replied with a yawn.

"Worth it. You're in the big leagues now." The excitement in Hollis's voice was infectious.

Our school had a secret society, and I had been hand selected to be a part of it. The idea of finding a book that had been lost, possibly for centuries, had my curious mind intrigued. But more than anything, we finally had a way to fight back against unwanted changes at Evergreen Academy, and that, more than anything else, stirred a fire deep in my soul.

Chapter Twenty-One

I was on edge all morning after my midnight waterfall excursion, waiting for Yasmin to say that she'd heard me showering in the middle of the night, but my friends acted like it was any other day.

During our last class period, when I couldn't hold it in any longer, I approached Callan. We were walking back to the academy from where we had been conducting soil health studies in the forest.

"Do you have some time to talk tomorrow. About... you know," I asked in a low voice.

"I'm going to be gone all day tomorrow."

"Is it a field studies thing?"

"No, something else."

"Wow, real forthcoming today, aren't you?"

Callan shook his head, but a slight smile tugged at the corner of his lips. "It's a hobby. Something I do with some local friends."

Local friends? I had no idea that Callan was friends with any of the nonmagical locals. "Since you're not going to tell me, I'm going to imagine the most embarrassing thing possible." I mimed a shocked expression. "Are you all going to ride unicycles together?"

"That's harder than it looks," Callan said, but his expression relaxed, and he ran a hand through his hair. "We're going rock climbing."

My eyebrows rose. "Really? Where?"

"Castle Crags. Some of the best climbing in the country."

I could picture it. On the weekends when I was at work or at my aunt's house, Callan had been out in the mountains, climbing rock walls. As if magical tree walking wasn't enough, he needed to push himself to new heights in a situation where his powers weren't in control.

My chest tightened. I had a feeling this was something Callan did when he needed an escape. When the realities of the impossible pressures his parents put on him were threatening to bubble to the surface. But I didn't say any of that because he hadn't said it.

"That's pretty badass."

"You want to come? It's remote out there. It could be a good place to talk."

I straightened, surprise coursing through me. "Is that a real offer?"

"Don't think your *tutor*"—he put a suggestive emphasis on the word—"could teach you how to rock climb?"

"I mean, my life would *literally* be in your hands, so I think that would be taking things to the next level. Don't you?" I said it playfully, but Callan's expression changed to something I couldn't read, and I felt a flush creep up my chest.

But then he took a step closer. "I guess it would be. In the tutoring sense."

"I'm in," I said before he could change his mind.

His eyes flashed in delight. "Okay then. Set your alarm, local. We leave at five a.m."

WHEN THE SOFT CHIME OF THE ANALOG ALARM CLOCK went off the next morning—well before the sun rose—I jumped out of bed. I wasn't sure if Callan knew I was a morning person, but if he was expecting me to roll into this activity a bleary mess, he was going to be disappointed. I stopped at the teahouse to fill a travel thermos of light roast coffee.

When I made it to the parking lot, Callan was loading gear into the back of his truck. As usual, my eyes were drawn to the tattoos on his uncovered forearms, which flexed as he lifted the coiled ropes into the truck bed.

"Need any help?" I asked then took a deep drink of my coffee. There was a hint of cinnamon to it that warmed my body like a fireplace.

"No, that's the last of it." He eyed my travel cup. "Trouble waking up?"

"Not in the slightest," I said brightly.

He eyed me critically, as if suspicious of my alertness. It was still dark—the sun not having risen yet—and the parking area was quiet except for the two of us. "I'm wondering if we should have been booking our tutoring sessions at the crack of dawn instead of the evenings last year."

"You live and learn," I said breezily.

We climbed into his truck, and Callan cranked the heater. I was wearing a bulky crewneck sweatshirt, prepared to remove it once we reached the trailhead.

We were quiet most of the drive, Callan's music playing on low volume. I sipped my coffee and pretended to be interested in the landmarks outside the window—ones I had seen hundreds of times—and tried not to get nervous about rock climbing. I typically liked new experiences, but this one felt well out of my wheelhouse.

At Castle Crags, we parked and began our hike in, Callan carrying most of the gear. The dramatic jagged rock formations that we would be climbing loomed overhead.

"Let's pause here for a second," Callan said after we'd been walking for about ten minutes. He stepped to the side of the trail and turned around.

I followed his movement and sucked in a breath at the brilliant sunrise peeking over the mountain. Swaths of orange, red, and pink crisscrossed the sky, illuminating the mountain and forests in front of us. "It's breathtaking."

Callan grinned. He was adorable, loaded up with all our gear. He looked like he could be a guide on a mountaineering show. A very young, cute guide.

"We get focused on the plants because of our connection to them. But they wouldn't exist without the sun. This is my favorite time to be out here."

"So you're a morning person too. Good to know we have something in common."

Callan gave me a sideways look. "You don't think we have anything else in common?"

"Besides our tree affinities? Let me think." I was teasing him a little. It was too much fun to watch his face while I did it. "I work at a café. You're destined to be the world's greatest physician. I'm an artist; you're a brilliant scientist. Right brain, left brain type of thing. Let's see..." I continued to list things as we began our ascent on the trail. "You're a founder's descendant, I was cursed by the founders—"

"You weren't cursed," Callan interjected with a lighthearted sigh.

"According to you. But is there a better way to put it?"

"You ran afoul of the founders. Something I've been actively trying to prevent from happening further."

"Speaking of... Has there been any movement on the whole senator front, or is your family still pretty dug in?"

"I've been slotted for a trip to Sacramento next week to meet someone at the capital, so their influence into my field studies assignment is about what I expected."

I deflated, upset on his behalf. "I'm sorry. That really drags. You're making me feel a little better about being the only person to not have received a field studies assignment yet."

"It's coming. I have a feeling something... extra special is being worked out for you."

"I hope so. If I don't have an assignment by the beginning of November, I'm going to talk to Professor East about it."

"I think that's a good idea," Callan said slowly before turning his attention to a fork in the trail ahead of us. "The group I usually climb with will be at the base. I told them you and I would be practicing on one of the small walls."

Nerves began to churn in my stomach. I eyed Callan again. He had strong, muscled legs and arms. I was fairly fit, but nothing like he was. What if I didn't have the strength for this kind of activity?

Once we reached the wall where Callan would be teaching me the basics, he introduced me to his friends, and then they began scaling a much larger slab of rock nearby. I had to look away, fighting a spell of vertigo.

"Let's get you into your harness." Callan put the harness on the ground, indicating the loops for my legs. I stepped into the loops and tugged the rest of the harness up, then Callan moved close and put his hands on my hips.

I focused on breathing and trying not to be taken away by the sandalwood and peach smell emanating from him and the fact that his hands were on me.

He tightened the waist belt so that it fit securely around my hips. As he settled the harness, his hands briefly skimmed my stomach over my shirt. We both froze for a heartbeat. So quickly that I almost thought I had imagined the moment, he whisked his hands away, breaking the contact. Did he think there were scouting plants all the way out here? Surely not.

Then, like he had been a professional rock climbing instructor all his life, he took the dark-green rope and tied it to my waist with a fancy knot before threading the rest of the rope through his belay device.

"All right, go for it. Let's see you climb to that platform right there."

I looked to where he was pointing, a spot about ten feet above. I could scale that distance in a tree without thinking about it, especially now that I had a tree affinity, but the rock seemed so harsh. I would much prefer to spend more time with him adjusting my harness. "And if I slip?"

"I'll catch you." A slight breeze kicked up around my midsection, and there was a subtle heat in his voice.

Callan had been right. Giving in, even a little bit, made it *extremely* difficult not to want more. Rather than address the spark passing between us in that moment, I took a steadying breath and focused my nerves into scrabbling up the rock.

To my surprise, I moved fairly easily after taking the first few movements, my arms and legs working together to hoist me upward. Despite my shaky arms, I was on the platform within a few minutes, and I turned to look back at Callan.

"Impressive. I'm gonna lower you down, and have you try something more difficult."

Great. I was being rewarded for success by more work. How very Callan-like.

Chapter Twenty-Two

An hour later, after Callan had shown me how to belay him and we had taken turns climbing up and down a few walls, my arms and fingers were aching. "Can we take a break? My forearms are on fire."

We stretched out our legs on a flat expanse of rocks, and Callan pulled some snacks out of his backpack. The sun on our backs and the exercise had warmed me significantly, but my hands still wrapped themselves around the warm thermos.

"So, about the *society*," I put a whispered emphasis on the last word even though no one else was around, and Callan shook his head in amusement. "Do you really think we have a shot at finding the *Vanished Compendium* after all this time? And what's the backup plan if we don't?"

Callan gazed at the view that was stretched out before us, endless forest extending for miles, with the snow-capped Mount Shasta in the distance. "I'll start with your second question. The backup plan is smaller acts of resistance. We can decide on those as a group, and we'll do them whether we get a lead on the book or not. If the board tries for a full-fledged takeover of the school, they won't find it easy. As for the book, you are correct that thinking we can find the book feels like a big swing. But sometimes, it's in times of greatest need that artifacts make themselves known again. Records indicate it's shown up a few times since it went missing. Perhaps, since the Root and Vine Society was on pause for a while, we will all come in with fresh eyes and see something that was missed before."

He spoke slowly, as if mulling over what to say. "I don't think we have any choice but to be bold in going after what we want. If certain other groups find the book, they will have even more control. And you can bet that they won't be sharing what they find with rest of the magical botanists in the world. If *we* find the book, we can stop that consolidation of power. A few elites already have enough. This knowledge belongs to all of us."

"Well, I'm with you on that one. The founders already put a nice little block on my powers at the academy. I can't imagine what people with that mindset would do if they controlled a whole new book of Floracantus."

Callan looked away, and I turned my head. "What are you thinking about?"

His Adam's apple bobbed up and down as he swallowed, as if he didn't want to share what he was about to say. "It's not just the academy that the founders weaved their magic into, Briar. There are other places for magical botanists around the country, including the nine magical botanical conservatories. All of those were safeguarded by the founders. When the founders cut you off from your powers on campus, they cut you off from it in those places too."

The reality of it hit me like a widow-maker falling from a tree during a storm. Callan and Professor East had been shielding me from this information, letting me think that my actions on the spring equinox last year had only impacted my magic at Evergreen Academy.

But it was so much more. There was a broader world of

magical botany that I had never explored, and now, it sounded like I might not get a chance to.

"That's... a lot to process." I tried not to let my face fall, but my heart was sinking to my feet.

Callan put a hand underneath my chin and tilted my face so that we were looking at one another, and the intensity I saw in his eyes caught me off guard. "We don't know that the magic that blocked your powers was irreversible. We know virtually nothing about the power that gave you all of the affinities. I've been thinking about this since last spring. Perhaps there's a way, if you get control of all your affinities and learn all the intricacies of them, that you could undo the hold."

His words sparked something within my subconscious that I couldn't place, and I bit my lip. "You really think so? Professor East hasn't said anything about it, and I haven't come across it in the research I've done."

He dropped his finger, gently releasing my chin. "Yeah, well, the founders wouldn't have wanted that information to be easy to access, would they? Besides, powers like yours were already rare at the time the academy was founded. Maybe they never anticipated someone like you."

I propped my hands on the harness at my hips. "It's a nice thought, but without knowing where to start... do you really think it's possible?"

This time he took my entire face in his hands as we stood, feet firmly planted at the base of the rock wall. His presence was so steady, his touch so reassuring, that I doubted even a hurricane could blow us away in that moment. "Your power is *yours*, Briar. No one gets to put limits on it but you. I won't rest until you have access to every ounce of what is yours. If there is a way to restore access to your power, we'll find it. And then no one will ever threaten to control you again."

Holy leaves.

We faced each other like that for a moment until a cloud

passed in front of the sun, and Callan took a step back. "One more climb?"

I nodded, unable to speak.

Callan scaled the wall, and I belayed him, watching his every move closely, trying to determine how he decided where to place his hands and feet for the most grip. Concentrating on his technique helped keep my mind off the bomb he'd just dropped.

Callan was willing to turn over every leaf, scour every page, exploit every loophole in order to help *me*. And I had never even had to ask for it.

Chapter Twenty-Three

"Not bad, local. You're built like a climber. We'll have you doing steeper pitches in no time." He belayed me from my final climb with ease, and I met him on the ground.

"Um, I don't remember agreeing to do this again."

Callan laughed. "We'll see."

We packed up and started back down the trail. But before we reached the car, Callan stepped off the side of the trail.

"Why'd you stop?"

"We're surrounded by forest. No one's around. And we're off campus, so your magic isn't blocked. Let's see how you've improved over the last few months."

"Don't get your hopes up." But I began to tap into the sensation of the trees around me, seeking their tissues and cells, feeling the water flowing in, the oxygen flowing out. Immediately, I was invigorated. Would this sensation of connecting with the plants like this ever become less than amazing? "What do you want me to do?"

Callan pointed to two small trees, barely saplings. One was

birch and the other cedar. "Try a Floracantus to graft those two trees together."

I shot him a look. "You can't be serious. Grafting takes months. Years."

"Not for magical botanists." Callan walked toward two other trees, muttered a few words in Latin, and within seconds, the cedar and birch trees were fused together, the two types of leaves sprouting off the branches in a brilliant synergistic display.

"Show-off," I mumbled. I hadn't heard his Floracantus, but bringing things together was a common task in magical botany. "*Colligate arbores.*"

The two trees I was connecting with moved near one another in the soil the slightest bit, but nothing else happened. "I'm rusty," I admitted.

"You'll get there. Try again."

We stopped into Vera's Café on our drive home from Castle Crags. As far as I knew, Callan had never been here before, and I watched him take in the cramped, plant-covered space when we entered. His eyes went to the closest wall where the pasture painting hung.

"My mom did that painting," I said, a beam of pride forming, as it always did, when I told people about it.

Callan stepped closer and studied it. "It's beautiful. Enchanting, even."

"I forgot you were an art critic," I teased. "But yeah, it is." We approached the counter, and I ordered two of the famous lavender scones then straightened a few of the fall leaf ornaments on the countertop tree. It was our cutting of Frank—the oldest tree in town—from last year's harvest celebrations and resembled a Charlie Brown tree. I loved it.

"Is your aunt here?" Callan asked.

I shook my head. "She's off today. She used to work seven days a week, but Bryce finally convinced her to take some time off now and then."

"Smart man," Callan said.

We received the hot, buttery scones, and I passed one to Callan, watching his face as he bit into it.

His eyes widened, and he studied the pastry. "Delicious. This could make Professor Sage jealous."

"That's what I've been saying! Vera's is famous for these."

"Can I order another one for the road?"

It was the best compliment someone could give. "Coming right up."

I ordered a whole box of scones, knowing that Yasmin, Aurielle, and Coral would devour whatever Callan didn't.

When we were back in the truck, a question occurred to me, and I pressed my luck, hoping Callan was sufficiently warmed up from the scones.

"Kaito said that if any of us had not accepted the invitation to the Root and Vine Society, you had ways of making us forget the location of the meeting place. What did he mean by that? How would he make us forget?"

"Don't ask questions you don't want to know the answer to, local."

I folded my arms across my chest and turned toward him in my seat, curiosity flaring. "Well, now I want to know more than ever."

"The night you each received your summons to Evergreen Conservatory, we sprinkled something in your dinner."

"Excuse me, what?"

"You asked."

My eyes had narrowed while Callan's face was firmly on the road ahead. A lock of loose hair played near his forehead, and his skin was even more tan from the day in the sun. His tattoos shimmered on his forearms as one hand rested on the steering wheel.

But even his current state wasn't going to distract me from *this* conversation.

"What did you sprinkle in our dinner? And what does that have to do with us remembering the location?"

"Just a simple, enhanced herb recipe that impacts short-term memory. The effects were undone with the toast we offered you all."

"You're kidding."

Callan shook his head.

"That's a little scary. I'm not sure I trust you and Kaito with the *Vanished Compendium*."

Callan laughed and put his hands up. "Hey, we didn't create the rules."

"And who did?"

"Those who founded the Root and Vine Society."

I broached what I'd been thinking about since our conversation at Castle Crags. "Are your parents part of the faction looking for the *Vanished Compendium*?"

Callan rolled his neck as if he had a stitch in it and nodded.

"So going for the book first... it means going against them. How about Hollis? Where do his parents stand?"

"Their views align with my parents. Consolidate power within affinity groups, bonus points if it means more power for the founders' descendants. Hollis is as angry about it as I am. His family might be even more controlling than my parents are, if you can imagine that."

That drew my eyebrows up. It was difficult to imagine boisterous, easygoing Hollis with domineering parents.

"So you two are like the protectors of all that is good?" I asked.

Callan barked out a laugh, and I smiled, the tension broken. "Sure, if you want to call it that."

"Oh, I definitely want to call it that. Just maybe not in public. And if you're a protector, I want in."

Callan studied me, his eyes roving over my face as if searching for any sign that I hadn't meant what I said. "Going against them could be dangerous."

"Then why'd you invite me into the Root and Vine Society?"

"Because I had a feeling if I tried to keep it from you, you'd end up finding out and worming your way in anyway."

"Hey!" I mocked offense. "No need to insult the worms. They're good for the soil. But thank you. I appreciate you looping me in, even if that wasn't your first instinct."

"My first instinct is always to have you around, local. I can count on you to keep things interesting." He glanced my way again, and his eyes locked on mine for a moment before returning to the road.

"Who knows? Maybe I'll end up protecting *you* from the scary elites. You and Hollis are inside men, which is good to have, but a fresh perspective never hurt a cause."

"That's true. Just remember, being a protector—as you call it —isn't all fun and games. Having the *Vanished Compendium* fall into the wrong hands could be very, very dangerous. And trying to stop it from falling into those hands... That could be dangerous too."

I studied him as I rubbed my hands together, not having expected such an honest answer. The tension in the firm set of his jaw was contagious, and I rolled my shoulders back and pressed my head against the headrest.

"Then if this book *does* still exist, I guess we're just going to have to be the ones to find it."

Chapter Twenty-Four

"When do you think you'll get your first call out to the coast?" Yasmin asked Aurielle as we topped off our evening tea.

"Hopefully soon. I'm ready to find out whether I'm going to love it or hate it. I wonder how things are going for Coral," Aurielle said.

Coral was away on her second field studies mission already, studying ferns alongside a secluded section of river deep in the woods outside of campus.

I was trying not to get concerned each time field studies assignments came up, but I was beginning to become genuinely nervous. It felt like it was all the second-years were talking about around campus lately. But I was sticking to my plan of waiting until the first of November to bring it up with Professor East.

Still, my stomach was unsettled. What if Callan had been wrong in his theory about the envelopes being prepared by the instructor's magic? What if I was never going to find one because my magic was blocked? Though, with the way Yasmin and Coral had both seemed less than thrilled about the direction of their projects, maybe it was just as well that I didn't have an assignment yet.

"I'm sure she'll be exhausted when she gets back. They left at, what, five a.m.?" I glanced at my watch. "It's almost nine now."

At that, Yasmin yawned. "And that's my cue to head to bed. Are you staying up for a bit?"

I sighed. "I have that pollinator study for floral affinities tonight."

"That's right. The bats," Yasmin made a face.

"Where's the study?" Aurielle asked.

"It's out in the north corner, near the Perilous Grove."

"Want me to tag along? I haven't explored that area with my cartography club yet. It could be interesting to see how the plants behave at night."

"Really?" I brightened. Waiting around for up to a few hours to observe bats would be much easier with a companion.

"Well, now I feel like a bad friend. Want me to come too?" Yasmin stifled a yawn.

"No way. You'll fall asleep on the walk over there. Aurielle and I have it under control," I said.

We packed a few supplies from one of the first-floor lab rooms, then Aurielle and I headed into the woods. The moon was nearly full tonight, but we both carried lanterns to have a clear view of our notebooks when we reached the research site.

"So, how is cartography club going? I wish I had time to join you," I said once we set out into the woods.

"It's been fun. There are maps of the campus, of course, but not to this level. The plant life is changing all the time, so that's what we've been documenting. I don't know if anyone will ever use it, but it's nice to have a record of the species here and the strange little microecosystems they create."

"Do you have a favorite area you've explored?"

Aurielle thought for a moment. "There's an interesting spot in the southeast corner where licorice ferns are growing over a bunch of stumps. They remind me of heads of hair on a mannequin."

I laughed. "That sounds awesome."

"Oh, and we did make one funny discovery, though it's not related to plants. We were surveying some grasses along the wall, and I spotted a miniature arch carved into it. It kind of reminded me of a fairy door. I'm guessing it was created by one of the moss affinities a long time ago. Seems like something they would do."

I nearly tripped on a root but steadied myself. "Where did you find it?"

"West side of campus, by the citrus orchards."

I chewed my lower lip. The arch I had seen at the petal portal was on the south side of campus. How many of those doors were there? And did they each allow passage if you had a pendant, or was that just a coincidence?

Somehow, the topic of *how* Meadow and I had snuck onto campus had never come up with my friends. They probably assumed we'd come through the front gate. After Callan's reaction to the pendant, I decided not to share that piece of the story.

"Interesting," I said. "Remember how I told you about coming to campus this summer? I saw one of those fairy doors along the wall where I parked."

"Huh," Aurielle said. "Maybe you could take me by it sometime? I'd like to map that one too."

"Sure," I agreed. "Okay, I see the marker." I reached out for the florescent green tag that had been left on the tree.

We trudged off the trail until I spotted the *M. evenia* vine I was going to be tracking, the tree it was hanging from denoted with another green tag. "Let's stretch out here."

We set up our blanket and readied our supplies. I handed Aurielle a pair of night-vision binoculars.

"Mind if I look around?" she asked, palming her cartographer's notebook and lifting her lantern toward a nearby tree. The freckles scattered across her nose were illuminated by the light, and her soft blond curls tousled in the gentle breeze.

"Not at all. I've heard it can sometimes take hours for a bat to come by." I was grateful we had a clear night, free of rain.

Aurielle began to walk a perimeter while I sketched the unique flowers, leaves, and nectar cup of the *M. evenia* vine by lantern light.

After about twenty minutes, Aurielle returned and flopped her notebook onto the blanket beside me.

"Find anything?" I asked, putting my pencil down.

"I saw some night-blooming phlox and caught a scent of their honey-like fragrance. It was amazing. Any sign of the bats?"

"Not yet."

There was movement down the trail, and I lifted my binoculars.

"The bats?" Aurielle asked.

I shook my head. "Students."

As they drew closer, the outlines became familiar. It was Callan and Hollis, floating some plant materials on leaves along the narrow trail that ran by where we sat. Glow stick lights were hanging from their belt loops.

Hollis glanced in our direction, saw us looking, and winked before continuing along the trail.

Callan's gaze caught mine as he walked past, and even in the dim light, I felt the intensity of it. Then he glanced at the tree where the *M. evenia* vine hung. "Pollinator studies?" he asked. There was a playfulness in his expression but a little heat too. I sucked in a breath.

"You got it," I said.

"I heard Professor East planted that vine himself, and he does something to increase the echolocation response on research nights so that students have a better chance of seeing the bats," Callan said.

"I hope you're right. I'm sure Aurielle doesn't want to camp out with me all night," I said.

Callan glanced down the trail where Hollis was already disappearing, only the flicker of his glow stick indicating where he was. Callan dropped his voice low, locked eyes with me, and said, "I could think of worse ways to spend an evening."

My stomach *flipped*.

He raised his voice and nodded to Aurielle. "Good luck, you two."

"Thanks," Aurielle called as I struggled to recover from the way his words had made me feel.

"*Fronds*, Hollis is a flirt. Did you see that wink? Too bad he doesn't realize his charms don't work on everyone," Aurielle said once Callan's light began to disappear.

Aurielle had never expressed interest in anyone at Evergreen Academy or mentioned a significant other back home. In fact, a few times she'd been vocal that she had no interest in romantic relationships.

"Coral might have tried to fling a fern at him for that wink," I said, and Aurielle laughed.

The heat of Callan's gaze was still lingering in my mind. I studiously tried to force myself to refocus on watching the *M. evenia* vine. I couldn't miss the bat because I was distracted by a certain *someone*.

A moment later, there was a soft graze against my outer thigh, and I looked down to see that a flurry of leaves had surreptitiously slid up the side of my legs where I sat.

Automatically, I set down the binoculars and pulled the note out of the pile. So much for being focused.

You look cute in reconnaissance gear.

I felt my cheeks flush. For a guy who wanted whatever was going on between us to stay under the radar, he sure knew how to play. I was debating what to send on a note back to him when Aurielle pointed into the trees above us to the north. She held her binoculars to her eyes.

"There! I see a bat."

My binoculars were back in place in an instant, and I focused on the nectar cup dangling from the vine like a succulent treat for the bats.

Time seemed to freeze as we watched the winged creature approach the *M. evenia* vine, attracted by its own sonar echoing back from the vine's disc-shaped leaves. We were lucky to be witnessing this since, outside of Evergreen Academy, this vine was endemic to Cuba.

The bat flitted in and got to the nectar in the cup hanging below the flowers, and the *M. evenia* vine successfully transferred its pollen.

The whole thing was over in seconds. I put down my binoculars and finished the anatomical sketch I'd been working on then listed the new observations while they were fresh in my mind. I had a timer and sonar sensor running, and I recorded each value.

"All in a night's work," Aurielle said as she closed her notebook and stood.

"I have to admit, that was worth the late night." I moved my pencil quickly across the page, putting the finishing touches on my notes.

A sensation like electricity began trickling up my arms, and I dropped the pencil. I loosely ran my hands over the blanket, trying to decipher where it had come from.

"Are you ready to head back?" Aurielle asked, not appearing to have experienced it.

The electricity rippled to the right, and I glimpsed a glowing moonflower off the side of the path, seeming to beckon in the direction of the Perilous Grove. "I'm going to make a stop first. You head back."

"You sure?" Aurielle asked, obviously wondering why I wanted to linger in the dark forest after midnight. "Oh, are you planning to meet up with C—"

I cut her off with a slice of my hand and a laugh. "That's not it! We're close to the Perilous Grove, and I haven't been out there yet this school year. I want to check it out while I'm here." I couldn't explain what was drawing me there to Aurielle, but it had to be a message from the Root and Vine Society.

Aurielle's face was uneasy, but I reassured her. "I'll be fine. Just a pit stop, and then I'll head back. You go and get some sleep."

"Okay. Good luck, B."

I was grateful for Aurielle's tendency not to pry, knowing I likely would have been peppered with a few more questions if Yasmin or Coral were here. I picked one of the two lanterns off the ground, and Aurielle lifted the other. "Thanks. And thanks for keeping me company on the bat mission. See you in the morning."

The soft earth crunched under my feet as I cut off the trail and ventured into the thicket deeper in the woods, holding the lantern aloft to light my path.

The moonflowers did indeed lead to the Perilous Grove, and when I got there, I turned around in a circle, unsure where to look. Why hadn't the message drawn me to the Evergreen Conservatory? There was a chill in the air that was a staple of the fall in Weed, and I tugged up the collar of my coat.

The sound of soft creaking set me on high alert, and I swiveled, anticipating seeing Kaito or possibly Callan. But the eerie noise had come from the ten-foot-tall corpse plant. It wasn't due to open for a few more months when it would emit the carcass-like smell that—in a human botanical garden—would draw a crowd of visitors a mile long.

But as I stepped toward it, the massive green exterior unfurled in front of my eyes. It folded outward to reveal a purple interior while the spadix remained standing tall, like a thick sword protruding from a flower.

I inhaled sharply and stepped closer. It wasn't until I was right next to the plant that I realized I didn't smell anything. Despite my lack of ability to perform Floracantus on campus, it seemed that some of my innate powers were still intact and my defensive plant affinity was kicking in to block the pungent odor. That, or this wasn't an official bloom and the plant wasn't producing the smell at all. I wasn't sure which possibility was most surprising.

My eyes landed on a letter made of green leaves, nestled in the giant open plant. With shaky hands, I reached out and removed it from the corpse plant.

Once the envelope was in my hand, the corpse flower creaked and slowly reversed its previous actions, folding up once more.

I stumbled to a nearby stump and sat down, dizzy from what had just occurred. I'd been attending Evergreen Academy for a year now. I'd seen magic. But that display had been *breathtaking*.

My hands shook as I broke the seal of deep myrtle-green wax and opened the letter that had been so elaborately delivered.

You have been invited to a field study in counterpoison development. This study is classified. If you accept, submit this invitation to Professor East for further instructions.

I let out a laugh of exhilarated disbelief. *Counter-poison development? Classified?* Was this why it had taken so long for me to receive an invitation?

I turned to the corpse flower and gave a small salute of thanks.

It was difficult to contain my awed smile as I walked back to campus, envelope securely in hand. I finally had a field studies assignment, and I had a feeling it was a good one.

Chapter Twenty-Five

When I woke the next morning, memories of the previous night came rushing back in a flood. The corpse flower opening before me. The envelope of green leaves waiting for me. The mysterious field studies assignment. Had I dreamed it all?

My eyes shifted to my nightstand, and I grabbed my notebook as I sat up. The green leaf-composed envelope was tucked securely inside. I let out a deep breath. *Not a dream.*

Yasmin was still asleep—the sun was just starting to creep over the horizon—so I bundled up in a coat and scarf and decided to take my books and art supplies out to one of the gazebos by the lake.

The field studies assignment claimed to be classified and mentioned Professor East. It was best if I didn't tell anyone else about it until after I had a chance to meet with him. So I would use my tried-and-true distraction—art—while I waited to speak with him.

Once at the gazebo, I settled onto a bench and spread my notebook on the table. Dragonflies flitted by then zoomed low to skim across the water. The morning air was cool, but the sun was beginning to deliver a touch of warmth. Morning glories bloomed in a circle around the gazebo, this variety emitting a sweet jasmine smell into the air.

For a late-fall day, it was going to be a beautiful one. By eight o'clock, I was deep in an annotated sketch that could function as colorful notes for the biodiversity section of my Advanced Ecological Studies class.

"Someone's an early riser."

I jumped slightly in my seat at the unexpected voice breaking the relative quiet of the morning but calmed immediately when I realized who it was. Callan was wearing a backpack and had a thermos in his hand, as if he was about to go on an expedition.

Hollis was with him, standing a few feet back, similarly outfitted.

"Look who's talking, Lewis and Clark." I nodded toward their attire.

Callan shrugged off the backpack and took a seat on the bench next to me, and I was immediately charmed by the ease of the movement. It was the way we'd sat for so many nights last year during my tutoring sessions.

"Did you see a bat last night?" he asked.

I had to hustle to remember what he was talking about. The discovery of the field studies invitation had almost made me forget the reason I had been in the forest at night in the first place. "I did. It was all over in seconds, but it was worth the wait."

"The best things usually are." He was quiet for a moment, then he nodded toward the gazebo. "I saw you sitting out here and thought I would tell you I'm leaving for a research mission for a few days."

Hollis busied himself with organizing something in his backpack, but he was watching us out of the corner of his eye. He was certainly roguishly handsome, his deep-brown skin catching the morning sun, but to me, he couldn't hold a candle to the level of attraction I felt toward the guy on the stool right next to me. And I smelled that cologne again.

I realized I'd been silent a moment too long and asked, "An actual research mission? Not Sacramento?"

Callan nodded. "Yes, it's a continuation of the medicinal research project I started last year. Someone may have inspired me." He bumped his knee into mine. "You told me to make my own opportunities, so that's what I'm trying to do. I reached out to my advisor from last year, and he was eager to have me back when I can squeeze it in. It's not technically sanctioned, but we're keeping it under wraps."

"I'm so glad you're doing that!" I exclaimed, feeling lighter by the simple fact that he was finally pursuing something he wanted.

"Me too. We're headed to a post on the mountain to evaluate the research site. We'll be camping out there."

That explained the outfits.

"That's great news." I caught Callan's eye for a moment, trying to silently convey that I was proud of him for making this opportunity. He met my gaze, expression soft.

The moment was broken when Hollis cleared his throat, and I immediately turned my head to look at Callan's friend. "And Hollis, you're going too? I thought you had a fern affinity."

Hollis eyed the ferns that were hanging from the gazebo, and they began to spin. "You are correct."

I startled, shocked at seeing the ferns do more than their usual shimmy.

"Hollis is doing his own extracurricular under the same researcher," Callan said.

"Are you interested in medicine then too?" I asked Hollis.

"Didn't Rhodes tell you? I'm a jack-of-all-trades. Plus, someone's got to keep an eye on this guy." Hollis winked.

I couldn't help but smile at the charm that came through when he spoke. No wonder Coral was suspicious. This man was as confident as they came.

"You're telling me." I leaned forward. "He might go around outshining everyone with his legendary powers."

Hollis raised his eyebrows, and his mouth opened in delight. "The wind will start blowing, and everyone will be—"

He was silenced by a loud groan from Callan. "Are you two ganging up on me now?"

I shrugged and made eye contact with Hollis. We both tried to suppress our laughter at the exasperated look on Callan's face. I saw a tug at the corner of Callan's mouth for a second, though.

"Maybe a little. Consider it initiation," I said. I thought of my own top secret field studies invite with my still unknown mentor, task, or location. My hands brushed across my notebook, where the invitation envelope was firmly tucked.

Something must have flashed across my face because Callan narrowed his eyes. "What is it?"

I didn't say anything but crossed my arms, as if warding off his inquiries.

Then his eyes widened, and he broke into a curious smile. "You got your field study invitation, didn't you?"

"How do you do that?" I asked, flummoxed. He could have so many secrets, but I couldn't even keep one.

"Do what?" His tone was innocent, but there was a devilish grin on his face. "So what is it? Which affinity group did you end up getting an assignment with?"

I squirmed on the bench, swiveling slightly to break our eye contact.

Callan positioned himself right back in my sightline, dark eyelashes framing steadily focused eyes. "Why so mysterious today, local?"

"I can't tell anyone about it until I talk to Professor East," I said finally. I cast an eye toward Hollis, who was pretending not to listen again.

Callan's eyes were still trained on me, and we sat locked in a staring contest for two heartbeats. Finally, he pulled back ever so slightly and said, "Interesting."

And, to my amazement, he rose. He wasn't going to try to get any more information out of me?

"That's it? You're not going to ask again?"

"No, because you would have told me. And I get the feeling you're not supposed to."

I pursed my lips. The man knew how I would respond to him better than I did. I shook my head, mildly vexed that he was right.

If he had asked me again, I *would* have told him. I didn't have that reaction to anyone else. For a year now, I had been able to keep being a magical botanist from my aunt and from Maci, and I regularly held off on telling things to Yasmin until I got the green light.

But with Callan, I wanted to share everything. I wanted his opinion. His approval. His support. I wanted the feeling I got when his attention was focused solely on me.

"When will you be back?" I asked, trying to tuck those thoughts away. They didn't lead anywhere good when we apparently had Callan's mom hanging over our heads.

Callan slipped his hiking backpack over his shoulders. "Two days, if everything goes well."

"Stay safe out there." I threw the words in Hollis's direction, too, and he nodded.

"I'll try to keep him out of trouble," Hollis said, voice full of humor.

"More like the other way around," Callan murmured. Then he eyed my notebook, where the envelope was stashed. "Good luck." He flashed me a grin that nearly knocked me off the bench, then he left the gazebo and began to stride across the field with Hollis, the grasses swaying out of the way as he walked.

There was no hope of studying or even of finishing my sketch after that interaction, and I headed to Professor East's office to meet him as soon as he arrived on campus. I was waiting outside his door when he crested the stairs.

"Hello, Ms. Whelan."

"Hi, professor. Do you have a few minutes?"

"Sure, sure." Professor East ushered me inside the spacious office, and we took our usual places. "What's on your mind?"

"I received my field studies invitation last night."

He nodded almost imperceptibly, and I removed the envelope from my bag. "The instructions say to talk to you."

Professor East took the offered note and read it over, expression unreadable. "I see. Nice work in finding this. I don't imagine its delivery was conventional."

I snorted, remembering the corpse plant and the way it had unfurled itself dramatically in the middle of the night. "Not exactly, no."

"So I take it you accept the invitation?"

"I'd like to, yes."

"Very well. This position is... unique. The botanist who extended the invitation has never taken a field studies student before."

I sat up straighter, waiting.

"She'd like to meet us in the park in Mount Shasta and continue to where you'll be studying from there. I will introduce the two of you for this first meeting."

My brain was working quickly, trying to piece together the information. If we were meeting in Mount Shasta, did that mean I'd be discovering another local botanist I didn't know about? Or was this person working in the area just for the duration of the field studies project?

"When do we get started?"

"I'll inform her of your acceptance and let you know when we are to meet. I'm guessing she will want to begin as soon as next week."

"Great," I said eagerly. Given that my friends had already begun their field studies, I was anxious to get mine underway. Plus, I was itching to meet whoever this botanist was who had never taken a field studies student. "Is there anything I should do to prepare?"

Professor East smiled softly. "Just be yourself, Ms. Whelan. That is more than enough."

"Oh, one other thing. The invitation said that the study is classified? What does that mean, exactly?"

"Aw, yes. You won't be able to share the work you're doing there with anyone else. But you can tell your friends that you've been assigned a field study related to defensive plants."

"Got it, thanks." My shoulders relaxed as my mind buzzed. This was confirmation that the field study was one for defensives. I had assumed as much, based on the mention of counterpoison development, but hadn't been sure until that moment. I was grateful I could tell my friends I had an assignment. Before the meeting, I worried I would have to keep the whole thing secret.

Professor East nodded, and a tendril from a trailing plant tugged the office door open. "Enjoy your week. I have a feeling that once you get started, your field studies advisor is going to keep you quite busy."

Chapter Twenty-Six

The day before my aunt's wedding, Yasmin and I met in the flower gardens at Evergreen Academy. Professor Tenella had granted me permission to take whatever I needed. The flowers I cut would grow back in no time, thanks to the magically enhanced soil and the skills of botanists with floral affinities.

"I feel so horrible that I had to cancel as your plus-one at the last minute. Who knew that these field studies assignments were going to be so spontaneous? I wanted to try to wiggle out of the last-minute project this weekend, but I need to make a good impression on my field studies advisor. With the whole career opportunities thing—"

I set a hand on her arm. "Yasmin, it's fine. I was looking forward to you coming with me, but I'll be okay on my own. Please don't beat yourself up about it."

"But you said you didn't want to be a third wheel with Maci and Alex all night."

I let out a puffy breath, and a wave of hair breezed away from my eye. "Yeah, that could be awkward. But I'll survive."

"*Fronds*. I'm a terrible friend. And Coral and Aurielle are both on studies this weekend too."

"Seriously, don't worry about it," I assured her one last time. "Alex and I were friends at one point. It will all be fine."

Yasmin continued to apologize as we walked through the flower beds with baskets, collecting huge bunches of chrysanthemums, dahlias, roses, anemones, and a smattering of luscious greens. The garden smelled heavenly this morning, and birds and honeybees flittered around us as we worked.

Once we had everything we needed, Professor Tenella used a Floracantus on the flowers for freshness, and we drove to the ranch venue where the wedding would be held. A large, empty commercial fridge was waiting for us.

We spent the next few hours assembling bouquets, boutonnieres, table arrangements, and a massive garland to decorate the arch my aunt and Bryce would get married under. It was more than a two-person job, but with my magic twisting flowers together into perfect displays, we completed the task in a few hours.

We saved my aunt's bouquet for last, and once done, we both sat back and admired it. "That is stunning, B," Yasmin said.

"I don't know if my aunt wanted a bouquet the size of Texas, but she's getting one." The arrangement was an explosion of whites, creams, pale pinks, and deep reds with a few pops of green, making it look like something from the cover of a bridal magazine.

"It pays to have a magical botanist for a niece, even if she doesn't know about it."

I laughed. "She's going to wonder where I've secretly been harboring this florist talent all these years. I'm going to tell her I had some help from people at the academy, which is true. Thanks again, Yasmin. Couldn't have done it without you."

"You most certainly could have. I worked at a snail's pace compared to you. Though I will say that the fern fronds I tucked into the garland really make the display pop."

"Absolutely. I can't believe tomorrow is the big day. And I want to hear all about your field studies project when you get back." Before she had a chance to apologize again, I continued. "Speaking of field studies projects, guess who finally received their assignment?"

Yasmin looked up abruptly, a grin spreading over her face. "You've been holding on to that bombshell all day? I knew it was coming! Which affinity gave you an assignment?"

"It's a study on defensive plants, and it'll be occurring somewhere in Mount Shasta, I think."

Yasmin's eyes widened. "Really? They managed to find someone with a project on defensives to take on a student? You're high rollin', B."

"Professor East said this botanist has never had a field studies student before."

"Not surprising, given how rare you all are."

"I guess so. Have fun out there this weekend. You'll have to share your tips when you get back."

"Will do. And I promise to make it up to you for bailing on being your wedding date."

"Please tell me you're going to make me a fresh batch of makeup?"

Yasmin pursed her lips. "Something like that."

I was debating between two miniature pies at the dessert bar that night when Callan approached me. He leaned a hip against the table and smiled mischievously.

"I heard you're in need of a wedding date."

"What?" I squeaked, swiveling to glance at my usual table. Yasmin caught my eye then looked straight at her food. *The little chicken!*

"Is your aunt not getting married tomorrow?" Callan folded his arms across his chest, and the corner of his mouth lifted.

"*In need* is a strong term," I said, stalling to gather my thoughts. I picked up one of the mini blackberry pies and pretended to examine it. For what, I had no idea.

"Really? Because I heard something about a former love triangle and—"

I cut him off with a gasp. Had Yasmin seriously spilled *all* the beans? "There is not a love triangle." I tried to say it firmly but couldn't be sure of my success, given how mortified I was.

"Well, if you *do* need someone, I happen to have a lot of experience at fancy events."

I tried to envision my options.

I could go to the wedding without a date and hang out with Maci and Alex all night, an awkward third wheel.

I could go to the wedding without a date and act like the strong, independent person I was and not be concerned about being a third wheel, but that sounded slightly exhausting.

I flipped the coin over in my mind.

If Callan came with me, I'd have to explain to everyone that we *weren't* dating, which might cause more problems than it resolved. My aunt was fully capable of being cool and not making it into something it wasn't. Bryce, on the other hand...

I suddenly had a vision of Callan spinning me around on the dance floor. Likely or not, it would only be possible if I agreed to let him be my date.

The coin flipped in my mind one last time, and Wendy Rhodes's face was engraved on it. *Fronds.* Callan had put distance between us because he didn't want me to have anything to do with his family. Did a stint as my wedding date serve as a departure from that? Or was this our chance to get away from the prying eyes that Callan seemed to think were at the academy and just be ourselves, together?

I realized I was still clutching the miniature pie, and I set it back on the table. I glanced around meaningfully, as if suspicious of listening ears. "What about, you know... not wanting people to think we're involved?"

"There won't be other magical botanists at the wedding, will there?"

"You make a good point, Rhodes."

"So you want me to come?"

"All right, yes. It could be helpful to have another magical botanist there in case the flowers start to wilt or something."

Callan smirked. "Well, if it's an official duty to keep the flowers from wilting, how could I say no?"

I rolled my eyes, though I was thrilled by this new development. "I have to go to the venue early to set up since I'm in the wedding party, but the ceremony starts at four. Meet me at three thirty? I'll text you the address."

At that moment, Hollis shouted to Callan from a nearby table. "Rhodes, come look at this!"

Callan glanced at him and nodded then turned back to me. "Any particular color I should wear?"

"Color?" I asked, thrown by the question.

"I know sometimes women like to color coordinate at these sort of things."

I had to work *very* hard to keep my expression neutral at that moment. "True. Well, my dress is maroon, so if you have something that goes with that. But if not, it's a Siskiyou County wedding. We're fairly casual around here."

"Okay, see you tomorrow. For this *casual* wedding." I didn't understand the teasing note in his voice on that word, but I smiled as I rolled my eyes.

As he turned to join his friends, I reached for his wrist, and he turned back around. "Thank you. While I'm not admitting there *is* a third-wheel situation, I'll be grateful to have a friend at my side."

The corners of Callan's eyes crinkled, and he said, "Anytime, local."

I forced myself to walk at a normal pace as I returned to my table, miniature pies abandoned.

"What did he say?" Coral asked. She, Yasmin, and Aurielle leaned toward me as I took a seat.

"He's coming to the wedding with me."

"Perfect!" Yasmin couldn't look more pleased.

"Yasmin! I didn't ask you to invite him."

"I know." She looked guilty now. "But I felt so bad that none of us could come. And then Coral suggested—" She cut herself off, eyes going wide.

I turned to Coral. *Of course.* "This was your idea?"

She raised her hands, completely relaxed. "Guilty. But you should be thanking me."

I covered an exasperated smile and kept my lips firmly closed. I didn't want to feed the rumor mill, even if it was just among my friends. I scanned the teahouse for real this time, wondering about scouting plants. How real of a threat was that? I shivered at the idea of plant spies listening in on our conversations, despite how innocuous they usually were.

"We're friends right now. And that's *all.*" I put an emphasis on the last word, hoping any prying ears would get the message. That was all we could be, at least as far as the world of magical botanists was concerned.

"Well then, a wedding sounds like the perfect opportunity for two *friends*"—Aurielle put the last word in quotes with her fingers—"to enjoy a romantic moment on the dance floor." My quietest friend wiggled her eyebrows.

I picked a chocolate-covered blueberry off Yasmin's plate and popped it into my mouth to cover my blush. "We'll see about that."

Chapter Twenty-Seven

The morning of my aunt's wedding flew by in a flurry of hanging decorations, straightening rows of chairs, and providing directions to the caterers. After I finished arranging the flower garland on the arch, I checked my watch and realized, with a jolt of panic, that it was already time for my styling appointment.

I rushed into the house and changed into my dress before planting myself in front of the hairdresser, who had just finished with my aunt and the other bridesmaids. Twenty minutes later, she'd transformed my hair with a braided half-updo scattered through with flowers.

"It's gown time!" Aunt Vera announced, reaching out her hands to collect me from my chair.

I clapped and let out a squeal. We went into a more private room, and I helped my aunt step into her gown then spent ten minutes lacing up the back. I was so focused on configuring the complicated laces correctly that I hardly noticed anything else around me. As I tied the laces into a bow at the bottom with a satisfied nod, I stepped to the side and finally looked at my aunt, who was gazing at herself in the floor-length mirror.

Out of nowhere, tears sprung into my eyes, and I covered my mouth with a hand. I had seen my aunt in her gown when she had purchased it, but seeing it now, when it had been custom-tailored to her body, emotions I couldn't name flowed through me. She was radiant.

"Aunt Vera," I breathed.

"How do I look?"

"Bryce is going to lose it."

She laughed. "I'm sure he's not expecting me to be in a big princessy dress. I never expected that either, but now that I'm wearing it, I can't picture myself in anything else."

"It's perfect."

My aunt looked me up and down. "Your maid of honor dress looks great. I think your 'not date' is going to like it."

I rolled my eyes but ran my hands along my waist and hips, feeling the smooth fabric of the floor-length maroon silk. "Fits like a glove. All right, let's get you ready to go meet your groom."

I helped her with the delicate tiara-like headpiece—she was skipping a veil—and a few other accessories, including a bracelet that had belonged to my mom.

"Something borrowed," she whispered, touching the silver chain.

My phone dinged, and I glanced away to look at it. The message was from Callan.

Just parked. Where are you?

Be out in a second.

The other bridesmaids filed into the room then, gasping as they saw my aunt Vera. "Don't forget, your first-look pictures start in ten minutes," I whispered to her.

I slipped into my kitten heels, promised the other bridesmaids

I would be back when it was time for the bridal party pictures, then headed for the parking area.

My heart stuttered for a moment when I saw him. Callan was wearing a gray suit with a burgundy silk tie that perfectly matched the shade and material of my dress. His dark chestnut hair was expertly coiffed. He looked like the picture of a prep school billionaire, not my date for a small-town ranch wedding.

"You made it." I was slightly breathless from all the rushing around.

"Barely. The guy directing the parking was like a pro car choreographer. I had to get my truck within six inches of the car next to it."

I laughed. "Yep, that sounds about right."

"I was going to say I'm a little disappointed you aren't wearing your plant lady dress. But... maroon is definitely a good color on you, local." He looked me up and down, eyes seeming to briefly flick to my emerald ring before returning to my eyes, which were lidded with sparkly gold.

I sucked in a breath, caught by his gaze for a moment. I lifted the front of my dress a centimeter off the ground, preparing to move again. "I'm sorry, I have to dash off. The wedding party is doing pictures. Feel free to sit anywhere you want, and I'll find you after the ceremony."

"Don't worry about me. I'm a pro at these types of functions."

I shook my head slightly and pressed my lips together as I walked away. Of course Callan would consider a wedding a "function." He'd probably grown up going to botanical garden openings and charity fundraisers that were fancier than the biggest event in my aunt's life.

Still, my heart leapt at the fact that he'd come at all. That gesture, more than any words, cemented for me that I meant something to him, as he did to me. Tonight, we could enjoy ourselves free of the burdens of the changes that were happening at the academy and the threat of scouting plants.

When the ceremony began, I sought Callan as I walked up the aisle to stand with the other bridesmaids and saw him sitting on the left side, near the center of the crowd. He immediately stood out. I thought my eyes would find him anywhere, especially in that suit.

He gave me a little smile and a nod as I walked past.

The ceremony went off without a hitch, and I heard more than one person comment on the flowers. I managed to keep my makeup in place despite shedding a few tears at the sight of my aunt walking down the aisle. There was an ache in my chest that my mom wasn't here to see her twin get married, and I knew that my aunt carried that with her today as well. More than once, I saw my aunt touch the bracelet she wore.

After the first kiss and the pronouncement of marriage, my aunt winked at me as the crowd cheered, and she and Bryce made their epic walk down the aisle as a married couple. It was more like a strut, given the way Bryce was dancing and preening to the music as if he'd won the lottery. I couldn't blame him. My Aunt Vera was the best person in the entire world.

When I looked out into the crowd, all of whom were whistling, clapping, and cheering as they watched the joyous moment, I saw that Callan's eyes were on me, and I couldn't help but smile.

Chapter Twenty-Eight

"That wasn't bad, as far as wedding ceremonies go. They kept it short and sweet." Callan offered me an arm, and I looped mine through his as we walked to the field where the tables for the reception were waiting.

"Have you been to a lot of weddings in your time?"

"It's a frequent occurrence within our circles, I'm afraid. When your aunt is a famous magical florist, you tend to get invited to a lot of events."

"Your aunt is a florist? She's not a botanical congresswoman or something?" I wasn't sure why the idea of a member of Callan's family doing such a normal job was surprising. Though I would wager a botanical florist didn't exactly have normal clientele.

"It's a shock, I know. But a few Rhodeses have managed to buck the family trend." His voice soured, and I knew a change of subject was coming. "Speaking of, I sense a magical botanist's touch here today. Nice work on the flowers."

"Thanks, I'm pretty happy with how they came out. But if you see any wilting, get to work."

"Want anything to drink?"

"Umm..." I hesitated, trying to remember what Aunt Vera had picked for the drink menu.

"I'll surprise you." He gave a deferential nod and walked away.

"You didn't tell me you were bringing your man candy as your date!" Maci whisper gasped, appearing at my side.

"Hey, Mace. It was kind of a last-minute addition. When did you get here? I didn't see you at the ceremony."

"Ugh. Long story. I'm super bummed that we were late. I misplaced the wedding present. We showed up and slipped into the back row to not interrupt the ceremony."

Maci looked over my shoulder, and I followed her gaze. Alex was standing at the appetizer table, loading two plates.

"How are things going with Alex?"

"I was kind of surprised he wanted to be my plus-one since things between us really aren't serious. But I'm happy he's here."

"Yeah, totally," I said, resolving to say hi to Alex and make sure there was no weirdness between us.

"Back to you. Holy swoon, Callan fills out a suit nicely." She fanned herself with a hand.

I choked out a laugh. "The guy does know how to dress. Come on, I want to say hi to Alex."

We made our way over to Alex, whose blond hair was slicked back for the occasion.

"Hey, Alex. How have you been?" I asked.

"B! Doing great. This wedding is really nice. Your aunt seems happy," Alex said, his comfortable smile easing any of my concern about seeing him.

"Thanks, she is."

"So, how has everything been with you? That's Callan, right?" He nodded toward the bar where Callan was waiting in line.

"That's right. You two met snowboarding last year. I've been well. Just busy prepping for this wedding and school and all that."

Callan headed our way then, hands full with two glasses.

"Hello, Maci," he said warmly. "Alex." He nodded in Alex's direction. So he remembered him too.

"Nice to see you again, Callan," Maci said. "Well, we better go find our dinner seats. I know you two are at the head table. Meet us on the dance floor later, okay?"

When she was out of earshot, Callan spoke, eyes on Maci and Alex as they walked away. "Speaking of dances, you owe me one." He handed me one of the glasses.

"I do?"

"Aside from the free food and drinks, the perks of being a wedding date are the epic dances surrounded by elderly relatives and neighbors." He pulled a test-tube-shaped vial of bright-orange liquid out of the inside of his coat. A bit of cork held it stoppered.

"What is that?"

"Just a little concoction of enhanced blood orange and blueberry. Nonmagical people are unfortunately dull in their drinking palate. Do you want to try it?"

"This isn't going to make me do anything weird, is it?"

Callan mocked a disbelieving expression. "You think I would mess with you like that? You won't *do* anything weird. But your sensations might be heightened, just a little. These are a staple at magical botanist weddings. Don't drink it if you don't want to."

That was a dare if I'd ever heard one. I took the test tube and poured half of it in my lemonade then chugged the drink. Callan tipped the remainder into his own glass and followed suit.

Within a few minutes, the pink and purple of the sky was so vibrant that I felt I was inside a fairy tale. Callan had been correct. I didn't act any differently, and all of my conversations and actions were normal, but there was the slightest sense that everything around me was a little bit *more*. The colors, the sounds, the warmth of the October breeze. It was as if we had taken a perfect evening and painted it with a brush of pastels and neons.

"It's called the Elixir of Bliss. Kind of a clichéd name but accurate. Some first-years accidentally invented it in a chemistry of plants class a decade ago."

"I'm surprised people don't take this all the time."

"Due to the nature of the chemical compounds involved, you can get sensitized to it very easily. It works best if you only take it once a year."

"And you chose tonight?"

"Why not tonight?" And then he took my hand and tugged me onto the dance floor.

The first few songs were fast, and we all danced together, Maci and Alex near us among the dozens of people boogying on the dance floor. Then a slower song came on, and Callan extended a hand like he was a British prince.

I arched an eyebrow but took his hand. Expertly, he slipped his other hand around my waist and tugged me just close enough to be decent then angled our intertwined hands together like a professional ballroom dancer. He began to move, taking perfectly coordinated steps that I followed, letting him guide me through the dance.

"I take it you learned this from all those functions you've attended?"

I could feel Callan smile from where his face was nestled above my head. "Something like that."

"And who do you dance with at those functions?"

"Mostly ladies old enough to be my mom."

I laughed, and Callan lifted my hand and spun me in a quick circle.

"I'm sure they all love your moves."

"My dance card's usually full."

"And what about girls your own age? Do you dance with them?"

"I've danced with Nevah a time or two, and Meadow. And a few other people from my parent's circles that you haven't met yet."

Yet. For some reason, the word lodged itself in my chest with a little bloom of warmth.

I could have asked then. I could have prodded more about his dating history, or what would happen if we found the *Vanished Compendium*, or any of the other million things I wanted to know. But when he pulled me in again and swayed to the music, I made the decision to tamp down my curiosity.

For this moment, I wanted to enjoy the fact that I was at my aunt's wedding, under a sherbet sky, dancing with Callan Rhodes.

Chapter Twenty-Nine

At lunch the next Monday, Professor East pulled me aside into a quiet corner of the teahouse. "I've been in contact with your field studies advisor. We'll meet her at the park in Mount Shasta after dinner. Let's drive separately since I won't be joining you the whole time."

I was surprised that we were getting such a late start but didn't question it. One of the many things I had learned from being around magical botanists was that, with plants, timing was important. If my advisor wanted to meet in the evening, there was likely a reason for it.

"Thanks, I'll be there."

I hurried off to class, where some of my fellow second-years were already getting to work with their microscopes. Throughout the class period, I cast a few looks across the room at Callan.

He returned them about half the time, giving a slight smile and gentle tilt of his head when he caught my eye. I was remembering how we had danced at the wedding, and the memory sent goose bumps arching on my arms.

"Would you two stop ogling each other? It's making me

blush," Coral said, carefully slicing a stalk of aloe vera open with a scalpel.

I jumped and refocused on the plants on our table. "I have no idea what you're talking about."

"Yeah, how was the hot date at the wedding?" Yasmin asked.

"Yasmin!" I gasped. "It was not a 'hot date.' Well, it didn't start off that way. We may have shared a slow dance or two, though."

"So you're not in denial that he's into you anymore?" Coral asked.

I considered what I wanted to share carefully. At last, I settled on, "It's complicated."

"What's making it complicated?" Coral pressed.

I spoke quietly. "He has concerns about his parents and the other founders' descendants groups. He thinks they're all sort of... competing for my interest. And his mom is at the top of that list."

"Fronds," Yasmin murmured.

"I knew that woman seemed scary," Aurielle said.

"Well, if Romeo and Juliet can manage it, so can you two," Coral said as she upped the magnification on the microscope.

The three of us turned to her, our faces variations of amused, confused, and shocked.

"Coral, you do know how that story ended, right?" Aurielle asked.

Coral waved a hand. "Such theatrics. You two obviously aren't going to *die*. But there is something romantic about fighting for love against the odds."

"Someone has been watching too many rom-coms," I said, hoping to turn the conversation away from Callan and me.

"All I'm saying is, you're powerful, B. You have every single plant affinity. And strong affinities, at that. Power like yours hasn't been seen in generations. If anyone can hang in the society of stuffy founders' descendants, it's you."

"Ahh, thanks for the ego boost, Coral," I teased, though I truly appreciated her belief in me.

"Look, you do you," Coral continued. "But if Waylon looked at me like Mr. Founder's Descendant looks at you, he and I would be making out in a treehouse right now."

"Coral!" Yasmin, Aurielle, and I all gasped at our friend then collapsed into giggles. Professor Variegata shot us a look from the front of the room.

Once I composed myself, I chanced one more glance at Callan and saw that his eyes were already on me.

Chapter Thirty

After a hurried dinner in the tearoom, I made my way to Mount Shasta's city park, wanting to arrive a little early. I tucked my car into an empty parking space. A canopy of trees spread overhead was blocking out the light from the stars. Aside from a few lights in the park, I might as well be in the middle of a forest.

I had grown up playing at this park and knew that, beyond the large grassy field and play structure, a stream snaked through the thin forest. It was the mouth of the Sacramento River and boasted some of the purest water in the world.

A few minutes later, Professor East arrived, and I joined him at a picnic table lit by a park light. He checked his watch. "She should be here any moment." He looked at something behind me and rose. "Ah, here she is."

I turned to see a woman approaching along the path from the parking lot. I likely would have recognized her even without Professor East to introduce us. She was wearing a soft brown backpack, hiking boots, and had sprig of lavender tucked behind her ear. She had magical botanist written all over.

"Petra, good to see you," Professor East said as the two shook hands. "This is Briar."

"Hello." The field studies advisor said kindly as she reached out a hand. "I'm Petra Mancini. You can call me Petra. It's nice to meet you."

"Nice to meet you too. Thanks for taking me on as a research assistant. Professor East said you haven't had one before," I said as I shook her hand. I studied Petra more closely, the dim light of the park lamp illuminating her face. I had noticed an accent—Italian, it sounded like. Her skin was tanned and lightly lined but vibrant, and she appeared fit in a lean way, as if she spent a lot of time hiking. I'd guess she was in her fifties or sixties.

"Professor East is correct." She was studying me, as if searching for something.

"Well, I just wanted to introduce the two of you and make sure you got connected. You have plenty of work to do, so I'll leave you two to it," Professor East said.

"I'll be in touch." Petra nodded to my instructor, and then Professor East headed toward his car.

"So is our research taking place here, at the park?"

"No, I wanted to meet here and have us drive together to my research area up on the mountain. I didn't want to make you drive that windy road alone at night. Are you comfortable with that?"

I sucked in a breath but quickly tried to display confidence. I knew exactly which road she was talking about. It was the one where my mom's car accident had occurred. I had been on it many times since—on school field trips, mostly, and more recently, on a trip with Callan last year. But I'd never driven it myself.

"Yes, that works for me."

"Okay then. Let's get going. I don't want to keep you too late. I'm sure you have many questions, but it will be easiest to show you rather than try to explain."

I agreed, and we got in her car, a sleek black outdoorsy SUV that was clean and tidy inside. Petra made small talk about the academy and asked how my studies were going as we drove on the road that led to the trailhead on the mountain.

We passed the bend where my mom's accident had occurred, and I tensed. Petra quieted and glanced my way, but then the moment passed, as it always did.

When we reached the parking lot, Petra handed me a headlamp before putting one on herself and switching on the light.

"I hope you're okay with a little night hiking?"

"Of course." I took the headlamp and adjusted it. I was glad I had dressed for research and was wearing comfortable clothes that would work for a hike.

"We're headed up to base camp, so not too far."

I nodded, familiar with the base camp area that housed a tiny alpine hut made of lava rock. We began our climb, mostly going in silence. I was grateful to be able to focus on putting one foot in front of the other. The hike wasn't steep at this low altitude on the mountain, but now that it was dark, I needed to look to ensure steady footing on the uneven parts of the trail.

Soon, though, I found myself distracted. The roots that stretched underneath the trail were like rivers of energy demanding my attention. The cells of the trees, shrubs, and grasses around the trail seemed to beckon me to examine them.

I let the sensations wash over me, and in some ways, I felt that they propelled me on the uphill hike faster than I would normally go. I was connecting with my power, and with field studies about to begin, the timing couldn't be more perfect. I was ready to learn.

Less than an hour later, we emerged in the base camp clearing, where explorers had once rested with their horses. The little stone cabin that was staffed by federal parks workers in the climbing season was straight ahead.

The cabin was tiny—more of a hut than a house—and the collage of rocks that built its four walls, plus the imposing stone chimney, harkened to something out of an early era of exploration. Or tribal displacement, depending on who was telling the story.

Petra made a beeline for it. I wondered what she was doing, given that I knew it would be closed right now. But Petra waved me on to follow, and then she pulled out a key and unlocked the door.

Right. So my field studies advisor had access to the historical alpine hut—the only structure this high up on the mountain. Interesting.

When we stepped inside, Petra closed the door then got to work setting up a few camping lanterns that were stashed in a crate in the corner. The hut had been built in the 1920s as a tiny shelter, and there was no electricity or much of anything inside.

"That's better," Petra said once the place was glowing with dim light.

"Umm, is this where we're going to do our research?" I asked, my curiosity finally spilling over.

Petra smiled and went to feel along the interior log wall. She pressed on it gently, and a panel fell open. My eyes widened.

"Yes, it is. This is why I only come up here at night. I need the cabin to be closed off to hikers."

She began rummaging through the materials that were stored behind the secret panel.

"How long has this cabin been your... workspace?" I asked, still awed that the cabin of my childhood field trips had secret panels inside it.

"It has been the workspace of others before me. I'm here on a temporary assignment. There is something about the ecosystem of this area that enhances a botanist's access to our magic."

Part of me wanted to reach out and skim the air to try to put a tangible feeling on what she was describing. Is that why I'd been so in tune with the plants on the hike in?

But what did she mean that our magic was enhanced? I had been studying botanical magic at Evergreen Academy for a year and had never heard of anything like that. "Enhanced access? What causes it?"

"We don't know for certain. There are a few areas like this around the world, though they are rare. We call them green zones."

"Green zones." I let the term roll off my tongue, reverent at the idea. "How large is the area?"

"The epicenter is about a two-hundred-foot radius around us, but the effects dissipate as they spread out beyond that, with less potent runoff effects seeping into the surrounding communities. It's the reason Evergreen Academy was built where it was."

I looked at her sharply, though things were snapping into place. "I thought it was because of the water here?"

"That was an added bonus, but the green zone is what drew the founders to this area to begin with."

"I see. Why haven't I heard about them?"

"The zones are classified information. It's a directive from the Magical Botanical Congress."

I began to open my mouth, and she sensed my question.

"I can tell you about it because this field study assignment comes with a certain level of clearance."

I swallowed. *Right*. The reason we were here. "The field studies invitation mentioned counterpoisons. Is that your area of research?"

"It wasn't always, but yes. As botanists with defensive plant affinities, it's as important to study how to guard against defensive plants as to wield them. Too many botanists fail to understand this."

I nodded, thinking of the incident the previous year where most of the student body had been drugged with *Scopolia* and had started spilling our guts due to the truth serum. Nevah, a founder's descendant who had attended the previous year, had helped me to work on my detection skills after that at the insistence of Callan. However, my training had been truncated when my powers had been cut off on campus.

"You won't have to convince me of that," I said honestly.

Petra nodded. "I didn't think so." She set a box on the picnic table that took up nearly half the room. "We'll start with the basics and see how you do. Do you have much experience detecting poisons?"

"Very little," I admitted.

"It's much like detecting any other part of a plant, except when you connect at the tissue level, you need to search for something hidden, almost as if reaching for a trap door." She held out a leafy plant I didn't recognize. "Give it a try."

I opened up my senses, filtering through the tissues of the plant down to the cell level and back up again. At first, the experience felt a little like the investigations I had done on campus last year. But it was amplified, and I wondered if it was the effects of the green zone allowing me to be so precise.

Then I felt something quietly knocking, as if asking to be let out. I zeroed in on the little pockets that were trapped. They were spread throughout the plant, but I felt them most acutely in the seeds.

"Ah, you've got it. I can feel them responding," Petra said. I opened my eyes to see her nodding encouragingly. "That's poison hemlock. More potent in the spring but still zesty enough in the fall for us to feel it. Try this one." She held out a different plant, and I noticed that there were a dozen samples in jars on the table.

I opened up my senses and repeated the process.

An hour later, I could zero in on each toxin and identify the plant without looking. Petra hadn't been exaggerating about the potency of our magic here. It was subtle, but I felt more connected to the plants I was working with than ever before.

"Excellent. Professor East told me you were powerful, but that's a subjective word. He was right to use it, though. You picked that up extremely quickly."

I glowed under her praise. Finally, I was working with an established magical botanist in a setting where I could stretch my powers. I hadn't known how exhilarating that would feel.

"Thank you, this is fun despite how difficult it is. Will we be doing this at every session? Is there something specific you'd like me to help research?"

Petra paused as she reorganized some of the plants. "I have a few goals in mind for us, but we will start with one that came on special request by Professor East."

"Really? What kind of request?"

"He would like us to find out the affinity of whoever poisoned the verdant shield."

Chapter Thirty-One

I sat in eager, slightly stunned anticipation as Petra began to explain the plan. "Professor East provided samples of the poisoned soil that he collected last year. While he's been running his own tests, he thinks that us defensives may be able to find something he hasn't, and I agree."

She removed a jar of soil from behind the secret wall panel and set it on the table. "I have been doing research in a niche field of detecting magical signatures. This is a skill that defensives are particularly well suited for."

"Magical signatures?"

"It's a new field of magical botanical science still in its infancy. But the theory is that using magic to modify a plant or soil leaves behind a trace. It doesn't sound groundbreaking since we know that if someone modifies a tree's cells, for example, they have to be someone with a tree affinity. But when it comes to soil manipulation, it's not obvious what affinity power the manipulator had."

"Professor East described some of the things that were added to the soil last year to poison the verdant shield. You're saying that there might be a way to trace the signature of whoever did that?"

"Correct. It won't lead us to a person, but it should lead us to an affinity power. Or multiple affinities, if that was the case."

I leaned forward. "Have you found anything so far?"

"I've gotten close to untangling the signature, but a small piece of the process keeps eluding me. I believe you could be of some help here."

"How so?" My mind was racing, excited by this possibility.

"Soil is—what is the word you use?—tricky. It is a combination of many things, and only part of it is organic matter. Professor East tells me you have some skill in sensing the properties of soil. Combine that with your access to all of the affinity powers, and you may be primed to untangle the magical signatures from the various plant material in the soil."

"What's the process?" I asked, eager to get to work but slightly nervous about my skill level and whether I would be up to the task.

Petra explained a complicated series of steps that involved activating the magical signatures in the soil sample then sorting through each and every piece to determine their origin.

As she talked and demonstrated the process on a clump of soil, I chewed on my lower lip and kept my eyes locked on every step, absorbing each word and trying to envision how it worked. This was far beyond any scientific or magical work I had done so far, but the thrill of finally getting a lead on the soil poisoner propelled me forward.

When Petra got to the final step, she said a Floracantus for illumination. "*Cellula illuminare.*"

There was a slight glow in a portion of the soil, but it died out before I could fully process it. "That's the problem I have been encountering. The signatures just won't hold for me. Even here, in the green zone, my power isn't enough."

"And you think mine will be?"

"I've never seen anyone pick up poison detection as quickly as you, Briar. If you're anywhere as in tune to magical signatures as to poisons, we stand a good chance." She scooped a dash of soil into a plastic petri dish and passed it to me. "Go ahead and give it a try. You can work on a small sample for now, so don't worry about messing anything up."

I nodded and dove in, careful to match the steps Petra had demonstrated. The process was as complicated as it looked, especially the sifting. I had to sense the plant material in the soil, separate it from the other components, examine it at the cellular level, and then prepare to activate the components that had been enhanced with magic.

While I was sliding portions of soil into piles, Petra was watching closely.

"Okay, I think I'm ready for the activation," I said, not taking my eyes from the soil that was between my hands.

"Go ahead."

I latched on to the particles of soil that carried a trace of something unusual. It was a task I had done before. Only this time, it wasn't poison I was detecting but the trace of magic.

"*Cellula illuminare*," I whispered. As if fireflies were coming to life inside the soil, a few patches lit up, glowing a soft chartreuse.

Petra let out a satisfied laugh. "Well done, Briar. The trace is holding. Now, we just have to feed these into the mass spectrometer and see what output we get."

She removed a machine the size of a video game console from behind the panel and hooked it up to a laptop I hadn't noticed her remove from her bag.

"I thought mass spectrometers were huge," I said, eyeing the machine.

"In the nonmagical world, they are. But we've developed a proprietary version that can be a lot smaller since magic does so much of the upfront work."

She slid the petri dish with specks of glowing soil into a slot in the machine. I strummed my fingers on the table as I waited for the results to process.

At the sound of a trilling *ding* from the computer, we both stopped what we were doing and gathered around the screen.

"All right, let's see what we've got," Petra said.

We were looking at a graph that was a series of thin spikes with numerical values above each. "This tells us the match of each compound in the sample," she explained. "We can compare them to known values. If there are any unknowns, by human standards, those will be our magical enhancements."

I watched as she made her way through the numbers, noting each item on the chart. She annotated four of them and high-lighted the peaks on the screen. "These are our four magical enhancements. Now, we just need to compare them to known values from our magical botanists' records." She pressed a few keys on the keyboard, and a report popped up.

Petra let out a breath. "We've got something here. These enhancements were all placed on leaf matter—of oak, pine, and cedar, to be exact. All extremely common in the forest around the academy."

My eyes grew wide at the implication. "Leaf matter. You're saying that whoever poisoned the soil had a tree affinity?"

"The evidence indicates that, yes. We can test a few more samples to see if they had multiple affinities that they used here. But this is good information. Excellent work, Briar."

I smiled my thanks, but my stomach twisted slightly. This was real evidence—beyond a doubt—that a magical botanist had manipulated the soil in a way that was harmful for the verdant shield and Evergreen Academy.

"Let's get back to it," I said, rolling up my sleeves in determina-tion. I would test every ounce of soil if it meant getting to the bottom of this mystery.

Petra and I worked for a few more hours, testing dozens of soil samples that I activated, but the only identification link we were able to make was to the trees. This meant the magical botanist who had manipulated the soil had had a strong tree affinity, and if they had any others, they hadn't used them.

I was desperate to tell Callan the news, so I asked, "Is this part of our study confidential?"

Petra thought about it for a moment. "Has Professor East allowed you to discuss the soil poisoning with anyone else?"

"There's another student in the loop, yes."

"Then I imagine you can share this development with them, but check with Professor East if you're not sure."

I nodded. "What are you going to do with this information?"

"I will pass the results along to Professor East. If there is more he thinks we can do, we'll follow his lead. Beyond that, until more information becomes available, we let the leaves fall where they may. This was great work for a first session, Briar. I have a feeling you and I have even bigger things in store."

Chapter Thirty-Two

I rushed to the treehouses the next morning, making an educated assumption that I would find Callan there. I used the slats to scale the tree to our favorite treehouse then ducked my head inside.

"Good morning," I said brightly.

Callan looked up. He had been leaning over a bench, test tubes and bark neatly organized on the counter.

I'd caught him mid experiment. "Sorry. Is now not a good time?"

"Now's fine, local. What's up? You're practically bouncing over there."

I made a conscious effort to curb my physical excitement and sat on the stool Callan slid in my direction. "I have news."

He waved a hand, signaling me to continue.

"I had my first field studies assignment last night."

He perked up. "How'd that go?"

"It was great! I think I'm going to learn so much from my advisor. She has a defensive affinity."

Callan whistled. "Defensives, huh? I'm surprised they found someone with that affinity power."

"Well, I think they had to look pretty hard because I don't think my advisor has been in the country for long. Her accent sounds Italian, but we didn't really get into that yet."

"That's not the only news you have, is it?"

I realized I was swiveling on my stool and forced myself to still. "My assignment is classified, but I was told I could share this piece with you." I didn't bother to say that, if pressed, I would tell Callan absolutely everything I learned in field studies. He already knew. And he wouldn't press.

I took a breath and dove in. "During our session, we examined some of the soil samples from the poisoning last year."

Callan raised an eyebrow. "Did you find anything?"

I nodded. "Ohhh yeah. We were able to determine that the person who manipulated the soil had, at minimum, a strong tree affinity."

Callan stilled. "Are you sure?"

"My advisor seemed to think the science was pretty conclusive. We were using a new field of magical tracing."

Callan nodded, as if that term was familiar to him. "Okay, this is good information to have. And really good work on the findings. Did you have to use all of your affinities to make the trace work?"

I filled him in on the scientific investigations I had performed with Petra, Callan nodding intently as he followed the science.

"Ahh, so it was the activating where your advisor was getting stuck. Interesting. Your different affinity lines must have allowed you to cleanly activate one signature at a time."

"That's what it felt like," I agreed. As usual, I marveled at how quickly he picked up what was going on at both the magical and scientific levels.

"Well, I have no idea what else your field study is going to entail, but you'll be kicking roots and taking names in no time, I'm sure," Callan said, and his smile was so playful that I couldn't even form a sarcastic return.

This moment felt like those nights we had spent studying in

the treehouse last year, only instead of him tutoring me on Calculus, we were discussing the future of magical botanical research. I didn't know what the year had in store for me, but the ease of these moments with Callan was one thing I hoped would never change.

Chapter Thirty-Three

"The last few sessions of creating antidotes to plant poisons has gone very well, Briar. I think we're ready to move on."

I took my usual seat across from Petra in the tiny stone cabin on Mount Shasta. "What's next? Are we going to continue researching magical signatures?"

"Not exactly. Professor East told me about your situation when I agreed to take you on as a field studies student."

"My situation?"

"He tells me you cannot access your powers on campus, due to the repercussions of trying to recharge the verdant shield last year."

I felt myself redden but nodded.

"A crafty bit of magic, that was. That piece of the shield would have been implemented by the defensives founder. Think of it like a plant with poisonous thorns, hurting one who didn't heed its warning."

"I hadn't thought of that before, but that makes sense." I remembered being expelled backward the moment I had touched the earth inside the charging circle and tried not to shudder.

Petra nodded. "I've never experienced it myself, but I imagine it wasn't pleasant. The defensives founder was an extremely strong and talented botanist, from what I've heard. Many have believed the tale that the effects of this spell are permanent. But I do not think so. If defensive magic was wielded on you, defensive magic should be able to undo it."

"Seriously?" I exclaimed, losing any pretense of trying to act professional in front of my field studies advisor. This was the first bit of concrete hope that the curse on me might be reversible. If Petra was right and we could remove my tethers, I would be able to have a normal experience at Evergreen Academy this year. I could grow my skills every day and push my powers to my limits, as I saw my classmates doing. This would change the game for me.

"It has never been done. At least, not this exact scenario. It's going to take a lot of dedicated work from you. But if what I have seen of your skills in detecting and countering poisons is any indication of your power, you have an excellent chance."

I beamed, a weight seeming to lift from my chest. I was willing to try anything. "I'll do my absolute best," I promised.

"Good. The first step will be to identify what poisoned you. I have a feeling that it was a mixture of things." She removed a mason jar full of soil. "Professor East provided this. It's from within the charging circle at Evergreen Academy. I've done some testing myself, and the defensives in the soil were cloaked so that I can't identify them. Since you have already been poisoned and have the effects running through you, I think you may be able to get around the cloak."

Hope was coursing through me, but there was a bit of hesitation as well. If the magic was implemented by the defensives founder, a literal icon at Evergreen Academy and beyond, what chance did I stand of getting around it?

"You really think we have a shot at this?" I asked.

"I wouldn't be here if I didn't," Petra said firmly. She nudged the jar in my direction and nodded toward the microscope. "The first step will be for you to examine the soil for poisonous plant traces. I have some suspicions on what is in there based on the results on your powers, but I can't know for sure. If you can sense it, we'll be able to start experimenting with antidotes."

I opened up my senses, drawing on the enhanced power of the green zone, and began to examine the soil. It felt like an hour passed as I painstakingly sifted through the various components, pausing to write down my observations. Finally, I landed on two pieces that I could immediately tell were from defensive plants. They were characteristic of the other defensive plants we had been practicing with.

"I think there are two different defensives here," I said slowly, not taking my eyes from the soil I was sifting with a toothpick under the microscope. I looked at it more closely then flipped through a reference book that Petra had provided.

About halfway through the book, I landed on the first defensive. "There is enhanced abrin in here. And"—I flipped through a few more pages—"black walnut."

I looked up at Petra, who nodded as if she wasn't surprised. "That combination makes sense. The toxins in the abrin would have paralyzed your own defenses long enough for the juglone in the black walnut to inhibit the use of your power. They reactivate any time you cross the boundary onto campus."

"Are there antidotes for those two poisons?" I asked, trying to temper my expectations.

"There are, but it's going to be the enhanced combination that will be difficult to account for. This is a fantastic start, Briar. I'll be prepared with some ingredients I think we should experiment with next week. And I probably don't need to remind you, but it's very important that no one else knows we're working on this besides Professor East. There are powerful people who have a vested interest in controlling the verdant shield."

I nodded solemnly, her words a stark reminder of the politics at play and the small piece I was within all of it.

As I drove back to Evergreen Academy, I buzzed with excitement. This was exactly the kind of solution Callan had been hoping we could find for me. If I could undo the block on my powers, I could truly be part of this world. Callan wouldn't have to be constantly concerned for me, and I could finally start to examine my power and determine what I wanted to do with it.

But all of this was classified, at least for now, so I would have to find a way to play it cool around Callan. Luckily, there were plenty of things to distract him, including the mission of the Root and Vine Society.

I'd just have to do my best imitation of a defensive plant and hide what was going on until the time was right.

Chapter Thirty-Four

"How are your applications going? I can't believe they're due in a few weeks," Maci said as we stood behind the counter in Vera's Café.

It was midday on Halloween, and children were already coming into Vera's in costumes, part of the progressive trick-or-treat through local businesses put on by the chamber of commerce. I was wearing my plant lady costume from the previous year and offering a decorative potted plant bowl filled with candy instead of soil to the kids.

"Applications?" I asked absentmindedly.

Maci gave me a bewildered look. "For four-year schools. What else?"

"Oh! Right," I said, trying to recover as a jolt of anxiety coursed through me. The truth was that all thoughts of applying to four-year schools had fallen off my radar, and that realization was alarming.

For years, all I'd planned to do was work hard to get into the art school program that my mom had attended but never finished. I rubbed my brow, realizing that I hadn't even thought of the school in months.

"I've submitted four applications so far. I have a few more to do. It's the essays that are killer. Do you have to do an essay for the art school application, or is it more of a portfolio thing?"

"Both. A portfolio plus a written statement." The words came out automatically. I had been tracking the admissions requirements for the school for years. How had the fact that the application window was now open completely slipped my notice?

A strange loosening occurred in the pit of my stomach, as if I could feel something slipping out of my reach.

"Are you okay? You look a little pale." Maci's forehead was pinched in concern.

"I'm fine," I assured her, taking a large sip of my tea. I was suddenly very glad I'd brought a potent calming chamomile blend from Evergreen Academy to Vera's Café.

Maci continued to fill me in on the status of each of her applications and the current rankings of where she was most hoping to get accepted. I tried to listen carefully and respond where appropriate, but my thoughts were elsewhere.

Without realizing it was coming, I had reached a crossroads. This was the point where I decided whether to continue chasing the dreams I'd had before learning I was a magical botanist—the dreams I thought my mom would want me to fulfill—or to take a new path that was completely unknown and see where it led.

With everything that I was invested in at Evergreen Academy, thoughts of attending art school had slipped my mind. What did it mean that I was no longer striving for that?

I needed to discuss this with someone, but no one met all the criteria. Maci and my aunt were obvious choices in the past, but they didn't know what was really going on at Evergreen Academy. Yasmin would be a supportive listener, but she'd grown up in the world of magical botany. Would she understand my dilemma?

And then there was Callan. I knew he could empathize. His parents wanted him on one path, and he wanted to be on another. But could I really compare what I was experiencing to his much more unpleasant situation? The only person who was forcing me to choose between these two paths was me.

I let out a deep breath and set an alarm on my phone to remind me to complete the art school application that weekend. I took another sip of my tea and reassured myself I didn't need to make any choices now. I needed to leave the door open and hope that, when the time came, I would know what to do.

"Ready to go get our Frank cuttings?" Maci asked, glancing at the clock on the wall. "Our candy shift is just about over."

"Right, let me make sure Mathew is ready to take over for us."

"My mom takes a cutting every year. Our backyard is starting to look like an orchard of mis-sized trees."

I laughed. "Aunt Vera took a cutting last year, and it's still in a little pot in her living room. It takes forever for those cuttings to become actual tree-sized."

"Some of my mom's oldest ones are a decent height now. A few are even providing some shade in the summer. My grandma once joked they must be magic trees since even my mom and her black thumb managed to keep them alive."

I went to the back of the bakery where Mathew was just finishing clocking in. Once we passed off the candy pot, Maci and I headed to the Wildflower Trail at SCC.

The parking lot was nearly full, and families were streaming down the trail to Frank, the oldest oak in town. I turned to my left and saw a truck I recognized.

"Callan's here," I breathed, surprised.

Maci raised her eyebrows. "This wasn't a planned meetup between you two?"

I shook my head, and we joined the others heading to the tree. When we got there, I spotted Callan hovering near the back of the gathering crowd.

"Hey, what are you doing here? Didn't you know this was a locals event?" I teased as I came up beside him.

"I'm emptying the tree boxes after this. Professor East said they fill up after this event. I offered since I figured you might be here." Callan's words were quiet so that Maci couldn't hear. She was busy greeting one of her neighbors and didn't notice.

"Good guess," I said, thinking of the time I had helped Callan empty the boxes the previous year.

"So, what's this all about anyway? Professor East just said it was a popular local event." Callan indicated the gathered people.

"Just an old town tradition. Every year, on Halloween, an arborist harvests cuttings from Frank. He's informally labeled Weed's oldest tree, and having a cutting from him is considered good luck. People take their cuttings home and grow them in pots until they're large enough to be planted."

The town's mayor raised her voice then, and we turned our attention to her. "Thank you all for joining us for the annual tree-cutting giveaway. Collect your cutting, and make sure to leave a letter for Frank if you have the chance. There are donuts and apple cider provided by Shasta Pumpkin Farm at the end of the trail."

Everyone clapped then began to collect their cuttings. I stepped forward and selected a sturdy looking twig. When I returned, Callan was eyeing the plant strangely.

"What is it?" I wondered if he thought the tradition was odd or if I had done something sacrilegious for a magical botanist with a tree affinity.

He surveyed the area and lowered his voice. "It feels like someone is using their power."

I looked around even though there was no point. By all accounts, Callan's ability to sense people using their magical botanist powers was extremely uncommon, and I didn't share it. I rarely had the opportunity to witness him use it since there was no reason for him to sense magic being used on campus.

"Huh," I said, not having much else to offer. This gathering seemed perfectly normal to me.

Callan's shoulders relaxed, and he shook his head. "Maybe it's nothing. Want to stick around and help me with the letters?"

"Sure, let me just tell Maci the plan. Can you drive me back to my car after?"

When Callan nodded, I informed Maci I was staying behind with Callan. She gave me gushy eyes, which I waved off.

Callan and I waited for the townspeople to continue along the trail for the cider and donuts, then we began to stuff the backpack he had brought with the letters from the letter box.

I paused to glance at one. "This one is a poem," I said, skimming the handwritten sonnet.

"I think some people find these boxes a way to express themselves artistically without having to share their work more broadly," Callan said.

I pulled out another piece of paper and opened it, my forehead scrunching together. "This one is blank. Should I throw it out?"

"No, we bring them all back. Professor B. ultimately decides what to store."

I shrugged and put the paper in the envelope with the others, resolving to stop skimming the notes so I could work more quickly. By the time we'd collected letters from every tree along the trail, a breeze had kicked up. I shivered.

"Here." Callan shrugged off his jacket and offered it to me.

"Oh, I'm fine. You don't have to—"

"I can see goose bumps on your arms."

"All right," I said, taking the jacket and slipping it on. The familiar sandalwood and peach smell settled in around me, and I tugged the jacket more firmly around my body. "Thanks."

His coat was warm and comforting, and I wondered if this was kind of what it would feel like to get a hug from Callan. I'd never seen him hug anyone, unlike the gregarious Hollis, who handed them out like candy.

We began to walk down the trail, Callan's backpack full of letters.

"So, going to any Halloween parties tonight?" Callan asked as we approached his truck. "I see the plant lady costume still looks great on you."

I glanced down at my dress underneath his jacket, having completely forgotten I was wearing it.

"Thanks, but I won't be wearing this tonight. You're lucky you even got a second chance to see it. I wasn't expecting to run into you here."

Callan grinned, and I bit my lower lip, knowing we were both remembering the dinner he had made for me on Halloween the previous year. That had been when the walls had first started to come down between us. Now, we were so much more than the near strangers we'd been then. Callan opened the passenger door, and I climbed in.

"I suggested a dress-up garden party at Evergreen tonight since you all don't traditionally celebrate Halloween. I'm doing a group costume theme with my friends. We could dress you up too. You *did* say you've never dressed up for Halloween before."

Callan eyed me sideways before putting the truck in reverse. "Do I even want to imagine what you would dress me as?"

"Hmm, let me think. You've got the tattoos. And you're slightly broody. So maybe a rock star?" I paused. "But your tattoos are very earthy, so maybe a hippie rock star? Ohhh, a lead singer from a seventies hippie band. We'd have to get a wig, though. Or maybe you'd be the drummer—"

Callan cut me off with a groan. "For the love of botany, remind me to never let you dress me, local."

I scoffed in faux offense, but a warm glow filled me as the weight of his jacket pressed into my shoulders and the comforting tingle of his presence cocooned me even more than his coat.

Chapter Thirty-Five

"Whoever had the idea for these fairy costumes was a genius. Oh wait, that was me!" Coral said as she put on her orange wings.

"We're not fairies. We're woodland sprites," Aurielle corrected.

The four of us were in coordinating costumes—with Yasmin in lavender-purple, Aurielle in cornflower-blue, and me in dark-green. We had vines and moss adhered to our outfits and earthy glitter tones highlighting our eyes and cheeks. For people who didn't celebrate Halloween, magical botanists sure knew how to do a costume.

"Don't forget your foliage." Yasmin settled a thin orange flower crown on Coral's head.

We gathered our moss-covered lanterns—the final piece of our attire—and headed outside. Callan had dodged the question of whether he would come out tonight, but I couldn't help searching the group, hoping to see him. As far as execution went, this costume far outdid my plant lady one.

When we reached the clearing where the garden party was

being held, glowing moonflowers encircled the ground as well as beeswax candlelit pumpkins carved with botanical shapes.

Most of the costumes around us were nature-inspired in some way. I jumped to the side when a student started walking toward us that I almost didn't see, their tree-person costume camouflaged so completely with the forest nearby.

"Gahh!" Coral shouted, apparently noticing the man a moment after I did. "You scared the spores out of me."

The tree-costumed botanist smiled, white teeth appearing from somewhere in the greenery. "Sorry," an amused voice said, and the tree continued on to join a group of students by the fire.

The four of us mingled with some of the other fern students and sampled the various snacks provided, all of which were served in tiny hollow pumpkins that my friends and I had prepared.

"Look at that costume! Wait. Is that... Hollis?" Coral's voice was low as I followed her gaze to one of the firepits.

Hollis was wearing fabric that looked like a terracotta pot around his waist and had fern fronds splaying across his stomach, chest, and arms. He wore a spiked crown made of fern leaves that somehow made him look manly instead of ridiculous. He was like a Greek god, if they'd ever dressed up in that much foliage.

"Coral, you might want to pick up your jaw before he notices," Aurielle said.

"I just wasn't expecting to see him in a costume, let alone one as good as that. He had to have put some real thought and planning into it." Her eyes shot to Waylon, who was laughing with friends at another firepit. He hadn't dressed up.

"Is someone acknowledging that the fern founder's descendant might not be a total jerk?" Yasmin asked, raising an eyebrow.

"I give credit where credit is due," Coral said.

Once we all managed to get over the shock of Hollis's incredibly detailed costume, we wandered around the field, chatting with classmates and admiring costumes.

After about an hour of socializing, there was a whisper of a breeze at the back of my neck. I turned, and a light glowing in the forest caught my attention. I wandered toward it, wondering if it was part of someone's costume. But then a swirl of leaves kicked up around my ankles, and I snagged a piece of paper from the air.

The paper had the familiar design of roots and leaves printed on it and was shaped like an arrow. As I held it, the arrow spun so that it was pointing deeper into the forest. I glanced back toward the clearing.

Yasmin was deep in conversation with a classmate, Coral was laughing with Waylon, and Aurielle was admiring the beadwork on a rainforest-inspired costume, complete with living butterflies flitting around it.

I clutched the paper and stepped deeper into the forest, knowing exactly what was going on. After weeks of wondering when it would happen, my initiation to the Root and Vine Society was about to begin.

Chapter Thirty-Six

I tried to step lightly as I crept through the forest, the darkness of the night feeling thick after all the festivities. I clutched my moss-covered lantern tightly. Aside from the moon and stars overhead, it was pitch-black in the forest.

The arrow formed by the paper note led me to the campus's wall, where I crouched and saw the now-familiar tiny arch on the brick. Another gust of leaves flew to me, and I opened a folded sheet of paper. Angling my lantern toward it, I began to read.

Your task is to collect one item from the academy's grounds that will be useful to our goal of preserving the academy from outside influences. What you choose is up to you. For the purposes of this exercise, we will call this your artifact.

My eyes moved further down the page, where text in a smaller typeface contained additional instructions.

*Each pillar will be assessed during your initiation task. These
include:
Pillar 1: Communication:
Send us a message once you have secured your item.
Pillar 2: Stealth navigation:
Navigate through campus to collect your artifact without
raising suspicion.
Pillar 3: Detection:
Secure the artifact, and bring it back with you.
Pillar 4: Distractions:
As needed, create distractions that would prevent someone from
following you or noticing what you are doing.
Note: For the purposes of this exercise, these should be small
distractions. We don't want to attract attention. See Pillar 2.*

I READ THE INSTRUCTIONS AGAIN THEN STOOD UP FROM
where I had been squatting by the fairy door to read the note. I had
to collect an item that could be useful in protecting the academy
from outside influences. What item would be useful if the Board
of Regents continued to flex its power?

I ran through the components of the school that made it the
most powerful. The verdant shield. The instructors. The research
we did here. The library of vast information and resources. Our
connections with the local community. The plants that were the
very soul of the school.

I couldn't exactly run off with any of those items, except for
maybe a few plants. I considered it further. What would be useful
to have if we wanted to do things without the board knowing? I
felt the Shasta lily pendant, which was hanging from a thin chain
around my neck and tucked into my top. Being able to sneak on
and off campus without detection was clearly useful. But bringing
the pendant the Root and Vine Society had provided me felt a
little like cheating.

My mind snagged on something. Aurielle had said she had

noticed a second fairy door in a completely different part of campus from where I stood now. If there was any chance that area contained a *second* petal portal and I could confirm it, that information could be valuable to us.

Aurielle, as far as I knew, was still at the Halloween party. I had seen the folder where she kept her cartography club materials many times. It was probably in her room right now. Going with my gut, I made my way back toward the academy and went inside.

The central vein and staircase were both empty, most of the students being at the party. Despite not seeing anyone, I tried to step nonchalantly as I went to the door next to mine. We rarely kept our rooms locked at Evergreen Academy unless you were Callan, who apparently warded his door.

I twisted the knob and let out a breath of relief when the door pushed inward and the room was dark and empty. I went straight for Aurielle's desk and found her cartography club folder sitting in clear view, secured with a rope of plant material. I opened the folder and scanned it for any indication of fairy doors, finding it on the sixth page.

Moments later, I had copied a rough sketch of the area and notes that Aurielle had included on a second piece of paper. I returned her map to the folder, tied it closed, and headed back for the door.

"I'm just grabbing my jacket. You wait here." Coral's voice came from the other side of the door, and I froze.

I scanned the room as I considered my options. I could make up an excuse for being in here on the fly, I could hide, or I could sneak out. My pounding heart was taking all the oxygen from my brain, and I couldn't come up with an excuse, so I squeezed behind Aurielle's bed and ducked out of sight just as I heard the door opening.

I nearly cursed when I remembered my lantern was glowing, and I hastily yanked a blanket from the bed to cover it.

The closet door slid open, and Coral hummed softly as she

presumably reached for her coat. Less than thirty seconds later, the door clicked closed again, and I heard talking on the other side.

I blew out all the air from my lungs as I emerged from behind the bed. I gave it a few minutes for Coral and whoever she had been with to get down the stairs, returned Aurielle's blanket, then I hurried out of my friends' room. Once outside, I lifted the mossy lantern, allowing it to light my steps.

Based on Aurielle's sketches and what she had told me before, I made my way to the west side of campus, where rows of citrus orchards lined the ground. I studied the hastily copied notes more carefully now, following the little details to the wall. I scanned the bottom as I walked, holding the lantern out to illuminate it.

Aurielle, the precise scholar she was, had included latitude and longitude values, but I had no way of checking those. I would have to use my eyes instead. After about five minutes of searching, the standard brick of the wall was interrupted by a tiny fairy door outline. It was at ankle height, like the other one.

"Now, to confirm if you're a petal portal," I murmured. I looked around, squinting at the thin citrus trees whose branches barely extended to the wall. Climbing them to get over the wall wouldn't be an option.

The ground didn't produce any options either. I saw nothing there but earth and grass. I eyed the trees again. The ruby red grapefruit was already producing, and an idea began to form.

I collected as many grapefruit as I could carry, stacked them near the fairy door, then went back for more. Eventually, I had a tall-enough fruit stack of stairs to climb and hoist myself over the wall. It didn't seem super secure to climb on a footstool made of orbs, but I didn't have any other ideas. I climbed the stacked stair set of grapefruit and reached my arms onto the top of the wall.

"Here goes everything," I said, grasping the pendant and stepping onto the wall. I sat atop it for a few moments, waiting for a sensation that would discourage me from climbing, or to set off some kind of alarm, but nothing happened.

I started to smile then realized I didn't know if the verdant shield only worked one way. To be sure, I would need to get off the wall and climb over it again from the other side. I hopped down and gratefully noted the California black oak on the outside side of the wall. I scaled it easily and sidled along one of its limbs then dropped down on the wall. I held my breath as I climbed over, but everything went smoothly.

"Well, well, looks like you *are* a petal portal," I said aloud. At that, a drop of cold water landed on my cheek, and I looked up. It was beginning to rain, and I needed to hurry back to the academy if I wanted to avoid getting soaked. It meant that the Halloween partygoers would likely be streaming inside as well.

I looked at the instructions from the Root and Vine Society again.

Each pillar will be assessed during your initiation task. These include:
Pillar 1: Communication:
Send us a message once you have secured your item.
Pillar 2: Stealth navigation:
Navigate through campus to collect your artifact without raising suspicion.
Pillar 3: Detection:
Secure the artifact, and bring it back with you.
Pillar 4: Distractions:
As needed, create distractions that would prevent someone from following you or noticing what you are doing
Note: For the purposes of this exercise, these should be small distractions. We don't want to attract attention. See Pillar 2.

For Pillar 3, the only artifact I had secured were the notes I had copied down in Aurielle's room. That would have to be enough. I hadn't created a distraction for Pillar 4, but I had successfully hidden from Coral. Did that count? For Pillar 2, as far as I knew, no one had seen me. That left Pillar 1, communication. I couldn't send a leaf message on campus. Should I try to climb back over the wall and send one from the other side?

The rain was increasing by the second, and I wanted to run back to campus, but the leaf messages were the only communication method I could think of. I turned around and used the unstable grapefruit stack to climb over again, noting that I should probably disperse that before I went back. Rain splashed my head, sharp and cold, as I faced the California black oak and examined its tissues.

"You are the most majestic black oak I've ever seen," I said. A moment after the compliment, her leaves floated down to me, and I readied my message. I kept the pencil Callan had given me in the small bag I carried at almost all times, and I used that to link the message to him and sent it off. Then I scaled the tree, said a quick thank you, moved the grapefruit so they would look like they had fallen randomly from the trees during the rainstorm, and began to run toward the academy building.

My heart was racing and my clothes were soaked through by the time I entered the central vein. Thankfully, no one seemed to notice my heightened state as they were all in the business of shaking off their costumes, getting their hair blow-dried by the tree affinities, or brewing extra-hot mugs of tea.

I joined my friends, who were waiting in line for their own hot beverages.

"B! There you are. We were worried when it started raining and we couldn't find you," Yasmin said.

"All good. Though I got soaked, obviously." I shimmied in my forest sprite costume, and water flung to the ground. An aquatic affinity walked by and, with the wave of their hands and a singsong Floracantus, the water flopped into a bucket they were carrying.

My heart was still racing as we collected our tea. It felt wrong not to tell my friends what I was doing, but I had a feeling there might be time for that down the road, if any of what the Root and

Vine Society was doing ended up being important. For now, I listened to their animated conversation about the social goings-on of the night.

My eyes locked with Hollis's as he entered the room half an hour later, shaking his head to the side to dispel a sheet of water from his fern frond crown. He grinned and winked at me, and I wondered what artifact *he* had acquired.

Chapter Thirty-Seven

The next morning, I was walking through the flowering gardens after an affinity studies session with the florals. After all the rain the previous night, the flowers were extra vibrant, and it had been a good time to conduct a study on nectar dilution.

As I neared the edge of the flower garden, the petals of a nearby honeysuckle began to shake, sprinkling pollen dust over the front of my dress.

"What on earth?" I looked around as I wiped the pollen from my outfit. Seeing no one, I turned back to the bush.

And that was when I saw the tiny piece of paper, folded into a flower shape and nestled into the plant. I carefully withdrew it and unfolded the paper. The typewritten font was familiar.

Come now. The usual place.

Without a moment's hesitation, I hurried to the first petal portal. As I was getting ready to climb, Hollis appeared.

"Can I join you? No tree affinity."

"Sure, but how did you do it the first time?"

"My lights led along the ground the whole way after I crossed over the wall. Tree walking is faster."

Together, Hollis and I tree walked the path I had taken before, him walking close behind me to catch the tree trail that was created for me.

"We were all impressed with your potted fern costume last night," I called over my shoulder.

I could practically hear Hollis's chest puffing out. "Who is 'all'?"

"Me and my friends Yasmin, Aurielle, and Coral."

"Good. It takes a fern affinity to truly appreciate the level of detail I went into."

"I think Coral will be talking about the symmetry of your fronds for days."

"That's one compliment I'll never forget."

"What did you get for your artifact?" I asked. "It must have been something from outside, given the state of your costume at the end of the night."

There was a soft clinking noise behind me, and I glanced back to see Hollis holding a velvet pouch. "Gemstones."

My eyes widened. "Wouldn't those come from Professor East's office?"

"Not if you know where the gemstone cave is."

"I'm sorry. Gemstone *cave*?" I asked, incredulous.

"You didn't think these were ordinary gemstones, did you? They're all formed here on campus."

I whistled. "Nice going."

"How about you? Ahh, fronds," Hollis moaned.

"What is it?" We had reached the waterfall, and I paused to look at the sunset that was blooming brilliantly around us like a field of poppies and zinnias.

"My path goes over the rocks on the side over there, but they're all slippery and treacherous."

"Maybe I can make a water bubble around you if you want to

pass through the pool instead," I offered. I had made a few small ones during my aquatic affinity studies the previous year. "It would keep you and the gemstones dry."

"Um, yes please," Hollis said, moving to the edge of the water.

"Okay, just give me a second." I recalled the Floracantus for trapping a bubble of air in water. "*Aqua tegmina*," I said firmly, swirling my hands to scoop the water around Hollis. I was concentrating too hard to smile, but Hollis's face broke into a grin as a shimmery screen formed around him.

"Hot fronds!" he exclaimed, and he sounded like he was underwater.

I laughed, then I dove in next to him.

We were the first ones in the cave, aside from Kaito. Callan was nowhere in sight. I felt a twinge of nerves, hoping everyone had managed to collect an artifact without getting caught.

Hollis—perfectly dry from my bubble—was the picture of confidence as he sat on a large boulder, legs crossed at the ankles in front of him, studying the eclectic assortment of plants in the Evergreen Conservatory.

Other students began to emerge over the rocks on the sides of the waterfall—or from the pool, in Nalin's case—the tension increasing as we waited for the final recruits to arrive.

Five minutes later, Callan finally joined us. Hollis stood and fist-bumped him as if he was already an accepted member of the club. Then, at last, Kaito got started.

"Welcome, everyone. We received each of your messages—well done on that," Kaito said. "Now, you'll each share your artifact with the group. Any volunteers want to go first?"

Hollis raised a lazy finger then poured some of the gemstones into his palm, where they glimmered by the fireflies and moonlight. There were many appreciative exclamations, and it was clear that the other non-founders' descendants hadn't known about the Gemstone Cave either.

Heath went next. "I brought the Wisteria Wind Chimes. Floral affinities swear they can calm any situation, and there's only one set on campus."

Kaito nodded. "Could be useful. Who's next?"

Ravenna, the grasses affinity, stepped forward. "I got the list of all field studies assignments from Professor Tenella's office."

I narrowed my eyes, wondering if my classified assignment was on there.

"Good find," Callan nodded appreciatively. "Those are valuable connections to know about."

Nalin from aquatics shared next. "I took some of our most sensitive research from the greenhouse research labs. I thought it could be used as leverage, at least."

Laurus lifted a slim book from inside his coat. *"Recipes for Deception.* It's an old book, and we're not really supposed to use it. It contains herbal recipes that can alter someone's response times, among other things."

"Devious," Callan said. "I like it."

"I also selected a book." Meadow pulled a much larger tome from her bag. "The collected histories of the founders."

Kaito's eyes widened. "Where did you get that?"

Meadow's voice was even as she said, "Professor East's office."

We all whistled appreciatively.

"Nice work," Kaito said. "Callan and I also wanted to contribute. I collected our contracts with local businesses."

Callan looked at me as if assessing whether I wanted to go next. When I shrugged, he walked to a dark portion of the cave and returned with a collection of small nursery pots with green sprouts growing from the soil. "Scouting vine seedlings. I think we should be prepared to set up our own countersurveillance."

That garnered a round of "Hear! Hear!"

All eyes turned to me. "Okay, I don't have anything physical to share, but I do have a location that could be useful."

"Location?" Kaito asked.

"There's another petal portal on campus."

Chapter Thirty-Eight

At my revelation about the petal portal, there were a few murmured gasps and plenty of eager faces as the questions rained down.

"A second one?" Nalin asked. "Does that mean there could be more?"

"How do you know? Did you go over it?" Laurus asked.

I answered each of their questions until Callan reeled the conversation in.

"That was an excellent find, Briar. I take it you didn't stumble upon the portal by accident?" he asked.

I shook my head. "Aurielle, one of the fern affinities, has been leading a cartography club this year. They are the ones who found it."

"Will she update you if she finds any others?" Callan asked.

"Yes," I said, certain that wouldn't be a problem.

"Okay, a successful initiation all around. Each of you produced items that could help our cause in some way. Very nice work." He nodded to Kaito.

Kaito surveyed the cave. "Congratulations, you are all officially members of the Root and Vine Society. We will work as a team to determine how to use the materials we have gathered as well as to share intelligence. We will also each be expected to research the *Vanished Compendium*." Kaito paced around the cavern, looking from face to face. "In this society, we consider it part of our mission to protect the academy from corruption and undue influence. If signs continue to point in that direction, we may up our efforts to support the school."

"I'm all for that, but do you really think the nine of us, and the items we gathered, can do anything against the Board of Regents?" Ravenna asked.

"Never underestimate the power of a small but dedicated coalition," Callan said, standing with his arms behind his back like a soldier at parade rest. "Each of us has unique gifts and influence that might be exactly what this group needs, if we're willing to use them when the time comes."

The fragrance of the floral varieties hanging overhead was the only thing keeping me slightly calm. The school's protective force was forming right in front of my eyes. And with Callan leading it, how could we fail? I still didn't know how deep the threat to our school truly ran, but I wasn't going to let grass grow under my feet if things got worse.

"Now, for the ritual that all members have taken part in since the dawn of the Root and Vine Society." Kaito waved to the abundant plant life around us. "Add your plant signature to the Evergreen Conservatory."

I studied the walls more closely, as Hollis had been doing before, seeing the plants dangling from them in a whole new light. While the flashier plants like wisteria dominated the scene, there were hundreds of species embedded into the walls of the cave, creating a tapestry of life.

"You can leave the cave to get your plant of choice," Kaito said. "Make sure your signature is embedded before you return to the academy for the night."

The botanists began to disperse, exiting the cave to choose a plant of their lead affinity.

I turned to Callan. "Where's your signature?"

"Take a closer look. Can you tell?"

I scanned the area again. There were tree bits grafted onto the cave all over the place. How to know which was Callan's?

I opened up my senses and searched the tree's cells. When my attention caught on a tiny tree growing out of the cave wall, there was a familiar sensation in the magic that tied it to the stone.

Callan had demonstrated his magic to me many times since we'd met. I knew it almost as well as I knew my own. That graft was his signature style. So simple. So clever. And unlike the other tree bits that were only a branch or two, he had managed to include the whole miniature tree there.

"That one," I said, pointing to it.

He nodded, a slow smile creeping across his lips. "Very good." Callan's voice dropped even lower, his eyes never leaving mine as he leaned in closer and said, "As much as I liked your plant lady costume, I think the fairy gave it a run for its money."

I startled, heat flushing my neck. I hadn't known Callan had seen my costume, but apparently, he had noticed me from some secret vantage point during the evening.

"Yeah, well, I hadn't intended on traipsing through the entire forest and scaling a wall in it. I'm surprised I didn't leave a trail of glitter from the scene of the crime straight to my room."

Callan's lips twitched, then he nodded toward the mouth of the cave, urging me to start my task.

I swam out of the cave, noting a little tug of pleasure deep in my belly. Each slow smile from Callan was like the first bloom of a dormant plant in spring. Sweet, assuring, and with the promise of something to come.

Once I was back on campus, I headed straight for the Perilous Grove. While I could have chosen from any of the plant affinities, I was starting to identify with the defensive plants much more since my training with Petra. Plus, I was the only one in the group with a defensive plant affinity. It seemed fitting to make that my contribution.

I scanned my plant options, wanting to choose something that would add to the beauty of the space despite its deadly qualities. Before long, I landed on lily of the valley. The delicate white bells drew the eye immediately.

By the time I collected a bunch of the flowers and returned to the cave, other botanists were already in the midst of attaching their plants to the damp floor or walls.

Studying the area, I noticed a spot that was typically dark but where a sliver of moonlight was beginning to shine through, illuminating the pool of water below. Perhaps it was where the name Moonlit Falls had come from. I got to work grafting my flowers to the wall.

I glanced at Callan, thinking of when he had me practice grafting on our rock climbing outing. Callan was watching Laurus attach a bundle of sage to an already overfull portion of the wall.

Once my lilies of the valley were grafted, I took a step back and admired them. They were shining in the moonlight, like little moons themselves.

"Interesting choice," Callan whispered in my ear, and I shivered, not realizing he had joined me.

"Exactly. It's unassuming. Only the people who know its power will ever see it coming."

Chapter Thirty-Nine

November rolled along, and I met Petra each week in the lantern-lit cabin on Mount Shasta to continue our development of counterpoisons. Tonight was our last meeting of the month, and I could tell we were both itching to make some progress.

"Okay, the yarrow- and comfrey-based concoctions didn't go anywhere, but maybe this sweet clover will give us something." Petra stirred a pot that was simmering on a camp stove. "Once this cools, you can test it out. Let me get the shield up."

Petra stepped outside, and I knew she was touching the earth, imbuing it with a shield that we hoped slightly imitated the one at Evergreen Academy. The only way to truly test if any of our antidotes worked would occur when I went back on campus, but we were both hopeful of some kind of breakthrough here under similar conditions.

A few minutes later, I felt access to my powers cut off. It wasn't as stark as it was at the academy. I could feel that they were there, but it was like they were resting behind a thin wall. Petra stepped back inside and closed the door. "It's ready. How's the antidote looking?"

I held up the drinking glass I had poured a portion into. "It doesn't smell great."

"Well, at least you've got the honey for taste. Okay, go ahead."

I lifted the cup to my lips and swallowed a tablespoon-size serving. The concoction was lukewarm and syrupy. Then as practiced, I began to test my magic at five-minute intervals.

"*Petale expandere*," I said, aiming the Floracantus at the wilted flowers on the table. After our previous tests, I wasn't expecting anything to happen, but Petra was rigorous with the scientific method.

Then I thought I saw a few of the petals twitch, and I jumped up excitedly. "I think something happened!"

"Try it again," Petra said, locking her eyes on the flowers.

"*Petale expandere*," I said, more heartily this time. Now, though, I didn't notice any twitching.

"Hmm, I didn't see anything. Did you *feel* a connection to the plant, like you would when your powers are unblocked?"

I thought about it then shook my head. "I don't think so. I might have imagined the twitching."

Petra nodded and recorded something on her data sheet. "Let's keep testing every five minutes for the next hour, just in case."

We finished out our testing, but I didn't see any further evidence of gains. I was trying not to get discouraged as we were still in the early stages of our research, but I couldn't help wondering how many more antidotes we would have to test. Would we ever find one that truly worked?

An hour later, as we cleaned up, my mind was on the *Vanished Compendium*. Could it have the solutions that we were looking for? Or was the issue of magical botanists poisoning each other's power a newer nuisance?

Members of the Root and Vine Society—and many others— had been searching for the book for centuries. I wondered, not for the first time, why no one had found it yet. I glanced at my field studies instructor, one of the most knowledgeable magical botanists I knew.

"Petra, what do you do when you're trying to find information but it's being elusive?"

Petra's forehead rippled. "Elusive?"

"You know, when you're doing research and combing through all kinds of books that are related to the topic but you aren't landing on exactly what you're looking for."

"Ahhh." She seemed to catch the meaning of the English word. "I get as close to the primary source material as possible. For example, if I were wanting to learn about how magical botanists used nightshade in the eighteenth century"—she nodded toward the nightshade in the basket of deadly plants—"I would try to find journals of defensive plant botanists of the era."

I mulled over her words. There were plenty of primary sources in the Evergreen Academy library, and various members of our group had been reading through them. But were we looking in the right place?

The Root and Vine Society had been seeking information on the *Vanished Compendium*, but if both books were created around the same time, maybe learning more about the known book would be helpful.

"Have you ever seen the original edition of the *Compendium Floracantus*?" I asked, keeping my voice casual even though I was sure my question felt out-of-the-blue to Petra.

"I have, in fact, on a trip to the Louvre. It's stored behind thick phytoglass and masked as an example of an old healer's grimoire. But even through the phytoglass, I could feel the power of the botanists who created it radiating from the pages."

I paused my work. "Really? You could feel it? How close were you?"

"I think I sensed it as soon as I stepped in the Louvre, but it got stronger the closer I went. Why? Thinking about making a trip?"

"Something like that," I murmured. I thought about Callan's ability to sense powers. "You don't have a special ability to sense when power is being used, do you?"

Petra shook her head. "No, that is a very rare gift indeed. What I experienced with the book is more like a magical signature. The book is a powerful artifact, and any magical botanist would be able to feel the magic coming from it if they got close enough."

So the original *Compendium Floracantus* emitted traces of magic. That shouldn't have come as a surprise. If there was a second volume, would it also put off a magical beacon? Would botanists be able to sense it if they got close enough?

This only made it seem more likely that the other book had been destroyed. If the *Vanished Compendium* was as powerful as its sister, some magical botanists throughout history would had to have sensed it.

I tucked the information away. Even if it wouldn't be helpful in the mission of the Root and Vine Society, every little detail helped inform my understanding of the society of magical botanists. And the more I learned, the more I wanted to know.

Chapter Forty

I asked Callan to meet me in the library the next night. Petra's revelations about seeing the original *Compendium Floracantus* had sparked something in me, and I wanted to discuss it with the person who could help me sort through my thoughts.

Callan came in with two mugs of delicious apple cider hot toddies, and he set one on the table in front of me. I was amazed that the library didn't have a rule against drinks besides water, but I guessed that most of the important books were protected with enchantments that would repel any spilled liquid.

"Midnight study sessions. Really, local?"

I shook my head ruefully. Around us, the library was perfectly quiet, the other students having migrated to their rooms or other parts of the academy grounds for the night.

"Nobody's ever in here this late."

"So you wanted some alone time with me?" Callan's voice was completely even, but there was a glint in his eyes.

I took a pointed sip of hot toddy. "Yes, actually. I want to discuss some theories about the book."

Callan raised an eyebrow. Behind us, the wind whisked the

library door closed, and there was a faint swirling sound that I knew was a light breeze creating a sound barrier around us.

He had been checking the library regularly for scouting plants, and so far had rooted out the only one he had found, placing it in a different portion of the academy.

"What's on your mind?"

It was incredible how he could switch from mildly flirty casual-heartthrob Callan to strictly serious academic-heartthrob Callan.

"My field studies advisor said that when she visited the Louvre, she could sense the *Compendium Floracantus* because of the traces of magic it contains. Why do you think no one has sensed the magic of the *Vanished Compendium* yet?"

Callan contemplated my words. "It's a good question and one I've thought about before. My best guess is that it's being suppressed somehow."

I frowned. That would throw a wrench in things. "Without the ability to sense it, it seems like it would be impossible to find."

"It would, unless there was something that could serve as a tracking beacon," Callan said casually, flipping one of the pages of a nearby book.

I sat up straighter.

He knew something.

"Spill."

He studied my face for a moment, as if he wanted to drag out whatever reveal was coming. Finally, he said, "One line of inquiry has been into the quills that were used to write the books. Obviously, the books were penned before the printing press was widely available. There is evidence that suggests the magical botanists around that time connected their books to their quills. It helped them identify who the authors were in case anyone tried to steal another's work. The quills would point in the direction of the book they authored."

"They connected their quills to their books to avoid plagiarism?" I asked.

"Stealing art was a thing even back then, it seems."

"So you're saying that scholars think the quills that were used to write the *Compendium Floracantus* and the possible *Vanished Compendium* are out there somewhere?"

"Not just somewhere. Many of the authors' quills have been preserved over the years. They give off magical signatures like the one your field studies advisor mentioned. Most of them are still accessible. There's even one that was said to have been used to pen the rumored *Vanished Compendium*."

I sat up straighter. "Has anyone tried to use it?"

Callan leaned back in his seat and took a slow pull on his hot toddy. "The Root and Vine Society has attempted it multiple times over the years. By their accounts, it just spins around wildly and doesn't point in a specific direction."

My hope deflated like an underwater fiddle-leaf fig. "So it's a dead end, then."

"Maybe. Unless we learn why the quill spins, and how to make it stop."

To console myself, I navigated to a section of the *Compendium Floracantus* that referenced magic that tied things together. Getting my brain around how the quills operated might take the sting off the letdown.

Across the table from me, Callan fell into quiet research as well, both of us reading and sipping our drinks. By the time I neared the end of the section I was studying, a warm buzz was filling my brain. I heard Callan sigh and flip his book closed, and I prepared to call it a night.

Then my eyes snagged on a footnote. I read it once, twice, then jumped to my feet.

"Are you okay?" Callan asked, clearly startled. The loose waves on the top of his head had extra volume now, as if he'd been running his hands through them while he read.

"Read this." I slid the book toward him and watched as his eyes began to scan the page. "The footnote," I clarified.

Callan spoke aloud. "'The magic tying two objects together that was used during this period required a piece of every affinity power the botanist wielded. Because most botanists at the time are believed to have had every affinity power, modern botanists are unable to replicate this type of Floracantus at the same level.'"

I waited with bated breath for Callan's reaction.

"What am I not seeing?" Callan asked, clearly sensing the excitement in me.

"Modern botanists can't create these strong tying spells because they don't have all the affinity powers."

"Right," Callan said slowly.

"So what if modern botanists can't use the quill's locating feature correctly because they don't have all the affinity powers?" I bit my lip, knowing he would get it now.

"Most modern botanists don't, but *you* do." He looked at me in awe, and I grinned.

"Maybe the quill would work for me. If we could get our hands on it."

Callan leaned back and linked his hands together behind his head. "I think I might be able to help you there."

"You know where this quill is right now?"

"I do indeed, local." The look Callan was giving me would normally have my insides melting, but I was too excited by this latest development to get trapped in how handsome he looked.

"Finding the missing book is like finding a needle in a haystack. But with a compass"—I pointed to the compass rose on a nearby map—"navigation becomes a lot easier." Rivers of excitement flowed through my veins as I watched Callan's eyes drink me in.

Callan stood and came around the table. He scooped me into a hug, picking me off the floor completely. "You're a genius, local."

"Finally, someone realizes it," I teased. I knew the hot toddies were making us both extra exuberant, but I didn't care. This was good news. This was a lead to chase. And we had found it—together.

I realized then that Callan's arms were still around me, and since I was lifted a few inches off the floor, our faces were level. My breath caught. He was wearing that cologne that was so delicious every time he came around with it on. It had been invading my senses all evening, and I had done my best to ignore it.

Now, I let myself breathe it in, enjoying the warm feeling it evoked.

Callan set me down and gently removed his hands from my waist. We were still standing close, and I wasn't sure if it was the hot toddy or the buzz from the discovery, but I whispered, "Did you get a new cologne?"

Callan pulled back, and a smile tugged at the corner of his mouth. "You noticed."

"I did."

"Do you like it?"

"A little."

"Well, scientifically speaking, you should."

I raised an eyebrow. "What are you talking about?"

"Remember last year when we did the phenols testing in class?"

"Yes," I said slowly, vaguely remembering the lab where we had tested and ranked different chemical compounds by smell.

"I may have seen a glimpse of your chart."

"You what?"

"Your chart. Where you listed your favorite scents."

I tried to contain my jaw from falling open. "And you... what? Made a cologne out of my favorites?"

"A few of your favorites. If I put them all in there, it would have smelled terrible."

"Peaches and sandalwood," I murmured, feeling like the heat of a fresh garden pepper was coursing through me.

"Those are the main notes, yes."

I had to suppress a huge smile and tried to grin coyly as I

shoved gently at his chest. "Callan Rhodes, were you trying to impress me?"

"I just thought, since we were spending so much time together, it wouldn't hurt if I smelled good to you."

He smelled more than good, but after this little stunt, I couldn't let that on. "Well, the jokes on you because I listed my results in reverse. You're wearing my least favorite aromas."

"Is that right?" he asked, voice and expression telling me he knew what a liar I was. "I'll have to keep experimenting then."

"You do that."

Chapter Forty-One

A few weeks later, we were exiting our lab room after Plant Adaptations when Professor Tenella raised her voice in the central vein.

"Botanists! Please gather in the tearoom. There is an announcement."

My friends and I exchanged looks but joined our classmates in the tearoom, which was dimly lit by the wall sconces and the roaring fireplace instead of the sun that streamed through the wall of glass in other seasons. It had been overcast all week, which matched the tone I was picking up on from the instructors.

Professor Sage and the Kitchen Botany rotation students were already there, doling out miniature pies that I suspected contained chamomile and citrus. What was going on?

Professor Tenella raised her voice. "We've had a declaration from the Board of Regents. Starting after the winter solstice, all campus clubs will require board approval to continue operating. All club hosts will be asked to submit evidence of scholarly contribution from their club, which will then be evaluated by the board."

Murmurs of discouragement ripped through the students

around me. I glanced at Aurielle, whose lips were smashed together as she focused on Professor Tenella.

"We understand that this may come as a surprise, as Evergreen Academy has long had a tradition of social clubs organized by our trusted student body and allowed to self-manage. At this time, our options are to pause all clubs or allow them to continue while the hosts submit their reports. We prefer to let you all continue. If anyone needs support in generating their evidence for the board, please reach out to any of your instructors, and we will be happy to help."

A first-year student walked by with a tray, and I took one of the steaming pies. The fragrance immediately took the edge off of the anxiety. Professor Sage was some kind of magician.

"Professor East is away, but you may direct concerns or inquires to him upon his return. The kitchen and hearth here will be open all night for those club members who would like to gather and discuss plans. Now, please get comfortable and enjoy your pies."

With that, the announcement was over.

"Aurielle, do you think they'll approve the cartography club?" Coral asked, obviously having the same question as me.

"I hope I can put together a strong case for it, but we've only been in place for a few months. I can submit the maps of the portions of campus we've evaluated so far, but that's really it."

Something stirred in me at her words. If Aurielle submitted her maps, it would contain the locations of the two known petal portals. Obviously, they wouldn't be labeled as portals in her documentation, but would the distinctive *fairy door* markings mean something to the Board of Regents?

"How closely do you think they'll even evaluate the 'evidence'?" Coral asked, putting the last word in finger quotes. "They probably already know which clubs they want to stick around and which they don't. This is getting ridiculous."

"I'm sure you'll put forward a great case," Yasmin assured

Aurielle. "Are your other club members here? Do you want to go talk to them?"

"Yeah, we'd better start preparing our game plan. I'll catch up with you all later," Aurielle said.

"I'm going to talk to Waylon," Coral said. "He's part of the Houseplant Curators Club."

"I'd like to meet with the Apothecary Arts Club. I've made most of my makeup and skin care with them. Maybe they'll need some help with their evidence," Yasmin said.

My friends went their separate ways, and I finished my pie in a few quick bites then went straight toward the table where Callan was standing with some fellow tree affinities. He stepped away from them and nodded toward the glass door. I knew that signal. He wanted to meet in the treehouses.

I left first, and he joined me at our treehouse a few minutes after I arrived. "I invited the others," he said.

"The rest of the Root and Vine Society?"

Callan nodded. "Some of them aren't available as they are in other clubs and don't want to raise suspicion. But Meadow, Ravenna, and Laurus should be out shortly. I asked them to stagger their arrival."

Once the five of us were gathered in the treehouse, I heard the familiar whooshing sound of Callan putting up a wind sound barrier around us.

I didn't waste any time with small talk. "What should we do about this? This is exactly the type of thing the Root and Vine Society would oppose, right?"

Meadow was the first to agree. "Total authoritarian overreach."

"Why do they care what clubs we have anyway?" Ravenna asked.

"They want to ensure botanists are using their time *effectively*," Callan said. "It's all part of the goal to get us into positions of more influence in society."

"Not everyone wants to run a government department or be CEO of a scientific start-up," Ravenna said.

"So, it's back to Briar's question," Laurus said. "What should we do?"

"Is there a handbook for the school where we could point to the allowance of student-hosted clubs?" I asked, hoping I wasn't letting on how ignorant I was of the structure of the school.

"Nothing in writing. The instructors have always been given wide latitude to approve clubs. Until now," Meadow said.

"I have the *Recipes for Deception* book I acquired for initiation. Maybe we could influence whoever comes to review the evidence?" Laurus suggested.

"Not a bad idea, though it's a temporary solution," Ravenna said.

I could tell Callan was holding his opinion back, waiting to hear what the rest of us had to say. When all of us turned to him, he finally spoke. "We could try to fight this, and I'll go along with whatever the group decides, but there could be some value in leaving it be."

Meadow narrowed her eyes. "What do you mean?"

"This is clear evidence of overreach. It's probably going to upset a lot of students, especially if their clubs aren't approved. Students will share their frustrations with their families. This may spread awareness of what's going on here and mobilize even more people against what the Board of Regents is doing."

We all sat silently for a moment, considering his words.

"You're suggesting that we give the board a small win now so that when the time comes for a bigger fight, people will be primed for it?" I asked, piecing together what Callan was envisioning.

Callan nodded slowly. "An illusion of a win, at least. Hopefully, all the clubs will put together strong evidence and be allowed to continue. We can show our cards early, or we can hold out until we have even more power." His eyes darted to me.

"The *Vanished Compendium*?" Laurus asked.

We had filled in the rest of the Root and Vine Society about our idea to attempt to have me use the quill as a compass to the missing book.

Callan nodded again. "In fact, I have an update on that."

The treehouse was completely silent except for the soft rushing of the wind outside and Laurus's rolling of a pencil along his pant leg.

"I've been tracking the location of the quill that is said to be linked to the *Vanished Compendium*. It is currently part of a traveling exhibit. The display was in Australia most recently, but it is headed to the United States next." Callan eyed me meaningfully.

So he had been waiting for the quill to come to us before making any further moves. That explained why things had been quiet since we'd discussed the theory about me being able to access the quill.

"Do you know where in the United States?" Laurus asked.

"Not yet, but it is scheduled to depart Australia before the end of the year. I should have more intel very soon."

My heart was thundering. The end of the year was weeks away. Were we that close to making our attempt at getting the quill?

Meadow spoke up first. "Then I think we go with your plan, Rhodes. We leave this alone, for now, and keep our focus on getting the quill. If the quill works for Briar and can point us to the book, we'll have much more leverage for whatever comes next."

Each person in the group nodded in turn.

Callan rose. "Then we have a plan."

Chapter Forty-Two

"Who's up for wreath making before the gingerbread house competition?" Yasmin asked as the four of us finished dinner in the tearoom three weeks later. Nearly everyone was eating inside now that the winter chill had fully set in. The courtyard connected to the tearoom was empty except for a few birds scavenging for morsels.

"I'm in," I said, and Coral and Aurielle both agreed. The winter solstice had completely snuck up on me, as it seemed to have a habit of doing.

I had been so busy the past month—with Evergreen Academy classes, field studies with Petra, my SCC coursework, and waiting impatiently for next steps on how we would get access to the quill for the Root and Vine Society—that a whole set of classes coming to an end was a bit of a shock. I wasn't ready for a break from my time here. I wanted to keep going at full steam ahead.

But as we settled into one of the large white-columned and glass-walled classrooms to assemble the wreaths, I found myself warming to the change of pace. This had always been a favorite time of year, when most families were celebrating holidays or simply soaking in the wonder of closing out another excursion around the sun.

I gathered a variety of evergreen boughs and began to weave them around the circular wire wreath frames. Bryce's house had a larger door than the apartment my aunt and I had lived in, so I decided to go for a bolder wreath this year.

"What's everyone doing for the winter break? Aurielle, is your family going to the fern conservatory again this year?" I asked.

Aurielle shook her head. "Sadly, no. We're planning to stay home this year. My parents are worried about the political climate right now. How about you all?"

"Baton Rouge or bust," Coral said, wrangling a large piece of cedar around the frame.

"I'm staying home too," Yasmin said. "To be honest, I'm excited for a break from field studies, which is something I never imagined saying."

My eyebrows pulled together as I looked at my friends. Aurielle and Coral were both nodding. I had been so thrilled with my field studies work I had forgotten my friends were less than happy with their own projects. "Has something happened?" I asked.

Yasmin shook her head. "Nothing major. It's just that the field studies I grew up hearing about were opportunities to train us in conducting real research and contributing scholarship to the field. What I'm doing now feels much more transactional. We're just handing off information that someone in a lab somewhere is going to use to make money."

Coral bobbed her fork up and down in agreement. "It kind of feels like our field studies projects have been weaponized for capitalist gain."

"And mine feels political," Aurielle piped in. "They're pressing our team for environmental data, but they're moving too quickly on wanting results. Studies like the one we're conducting take years to draw any conclusions from, even by magical botanist standards."

"I'm going to bring it up with my parents over the holidays. It will be interesting to hear if they have any concerns about the direction the school is going. Neither are on the board, but with the ferns' annual strategic meeting happening soon, there is sure to be talk," Coral said.

"Fill us in on everything they say," Yasmin said. "Maybe it will help calm the strange feeling I have about all this."

A second-year harvester student named Brie approached our table. "We're looking for volunteers to judge the gingerbread house competition. Any takers?"

I thought about it for a second. If anyone was able to be an impartial judge, it was me, who had no commitment to any particular affinity. "I'll do it."

"Great, thanks," Brie said. She looked around the table.

"I want to participate," Coral said, rubbing her hands together.

"Ferns are going to dominate, quietly and calmly," Aurielle said.

"The materials are on the table over there, so get started whenever you want. Entries have to be in by five tonight. Briar, can you stop by at five to judge?"

"I'll be there," I said.

"Well, ferns, are we ready to do this?" Yasmin asked, looking between Coral and Aurielle.

"Good luck. Though you three are going to make it difficult to be impartial in the judging," I teased.

"I'm sure we'll win on our own merits," Yasmin said sweetly.

"I'll be in the library until five then. I just need to add the final bow." I secured the velvet fabric to the evergreen boughs and gave a satisfied smile. Bryce and Aunt Vera would love it.

As I was heading to the library to sketch while my friends created their gingerbread house, Callan called out to me from the bottom of the stairs. "Wait up!" He bounded up the steps then ushered us both into the library. With a quick look to confirm it was empty except for a couple that was on their way out, he drew me to a far corner.

"I have another update for you regarding your *theory*." He put an emphasis on the last word, and I instantly knew he was talking about the quill.

"Well, don't keep me in suspense forever," I whispered. I had already been waiting weeks for this.

"I've found out where the new display is going to be. Since the ink used with the quills was made of tree gum and oak gall, it will be on a special display at the tree conservatory," Callan said, and my heart began to race.

"And we get to go there?" I was so excited that my voice lifted, and Callan softly touched a finger to my lips, though a smile tugged at the corner of his mouth. *Fronds*, we were standing close in this little corner.

"Yes, I'm still working out a few details of the plan, but it looks like we're going to have a narrow window of opportunity right after Christmas. Meadow's mom works at the moss conservatory, and there's an annual strategic meeting there that can serve as a guise for us to fly to Washington. Meadow will secure us invites as part of a project for school. I'm still formulating how we'll get into the tree conservatory undetected, but at least our trip to Washington won't have to be full stealth."

Energy was buzzing through my veins. "Does everyone else know?"

"Kaito has been spreading the word. The mission will only consist of critical members. It'll draw less attention to have a smaller group."

"Please tell me I'm a critical member."

"The girl who might be able to use the quill?" His eyes were crinkling at the corners, and a warm breeze touched the back of my neck. "I wouldn't dream of leaving you behind."

I smiled so wide I felt it in every corner of my face. I dreamed of seeing one of the conservatories one day. And to get to see the tree conservatory—Callan's lead affinity—the thought was overwhelmingly appealing.

"Good. Because there's no way I'm missing this."

Chapter Forty-Three

"They badgered you into judging too?" Hollis asked as we gathered in the tearoom an hour later.

Brie had had to force some of the students out at five o'clock, my friends included. Who knew magical botanists were so competitive when it came to gingerbread?

"I volunteered."

"Lucky you. A harvester accosted me when I was trying to get some spiced cider," Hollis whispered, leaning sideways toward me but keeping his eyes on Brie, who was pacing in front of the gingerbread houses as if they were precious gems. There was one per affinity group, except for the defensive plants, which didn't have a house.

I laughed and turned to Brie. "So, what are the rules?"

"The categories for evaluation are composition, unique elements, and overall aesthetic," Brie explained. "There are no criteria for taste, so please don't attempt to eat them."

"What a shame," Hollis whispered. "I was planning to eat as many as I could get my hands on."

I rolled my eyes.

Brie handed us each a clipboard with a fancy scoring chart attached. "All right, let's get started."

I walked to the first gingerbread house, which had clearly been created by the tree affinities. The gingerbread had been styled into a treehouse, and fondant leaves and twigs had been magically attached to imitate the look of the treehouses in the forest. Impressive. I made a few notes on my clipboard, marking scores within Brie's complex scoring matrix.

The floral house was up next, and it had been transformed into a magic flower shop, with a mix of real and fondant blooms in vibrant colors exploding from the house.

I moved from display to display, stopping to examine the ferns last. My friends had made the house look like an enchanted fairy garden made mostly of edible fern leaves. I hid a proud smile as I began to score it.

"Clearly the winner." Hollis nodded toward the fern display as he sidled up next to me.

"Says the fern founder's descendant."

He tapped the clipboard with his pencil. "They should have thought about that before roping me into this role."

I laughed but said, "It's impossible to choose. The aquatics one has a glass-bottom boat floating on sugared jelly. I mean... come on. It's pretty fantastic."

"Do what you must. I promise not to rat you out to your friends if you don't give them top marks."

"No collusion!" Brie called from where she stood, leaning in to look at the grasses display, which was somehow swaying as if there were a slight breeze in the room.

Hollis made an affronted face that was still charming, and we went back to marking our scorecards.

At the sound of footsteps behind us, I turned to see a tall man, at least six feet five, with an athletic build and a fancy-looking navy suit enter the room.

"Hollis, there you are."

Hollis stilled but then quickly rolled his shoulders and turned around, the picture of casual indifference. "Dad, what are you doing here?"

Dad? Now that I knew, I could see the resemblance. Same medium-brown skin tone, similar straight noses. The lips were different, though, and I assumed Hollis favored his mom there.

"I've been asked to oversee the verdant shield recharging tonight."

"Oversee? Why?" Hollis asked, voice still sounding bored.

I cast my eyes between them, not sure where the conversation was headed.

"New standard practice," Hollis's dad said.

"Seems like a waste of resources, but whatever floats your fronds," Hollis said, tapping pencil to clipboard.

"That's a matter of opinion," his dad said. "Each affinity group would like to make ourselves a little more present here at the academy. Is this a fellow fern affinity?" The man turned his attention to me.

Hollis didn't look at me as he said, "Yes."

Well, that was *technically* true.

Brie had finished marking then, and she walked toward us. "Briar, Hollis, are you two done scoring?"

"Briar?" Hollis's dad said, his tone much sharper now. "Briar Whelan?"

"That's me," I said, trying to smile politely, though it was strange that someone knew who I was before I knew them.

The man glanced at Hollis, a tinge of irritation in his lips. "You don't say. I'm Nash. I'm glad to see you hanging out with my son. Perhaps he could give you a tour of the fern conservatory some time. Have you ever been to Alaska?"

"Oh, no, not yet—" I began, but Hollis let out a loud sigh, cutting me off.

"Dad, this is not the time and place. Can't you see Briar and I are busy with a project?"

Nash straightened at his son's words but relented. "I'll let you get back to it. Briar, I'd love to speak with you more if you have some time today or tomorrow."

"Nice to meet you," I said, and Nash turned to leave the teahouse.

"Fan-frondin-tastic," Hollis said. "There's no getting away from them."

Brie cleared her throat. "Ready to calculate the winner?"

Hollis's face was as smooth as butter, as if his dad hadn't arrived to supervise the winter solstice events. He turned to Brie, "Yes, chef."

One thing was for sure. The board's influence at Evergreen Academy was continuing to expand, and the younger founders' descendants weren't happy about it.

Chapter Forty-Four

The next night was the winter solstice, and we donned our warm coats, picked up our lanterns, and made our way into the woods for the evening meal.

The long rectangular table that ran the length of a large clearing in the woods was even more spectacular than I remembered. It was covered with flickering candles, greenery, and of course, mountains of freshly prepared food. I had helped my fellow harvesters bake bread earlier that day, and the aroma of the fresh loaves had my stomach growling now.

The gingerbread houses were on display along the table, and Coral moaned as she looked at it. "Beat out by the herbs. Seriously, how?"

All three sets of eyes shot to me, and I lifted my hands. "They made spices fall from the top of a snow globe like real snow. It's incredible. But why are you all blaming me? I wasn't the only judge."

"With Hollis and you, we thought ferns would have it in the bag," Coral said.

"I loved the fern house and marked it high, but Brie provided an entire spreadsheet scoring system with weighted values and *math* involved. I didn't even know what winner I picked, just the various scores I gave."

"The herbs one *is* really creative," Yasmin admitted.

I glanced around and spotted Callan near the other end of the table, sitting with Hollis and some of his tree affinity friends. Meadow was two seats over, swatting something out of his hand.

Professor East rose, and everyone turned their attention to him. My eyes briefly flicked to Nash, Hollis's dad, who was seated near him with the other instructors. "Good evening, botanists. Normally, I give a speech about enjoying the season we're in or about the changes our plant friends undergo at the tides of the year, but tonight, I want to thank you all for the unique spirit each of you brings to our academy. There is no academy without our wonderful students, our dedicated professors, and the spirit of collaboration and scholarship that we all share. As the seasons shift, I encourage you all to remember these things and that there is more that unites us than separates us. Now"—he lifted his glass —"for the toast. To the returning of the light."

We raised our glasses in return, each of us calling, "To the returning of the light."

I leaned over to whisper to Yasmin. "Did that feel ominous to you?"

She nodded. "And we have another visitor from the board."

"They seem to be rotating through. That's Hollis's dad. I met him at the gingerbread competition yesterday."

"He talked to you?"

"He said he hoped Hollis could give me a tour of the fern conservatory."

Yasmin nearly choked on her drink. "Guess he doesn't know you're basically taken. If the undertones weren't so possessive, I would encourage you to take him up on the offer."

"All the interest from the board is giving me the creepy-crawlies. Can't they just focus on saving the Earth or something like that?"

"I think that's what they're all hoping to get *you* for," Yasmin said pointedly.

We didn't discuss it further as students reached for the bounty on the table, and the feast began. I listened to the conversations of those around me while occasionally shooting glances in Callan's direction.

With the verdant shield recharging happening tonight, I couldn't help but remember with a spark of excitement and longing that it was exactly a year ago that my magical powers had been identified. I thought about my field studies with Petra and the dozens of antidotes we had tried. If we could only find one that worked, I could experience that magic here on campus again.

"Boy, if you say that one more time!" Coral roared with laughter, and I saw that her mirth was directed at Waylon, who was shaking his head with a self-satisfied grin on his face.

"Looks like things are going okay between those two?" Yasmin whispered. I glanced over and saw Coral's hand on Waylon's arm, their legs pressed together under the table.

"Seems like it," I said.

"I guess it's just us three," Yasmin said a few minutes later as we noticed Coral and Waylon head to the pools together.

I glanced toward the other end of the table to see Callan, Hollis, and Meadow breaking from the other students, presumably off to charge the shield.

I tried not to let a hint of unnecessary jealousy creep in at not being part of that particular group. They were a tiny percentage of the student population at Evergreen Academy. I was hardly the only one left out. And besides, wasn't I just bemoaning being the center of a board member's attention? Staying away would put space between me and Nash, who I had been avoiding all night.

Once at the pools, we changed into our bathing suits in the

trees then climbed into the whirling springs, steam and citrus filling the night air around us. I let my body relax into the warm, bubbling water.

"Let's hear everyone's New Year's resolutions," Yasmin said before rattling off items on a list of her own, all of which were practical and attainable. "And finally, I want to drink more green tea. The health benefits are unmatched."

I smiled at that one. As if the students at this school couldn't drink the English under the table with their tea habits.

"Mine's to keep the cartography club open. We've put together a thick file to justify it, but I'm nervous," Aurielle said.

"There's no way they could deny that your documentation of the microecosystems around campus isn't valuable," Yasmin said. "I think you have a really good chance of approval. Apothecary Arts, on the other hand? Depends who from the board evaluates their evidence and if they care about skin care or not."

We all sighed, and I sank deeper into the hot spring, letting it massage my shoulders.

"B, did I tell you that we found another of those fairy doors? That's three total so far," Aurielle said.

"You did?" I asked, keeping my voice casually interested.

"Let me guess. There was moss growing around each of them in a cute little arch?" Yasmin asked.

Aurielle nodded.

"Had to be created by the mosses. Maybe it was an art installation one year," Yasmin said.

I considered Aurielle's findings, not letting on how invested I was. If the pattern held with this one, that "fairy door" was another petal portal and another entrance to the academy that very few knew anything about. Even the Root and Vine Society had only been aware of one portal until our initiation. How many were there? And did the Board of Regents know about them?

"Did you include those in your evidence for the submission to the board?" I asked, hoping the twinge of anxiety in my voice didn't come through.

"No, do you think I should? I thought they might find that too fanciful and have a reason not to approve us. I kept it very scientific and ecosystem based."

"Good," I said quickly. "I think that was the right call."

"What about you, B? Any resolutions?" Aurielle asked.

I wrenched my thoughts from the petal portals and struggled to form an answer. My goals were all over the place.

Make Petra proud in my field studies work.

Decide if I was still going to pursue an art degree.

Try to make the quill work for me.

Find the *Vanished Compendium*.

Get my powers back on campus.

Prove to Callan I could handle myself so that he wouldn't have to protect me and we could finally be together.

Okay, a few of those were a stretch, but with the upcoming mission for the Root and Vine Society, they weren't impossible. But I couldn't tell Yasmin and Aurielle about those particular goals.

"Just figure out my future, I guess. I know, it's not exciting," I added before either of them could protest.

"How about *keep the tendrils of all board members off of thyself*," Yasmin said before closing her eyes and sinking deeper into the pool.

She wasn't too far off the mark.

Half an hour later, I felt a surge of energy through my emerald ring, letting me know that the verdant shield had been successfully charged.

We climbed out of the hot springs, and a tree affinity classmate walked by and swooshed some warm air in our direction, drying us completely. Then, as I was slipping my clothes over my bathing suit, I heard a rustling. Twisting around, my eyes fell upon a small pool of leaves swirling around my feet.

I leaned down and picked up the paper that was floating with the leaves. On its crinkled surface was a note in handwriting I would recognize anywhere.

Meet me in the treehouse?

Chapter Forty-Five

My stomach flipped in surprised delight at the message that had come in the leaves. It had been months since Callan had sent me a personal message like this.

Yasmin, spotting the note, said, "I'm guessing we'll see you later tonight?"

I nodded, said a quick goodbye, then peeled off from the group and went straight to the treehouse that Callan and I frequented. When I climbed inside, he was already there.

"Hey," I said, moving to take a seat next to him. "Did everything go okay with the shield?"

"Successfully charged. How were the hot springs?"

"Heavenly, as usual. Too bad you miss out on that every year."

"Solstice isn't the only time one can visit the hot springs, you know, local."

I briefly imagined a shirtless Callan in the pools with the rest of us. Or maybe with just me. Clearing my throat, I averted my eyes from his face and scanned the room, looking for a distraction.

I didn't need to look for long because Callan reached behind him and brought forth a rectangular object wrapped in brown paper.

"What's that?" I eyed it curiously.

Callan looked slightly sheepish. He flipped it around, and I saw a small red bow in the center of the paper.

I felt a surprised smile form on my face. "Callan Rhodes, did you get me a Christmas gift?"

He passed it to me. "It's just a little something."

I shifted the present in my hands then gave it a shake.

"Careful," Callan said, reaching a hand out as if preparing to steady it.

"So it's fragile?" I fished.

"More like precious."

I cocked my head. "Should I open it now or wait until Christmas?"

"Now, if you want."

I tore into the paper, and a familiar sight came into view. "Wait. This is my *In Bloom* painting from last year's Floral Fete." But my eyes were drawn to the frame around it, dainty and silver. I'd seen it before. Shocked affection flooded me. Unexpectedly, tears pricked my eyes. "This frame... where did you get it?"

"I saw it when we visited your aunt's café. You pointed out the painting of your mom's, the one of the pasture. It seemed important to you, and it was in a frame just like this. I thought you could hang your painting next to hers."

I swallowed a lump in my throat and took a moment to collect myself while I ran my fingers over the pattern engraved on the frame. I don't know what I had been expecting when Callan had handed me the gift, but this was more than I ever could have imagined.

"That was just a random frame my mom found at a garage sale years ago. Apparently, it had been made by a regional artist. She loved the little details in the ridges."

"It took some work to track down, which may have involved an extensive internet search. There were quite a few frames that looked *almost* like that one but weren't the exact same. And then there was the matter of the siz—"

Before he could say another word, I interrupted him by gingerly setting down the painting then flinging my arms around his neck. "Thank you, Callan. Seriously, this is the perfect gift I didn't even know I needed. My aunt Vera's going to love it, and my mom would have..." I trailed off, the words catching in my throat. My arms slid from around his neck, but Callan slipped his hands onto my forearms, holding me tenderly.

"I've never been much of a gift giver. That's a transactional act in my family. But when I saw that frame, I just knew I had to find one for you."

"Well, you get an A-plus in gifting, for a novice."

Callan was turning uncharacteristically flush from all the praise, so I took a seat and asked another question. "When do you head home for Christmas?"

"Tomorrow. And then I'll be back in time for our mission."

"Who is going? You, me, and Meadow, obviously."

Callan nodded. "Just us and Hollis. We need Meadow for the premise of traveling to the moss conservatory. We don't want to be linked to the tree conservatory while we're there, if we can help it. Hollis will be there as... backup."

Backup? What did that mean? "I can't believe I'm going to see two of the magical botanical conservatories. Is there anything I can do to help before we go?" I asked.

"Read as much as you can about the connecting Floracantus the ancient botanists used. We don't know exactly what you're going to need to do to make the quill work. And another request —if you're up for it."

"Sure."

"If I manage to get some pictures of the quill, do you think you could make a fake?"

I thought about it for a moment. Three-dimensional objects had never been my specialty, but with the prop design class I was taking this year, my skills were improving. In fact, there was a chance I could use the prop lab undisturbed while it was closed over winter break.

"I think so," I said. "I take it that plays into the ideas you have about getting our hands on the quill?"

"Yep. Ready to hear more?"

"Talk to me, tree prodigy."

Callan rolled his eyes as he laughed, but then we got to work. Plans to secure the quill that could lead us to the *Vanished Compendium* were underway.

An hour later, we climbed down from the tree. Callan surprised me by doing it the old-fashioned way, though expertly. We walked back to the edge of the woods near the academy and prepared to go our separate ways.

I was reluctant for the night to end. Callan and most of the other magical botanists were leaving in the morning, and I felt a little ache at that even though I knew he wouldn't be gone for long.

"Well, have a great Christmas," Callan said. He leaned in closer and cradled a piece of the winter leaf crown I had worn for the night, which was undoubtedly looking unruly after the festivities. "Winter looks good on you. Every season does."

I shivered at the proximity and at the sweetness in his words. How did he still have the ability to make me nervous after I had spent so much time with him?

"Really? Are you sure I don't look like a wilted flower?"

"That's impossible," he said, eyes gleaming in the moonlight.

I held my breath but didn't move, completely rooted to the spot. In that moment, I didn't care whether there were scouting plants on every tree. I wanted Callan Rhodes's arms around me.

After what felt like an eternity under the glistening winter stars, Callan took a step back then continued to walk backward toward the academy. "See you in a week, local."

"Have a good Christmas," I squeaked, and I thought I saw the tiniest twitch of his lip before he disappeared into the darkness.

Chapter Forty-Six

A few days later, on Christmas Eve, I dressed in a deep-green sweater, black skirt and tights, and warm boots before driving to Bryce's house. His home was fifteen minutes away in a housing community slightly outside of Weed proper.

I smiled as the giant wreath I had made for them came into view as I approached the house but shivered a little at the red berries that adorned it.

My session with Petra the previous night had involved a concoction of red berries and had been more strenuous than any before. So far, there were no signs that we were breaking down the binds on my magic, but Petra had a plan to take things a step further, which we would be testing after Christmas.

I scanned the rest of the front porch before knocking, noticing Aunt Vera's touch everywhere. Rosie—our family rose bush—was climbing up the front of Bryce's house as if it had been there for years, not months, and was blooming the softer hue of pink that it took in winter.

"Come in, come in." My aunt somehow managed to hold open the door and pull me in for a hug all in one movement.

"These are for you and Bryce." I handed her the wrapped gifts

—perfume and cologne I'd made at the academy. I used what I knew about my aunt and Bryce to create scents that I hoped would make them always crazy for one another. I might have been a little inspired by Callan's nefarious activities with my pheromone profile.

"Put them under the tree," Aunt Vera said.

It was strange seeing such a tall tree with my aunt's ornaments on it. We had only ever had small or fake trees in her apartment. But Bryce's ceilings were twelve feet tall, and the tree extended nearly all the way up.

"Hey, B. Merry Christmas." Bryce extended his arms for a hug.

"I hope you're ready to be the judge of the Christmas cake decorating contest this year. It's not for the faint of heart, but since you were brave enough to marry into the family, I'm sure you're up for the task."

My aunt called out from the kitchen, "If I don't win, you're sleeping on the couch tonight!"

"And if *I* don't win, we'll know it was rigged," I shot back.

Bryce stuck up his hands. "You two are making this sound real appealing."

I laughed and placed my tiny presents under the tree. "It looks like Rosie is doing good outside there. Did you have any trouble moving her?"

"I was terrified to unclip her from the trellis on your balcony," Bryce admitted. "We got a couple friends to help, but once we attached her over here, she seemed to do great. One of the friends that helped is a gardener, and she was impressed with how well it transferred."

"Did your gardener friend know what kind of rosebush it is?" I asked.

Bryce and I moved into the dining room.

"I don't think so. She did say she thought it was a rare variety."

"Are you talking about Rosie?" Aunt Vera asked.

"Yeah, do you know what species it is?" Bryce asked.

"I'm not sure. We've always just referred to it as a trailing rosebush."

"Do you mind if I take a cutting of it?" I asked. I had forgotten all about trying to identify it with the books at Evergreen Academy.

Aunt Vera shook her head. "Of course not. I think Rosie is indestructible."

I glanced across the room to where my aunt was doing the dishes. The poinsettia I'd given her was on the counter next to her, its leaves subtly arching toward the light from the window above her.

My aunt and Bryce thought the poinsettia was a fresh one I purchased this year when really it was the same one I had accidentally enchanted last year.

"Ready for this competition?" my aunt asked, drawing my eyes away from the poinsettia. Two cooled cakes were on the counter before her, waiting to be decorated.

"Born ready," I said.

An hour later, as the timer dinged, I examined the nutcracker theme I had attempted to pull off. The grandfather clock was my favorite part, but I thought the mice had come out pretty great as well. When I turned around to see what my aunt had come up with, I grinned.

Aunt Vera had covered her cake in three-dimensional blooming flowers. To tie it into the Christmas theme, she had made them all in shades of red, green, and white.

"Went with a floral theme this year?" I asked as my aunt dusted her hands on her apron.

"I think you inspired me with your floral creations at the wedding."

"All right, Bryce. You're up."

Bryce walked into the kitchen, putting on a dramatically scared expression. He looked over both of our cakes, walking circles around them like a baking show judge, then said, "Can I call it a draw?"

My aunt and I both let out an exasperated gasp and shook our heads.

"Come on, Bryce. We thought you were up for the task," I teased.

"Are there any criteria for this? Choosing which is *better* is a little subjective." Bryce wasn't wrong. I had become much more scientific in these sorts of things since joining Evergreen Academy, and our judging methods would never hold up against Brie's and her complex matrix for scoring the gingerbread house competition.

Bryce began pointing back and forth between the two cakes and murmuring.

"You're doing eeny meeny miny moe, aren't you?" Aunt Vera rolled her eyes, though a smile graced her lips.

"Moe," he said, landing on my cake. "You're the winner, B. Congrats."

Aunt Vera looked pointedly toward the couch. "Hope you'll be comfortable there tonight, sweetie. Don't interfere with Santa."

When I laughed as Bryce retreated to the living room, my aunt turned to me and lowered her voice. "Just between the two of us, I think Bryce picked the right cake. Your skills have been majorly growing. Maybe you should consider culinary school instead of art school."

Her tone was light, but I bit my lower lip, and she noticed. "Or do you have something else in mind?"

"I'm not sure," I said, responding slowly to buy myself time. I couldn't explain the real reason I was conflicted, but I had always been able to share things with Aunt Vera, and this didn't have to be any different. "Up until I started at Evergreen Academy, I was so sure of my plans. And now..."

"Plans change, Briar Rose. In fact, I was considering law school before I started apprenticing at the old bakery."

"What?" I leaned my elbows onto the counter. "You never told me that."

"It's true. When your mom was getting ready to transfer to art school, I was thinking about attending a university and then studying law. I was the top student in debate class in high school."

I snorted. That was no surprise. "So what happened? Why didn't you pursue it?"

"The bakery apprenticeship sort of fell into my lap, and at the time, it just felt right. I've never looked back."

I pressed myself backward, leaning so hard against the back of the barstool that its front legs began to lift off the ground. I straightened up when I noticed. "Wow. It's so hard to imagine you doing something else. The café feels like an extension of who you are. You would have been a kickass lawyer, though."

"I've never had any regrets. Sometimes different options present themselves for a reason. The thrill of life is the choice in what path you take."

I nodded, considering her words. If I didn't go to art school, what would my path be? I thought of the work I had been doing with Petra. Were there careers for magical botanists with defensive affinities? It was hard to even think about that when we were still working on un-poisoning my powers.

My aunt Vera spoke again, and this time her voice was soft as her eyes searched my face. "You know your mom would be proud no matter what you do, right?"

I hurried to nod even as I swallowed a lump in my throat. She'd hit on the crux of the matter. I had always loved art, but the driving force for pursuing art school was because it had been my mom's path. It was my connection to her and a fulfillment of her dreams. What would she think about Evergreen Academy and magical botanists and affinity powers? What option would she have chosen, if she were in my shoes?

"And no matter what you decide, you can rest easy knowing that you have the coolest aunt in the land," Aunt Vera said.

I laughed at what was obviously a joke but what meant so much more than she realized. I *did* have her to fall back on, and that reassurance meant more than she knew.

"Without a doubt," I agreed. "Dibs on picking the Christmas movie!" I called so that Bryce could hear. And then I focused on being present in this season with these two people who cared about Briar the girl, not Briar the botanist with all the affinity powers. That identity would be back soon enough.

Chapter Forty-Seven

The day after Christmas, I bundled into my warmest jacket and gloves and headed to the SCC campus. I was still feeling festive, so on impulse, I peeled a pink rose from my cutting of Rosie and tucked it behind my ear. There was a light dusting of snow on the ground, giving the streets the appearance of frosted sugar cookies.

The lampposts along the sidewalk in Weed were adorned with light-up wreaths, and window art decorated the glass panes of a few of the businesses along the way. None of the displays rivaled the festiveness of Vera's Café, but they were magical all the same.

When I arrived at SCC, I headed straight to the prop design lab. While the fall semester had ended, prop design was a two-semester commitment so that we would all be available to finish the designs and assemble the set when the play went live in the spring. I was beginning to see posters for the spring production of *A Midsummer Night's Dream* cropping up around campus and felt a little swell in my chest that I would be a small part of it.

The instructor was offering open lab hours for any of us who wanted to work on projects over the break. I found my instructor in another room, working with clay on a kiln.

"Go right ahead, Briar. I'll be in here if you need anything."

I thanked her and went to the worktable where Yasmin and I usually sat. My goal for the day was to create the fake quill needed for our trip to the tree conservatory. I pulled up the pictures Callan had provided me and examined them closely. Once I had a feel for the overall look, I reopened my bag and removed the feathers I had tracked down to serve as the quill's base.

Thankful for the solitude, I slipped in my earbuds and put on some melodic music to help me create. I checked the door occasionally for signs of my instructor or anyone else, but for a solid two hours I was left alone, and I worked diligently to modify the feather, completely in the zone of creating something new. I stretched the bounds of my power, implementing many of the strategies from my growing defensive skills to subtly shift the appearance of the feather.

When I finished the process and was satisfied with the result, I started again on a new feather. This had to be perfect, and I would make sure that it was.

After moving from drawing to painting to prop craft, I realized it wasn't necessarily just art that I loved... it was *creating*.

By the time I said goodbye to my instructor and exited the prop room that evening, I was hopeful that what I had made would suit our needs at the tree conservatory. I checked my watch and realized that it was almost time to meet Petra. We were squeezing in one last field studies session before she returned to Italy for an extended winter holiday.

I turned my car toward Evergreen Academy. For the first time, we were meeting on my school's campus. Petra had recently become concerned that the shield she was creating in the cabin on Mount Shasta wasn't close enough to the actual conditions at the academy to make our tests valid. With most of the students gone for the break, it was a good time to test if any of our antidote combinations worked on the academy grounds.

Petra was waiting in the flower garden when I arrived, sniffing a cluster of snowdrops. "Good evening, Briar."

"Hi, Petra. Have you been here before?" Since Petra was from Italy, I didn't know whether she had reason to visit Evergreen Academy before today.

"A couple of times," Petra said. She held up her hand, showcasing a beautiful ruby on a delicate silver bracelet—her gemstone that gave her access. "Enough to know that the Perilous Grove will be a discrete place for us to practice."

I nodded, and we walked toward the luscious grove, stars twinkling overhead in the twilight sky.

"What's this flower?" Petra asked.

I touched my ear, having forgotten the bud from Rosie was there. Miraculously, it had managed to stay in place the entire time I had worked on the quills at SCC.

"You know, that's a good question. It's been in our family for generations, and we've always referred to her as a rosebush. One of my friends from the academy saw it and pointed out that it doesn't have any thorns. So now I'm not so sure."

"May I?" Petra reached out a hand, and I gave her the flower.

"Hmm," she said. "I'm unsure about it, too, though flowers aren't my specialty. Have you had any of your instructors look at it at the academy?"

"No, not yet. Maybe after the holidays. Here we are." I stepped into the Perilous Grove.

Petra handed me back the flower, removed her backpack, and began settling mason jars of antidotes we had concocted onto a log that was covered in moss. "Which one would you like to test first? I brought some tea to soothe your stomach between tests, if needed." She pulled a travel carafe from her backpack.

"How about the sweet clover mix?" That had been the only time I thought I had noticed a small difference, even though it had turned out to be a hallucination.

I took a swallow, and we began testing my powers. After an

hour and four different recipes, I shook my head. "The plants here still feel as blocked off as ever."

Petra's forehead creased. "These were my top candidates for antidotes against the abrin and black walnut effects that are impacting you. There must be something we're missing."

"Maybe the stories are right, and the poisoning of my powers was irreversible." I tried not to show her how much that idea disappointed me. I was headed to a magical botanical conservatory within days for a mission with the Root and Vine Society. A small but overly hopeful part of me had thought there was a chance we could unlock my powers before then. If we could, I would be much more of an asset on the mission.

Petra extended a hand toward the flower behind my ear again. "I wonder... You said it's been in your family for generations?"

"Yes," I said slowly, wondering where she was going with this.

"The poison used on you when you tried to charge the verdant shield latched onto your magical pathways, inhibiting your abilities. I wonder if something you have a strong connection to might be able to force the inhibitors off those pathways."

I held up the flower. "You think this might be that connection?"

"It's too risky to have you consume it without knowing what kind of plant it is. Do you mind if I take it with me? I can study it over my travels the next few weeks. If I can identify it, then we can attempt a concoction."

"That sounds great," I said. This was good news. Even though it meant I wouldn't get access to my powers before the conservatory trip, there was still hope that my condition wasn't permanent. "Is there any way for me to continue our research while you're gone?"

"I have a feeling you'll be busy enough without me assigning homework," Petra said, beginning to put away the glass jars.

For a moment, I held my breath, wondering if she somehow knew about the mission we were planning.

But the fleeting concern passed as she asked, "Ready to walk back?"

"I think I'm going to stay out here for a bit," I said, having an urge to draw for the first time in a while. With the empty grove in front of me, this felt like the perfect way to clear my head and mentally prepare for the mission to the tree conservatory.

"Very well then. You've been very resilient through all of this, Briar. Enjoy your break, and I'll see you in a few weeks."

"Have fun in Italy," I said.

When she was gone, I turned to the variety of plants that made up the Perilous Grove, searching for the right vantage point to sit and sketch. I found an angle that felt right and took a seat on the log.

I considered everything I had been asked to do with Petra so far these few months. We were attempting something that had never been done before, at least not according to modern records, and there was a thrill in the testing and discovery. I mentally worked through the steps of creating an antidote as I sketched the view in front of me.

Study.

Assess.

Change.

Create.

These, I could do.

Chapter Forty-Eight

"Here she comes," Hollis said, standing from where he'd been squatting to unfurl a fern leaf beside Callan's truck.

"Awww, did you two wait for me?" I teased, knowing that had been the plan.

"Wouldn't think of leaving you behind, B," Hollis said.

"All right, let's review the plan one more time, and then get this show on the road," Callan said, reining us in. He turned to me. "Do you have the quill?"

I nodded and reached into my bag then carefully drew out the prop quill.

"What do you think? I used the pictures Callan gave me and tried to match the aging on the feather. I also used my tree affinity powers to make some magical adjustments to the oak gall ink we procured in case anyone thinks to check it for traces of magic."

Hollis took the prop quill from me and nodded. "I'm impressed. To an untrained eye, there would be no reason to be suspicious of this."

"And to a trained eye?" I asked, looking nervously between them.

Hollis was still eyeing the quill, a contemplative look on his face. "Do you feel that?"

"Feel what?" I asked, shifting my weight on my feet.

"There's magic in it," Hollis said.

Callan, who had been farther from the quill as he loaded bags into the truck, stepped closer now.

"There is." Callan turned to me, expression curious and surprised.

I tried to keep my face straight. The truth was, I had held back on letting them know the final piece of my plan. I hadn't been sure I would be able to pull it off. Now, it was clear that I had.

"It wasn't all me. You told me some of the protections you thought might be on the real quill. I thought I could try to imitate those here. That way, when the botanists put this quill out for display, it won't be so obvious they have a fake."

"Good thinking." Callan's voice was calm with a tinge of awe. But he didn't sound shocked, and I realized it didn't come as a surprise to him at all that I could figure this out. That sent a little thrill of joy through me.

"I doubt it would fool an expert, but it should buy us some time."

"You're brilliant, B," Hollis said. The ferns surrounding the parking lot shimmied at his words.

"He's right. As long as there are no historians of magical botanical artifacts monitoring the exhibit this week, this prop quill should be the perfect disguise," Callan said.

I nodded, glad to have done my part.

"On that note, I think we have everything we need. Meadow will be waiting up tonight to let us in. Let's head to the plane." Callan shut the tailgate with a soft shove.

I placed the quill back into its carrying bag and slipped it into my backpack.

Hollis clapped Callan on the shoulder and saluted. "Lead the way, captain."

I raised my eyebrows and tried not to react too visibly. *Callan* was our pilot?

"You have your pilot's license?" I asked.

"It's pretty common for us to learn how to fly small planes since it's the easiest way to get around between the conservatories or for field research. The magically enhanced biofuel makes it so that we rarely have to fuel up."

"Okay but... you're experienced, right?" I asked.

"I can vouch for him. He's only crashed once or twice," Hollis said with a wink.

Well, Callan Rhodes, aren't you just full of surprises.

A COUPLE OF HOURS LATER, AFTER I BRIEFLY NODDED off during a surprisingly smooth flight in the four-seater plane, there was a shift in our equilibrium as we began our descent, and I peered out the window to see giant, lush trees looming below us in the dark and mist. A few minutes later, the glowing lights of moonflowers lining a small landing strip came into view, and with the grace of a leaf settling to the ground in the fall, Callan landed the plane.

I squinted around at the inky forest as we climbed out—the humidity clung to my skin instantly, even in winter—and I realized that, unlike the small public airport we had departed from on the outskirts of Weed, this must be a private airport just for magical botanists. Aside from the moonflowers, there were a few other species of glowing plants guiding our way to a parking lot.

We gathered our bags, hopped into a black SUV, and headed deeper into the woods. There was no one else around, and when I glanced at the time in the vehicle, I saw that it was just after eleven p.m.

I knew the loose plan. We would crash at Meadow's house

tonight then head to the tree conservatory in the morning. I yawned, body tired despite how curious I was about this new world around me.

Despite my research into the tree conservatory over the past few days, there were no pictures anywhere, and I wasn't sure what to expect. All I knew was that we were somewhere deep in the Hoh Rainforest of western Washington.

As we drove, my magical connection with the towering trees, mosses, and ferns was like rivers of liquid sugar rushing through my veins, sweet and comforting. The sheer volume of it was staggering, and I had to force myself to concentrate on the plan Callan and Hollis were discussing as we drove.

"You really think the two of you will be able to get in unseen?" Hollis was asking.

Callan cast his eyes to me in the rearview mirror then returned his attention to the road. "We are going to give it our best shot."

"Well, you'd know better than I do. I've always heard the tree conservatory is tight on security."

"You heard correctly," Callan said, turning the steering wheel. We shifted onto gravel as the car pulled up to a dark-green house with a large glass front exterior and Callan parked the SUV. I couldn't see much in the dark, but I grabbed my bag and followed Callan around the back of the house, our shoes crunching over pine needles and soft moss.

A figure emerged underneath a porch light, and I recognized the heart-shaped face of Meadow. She was wearing a baggy sweatshirt and leggings, her feet stuffed into fuzzy black slippers. "Look who finally arrived. My stowaways. Rhodes didn't get you too airsick on the flight, did he?"

"I have to admit, it was pretty smooth," I said.

"You all have a plan for the trees, right? I'm telling my parents you'll be doing studies in the rainforest in the morning."

"Rhodes thinks he has it covered," Hollis said, joining Meadow on the porch.

"Just make sure you're back in time for the annual strategic meeting." Meadow directed those words at Callan. "Remember that we have to hike in and then change up there, so give yourself plenty of time. My mom thinks you're all coming as part of a group project for school. Personally, once we're there, I don't care what you all do, but we have to make an appearance."

"Annual strategic meeting?" Hollis scratched the back of his neck. "I think I'll fake an illness tomorrow night."

"Don't let the name fool you. It's the gala I was telling you about," Meadow said as she opened a sliding door and ushered us inside. "Which, to be honest, is even more of a reason to play sick. But you all needed a cover for coming here, and I found us one."

Chapter Forty-Nine

I glanced at the four bunk beds at the spare room in Meadow's house, realizing that I was going to be sharing the space with the two guys in the group. Still, I was too tired to care, and I quickly claimed the bathroom. I washed up and changed then went to choose a bunk.

Callan came to stand by me as Hollis closed the bathroom door. "Chat outside?"

I nodded and followed him to the porch. There were a few bamboo chairs on the knotted white pine wood, and we each took a seat.

"I know you've been wanting more details about the plan tomorrow. The truth is, what we don't know is almost as much as what we do. I have a plan for getting in that should only leave a small footprint, and we have intel on where the quill is being stored. What we don't know is how many people will be working at the tree conservatory tomorrow, if any atypical protocols are in place, or if there has been any change of plans related to the quill."

"You're making this sound like a piece of cake, Rhodes," I quipped, though my stomach was tightening. We were really doing this.

Callan's smile was almost a laugh. "I think our chances are decent. I wouldn't be risking it if I thought the situation was unsafe. But I wanted to give you one more opportunity to stay here or go to the moss conservatory early with Meadow. I can go in myself or take Hollis off patrol duty outside and bring him with me."

I was shaking my head before he even finished his offer. "No way. I agreed to be one of the protectors, remember? That involves taking risks. Besides"—I cast my gaze out at the trees in the dark woods surrounding us—"who knows when I'll have another opportunity to see the tree conservatory. Do you think I would miss out on that?"

Callan shook his head. "No, I don't think you would. A little risk has never scared you, though."

I glanced at Callan and saw his hand was rubbing a small circle in the center of his chest.

"Is that your gemstone?" I asked. I knew Callan wore his gemstone on a necklace since I'd glimpsed the chain a few times, but I had rarely seen the stone.

After a moment's hesitation, he pulled the necklace from under his shirt.

I leaned in closer to look at it under the porch light. "It's beautiful. Peridot, right? We're both greens."

Callan's eyes shifted to my emerald ring, and I held it up, letting it glimmer as the light caught it. "Pretty fine handiwork. Do you make the jewelry for everyone on campus?"

"Any of the founders' descendants can do it. It's something we learn growing up. My aunt taught me."

"Your aunt? The florist?"

Callan smiled, seemingly surprised that I remembered. "Yes, she'll try her hand at any craft. She became a bit of an amateur jeweler, and she taught me. Her lessons were more fun than my parents'."

"How so?" I was eager, as always, for more about Callan's

home life.

"Let's just say my aunt is more into the... mystical side of magical botany."

"Mystical? Like having plant affinities isn't mystical enough?" I laughed.

"Some theories are a little more out of the mainstream, I guess you could say. She's a big fan of a fringe theory about birthstones."

I nodded for him to go on. "What is it?"

"You'll think it's silly."

"Well, now I really want to hear it."

"Some botanists believe that certain birthstone combinations are nature-blessed matches."

I raised an eyebrow. "Nature-blessed matches?"

Callan sighed like he regretted bringing it up. "Like something about their unique properties complements each other."

"Huh. I've never heard of it."

"There's not much evidence behind it, so it wouldn't be taught at Evergreen Academy, which prides itself on its scientific study of magic. But there are some circles where it has a huge following."

"So does your birthstone have any nature-blessed matches with other stones?" I eyed the soft peridot stone around his neck again.

"According to the theory, similar colored stones meant their wearers had a connection. Ruby and garnet. Turquoise and aquamarine."

I noticed he hadn't mentioned our stones. "Emerald and peridot," I breathed, gazing at the clear pale-lime hue of his stone.

He glanced toward my ring again. "Because emerald and peridot are the only two green birthstone rings—and green is the base color of plants and photosynthesis—the theory says their combination is extraordinarily powerful."

I glanced down at my ring then too. "Powerful, how?" I spoke softly, lost in the magic of this moment with Callan, in the middle of the forest, discussing the ring that had brought me into the world of magical botany.

Callan let out a soft laugh. "I told you, it's silly. What's reality is that we have an early day tomorrow." He ran his eyes over my pink pajama top and shorts. "And we both need to get to bed."

I crossed my arms over my chest, having completely forgotten what I was wearing. "Well, I, for one, don't think we'll have any trouble tomorrow," I said as I rose. "After all, we're destined to be *extraordinarily* powerful together."

Callan shook his head as if he wished he'd never told me, but there was a little spark in his eyes that twinkled in the porch light.

Chapter Fifty

In the morning, Meadow allowed us to raid the fruit and oatmeal in the kitchen, and then we loaded up our packs.

"You three good?" she asked, shrugging into a raincoat the color of peas.

"I think so. Thanks for giving us a place to crash, and I promise we'll be back in time for the annual strategic meeting tonight. You'll meet us here?" Callan asked.

Meadow nodded. "Enjoy your little covert operation," she said wistfully. "I get to spend the entire morning shadowing my mom at work." She lifted her travel coffee cup in a *cheers* gesture, grabbed a pair of trekking poles, and we followed her out the door.

In the light of day I could see that Meadow's home was the only structure around. Its architecture was designed in such a way that the walls reflected light and blended into the forest. Someone could walk by a few feet away and might not even notice it was there. I imagined that from a short distance, it was practically invisible.

"Is this a special home for the caretakers of the conservatory?" I asked.

"You got it," Meadow said.

"Is there one like this for the tree conservatory?"

"Kind of," Callan said. Then, more quietly, "I'll show you sometime, when all this is over."

"Is that a promise?" I asked.

Meadow looked over her shoulder and raised an eyebrow.

I hurried to change the subject. "How close are the two conservatories?"

"Very. They even have a research area that overlaps. But the entrances are a few miles apart, and we can't cross between the two without the proper credentials," Callan explained.

Meadow came to a halt and pointed to a golf cart that was parked under a tree near the house. "I know you all probably wanted to tree walk, but that will be faster, and Hollis will be less likely to die."

Hollis tipped an imaginary hat in Meadow's direction.

"Good luck. I don't want to bail any of you out if things go south." Meadow waved with her trekking pole and continued onto an almost-imperceptible trail in the forest and disappeared into the woods.

The outside of the golf cart was covered in moss so that it was nearly camouflaged with the forest. The three of us climbed aboard, with Hollis immediately jumping into the driver's seat.

Callan leaned toward me where we sat in the back, and his forearm brushed against mine. "Ready?"

I smiled. "Let's do this."

As Hollis steered us through a narrow trail through the trees, I took in the majesty of the rainforest in the daylight. Moss clung to each tree like scarves.

It was chilly in the morning, but we all wore layers, and I enjoyed the humidity in the air as it soaked into the skin on my face. That feeling hit me again—the sensation of being hyperaware of every plant around me, from the tallest of trees to the tiniest of wood sorrels. I stretched out my connection toward a nearby moss and murmured a Floracantus for growth then smiled in delight as it filled in a small empty patch on the tree.

I noticed Callan watching me out of the corner of his eye, but he didn't say anything.

The ferns along the trail were shimmying as we drove past, an obvious nod to the presence of Hollis, who was periodically whistling.

"Pull over here," Callan said after about fifteen minutes, and Hollis parked on the side of the trail. When we stopped, I looked around in confusion.

We climbed out of the golf cart, and Hollis and I studied the towering trees and fern-covered forest floor around us, the mist settling around our ankles like touches of unscented smoke.

"Where do we go?" I asked.

Callan pointed up, and a smile spread over my face as realization dawned.

"Of course," I murmured, already itching to scale the nearby maple.

"And this is where I leave you?" Hollis asked.

I glanced down at a slight movement near his feet and noticed that fern sporophytes were uncurling at a rapid rate around him. Would this entire trail be covered in ferns when we got back?

Callan nodded. "If you see anything unusual, send word."

"You got it, boss." Hollis put the shuttle back into gear and sped off. I had a feeling he was going to have fun *patrolling* the forest. We weren't expecting anything unusual, but being prepared was always better than the alternative.

I scaled the tree after Callan, and when we reached the canopy, the branches automatically formed a trail for us, as if they were used to doing this, perhaps with more demanding botanists.

"How is Hollis going to send word?" I asked absently, marveling at the canopy as we walked. Everything was so lush and *green*. I thought I was used to green—growing up in Weed and then living at Evergreen Academy—but nothing could have prepared me for this. With no manmade structures to be seen, I felt like I had been transported back in time. This could be a Jurassic-era world, not the twenty-first century.

"I primed some leaves for him. They're already connected to me, so all he has to do is write down a note, and they'll come to me."

The air smelled prominently of pine, crisp and refreshing. As we tree walked, I let my hands skim the leaves, marveling at the variety of soft, smooth textures ranging from the size of my thumbnail to as large as one of the baskets we used to transport food from the fields at the academy.

We walked for about ten minutes, with the only sounds around us being the tweeting and singing of birds, and then Callan slowed. I followed his gaze and stuck out my arms to steady myself as the vision ahead formed in front of my eyes.

A perfectly camouflaged, slightly oblong door with rounded edges was embedded in the trees, right here, twenty feet off the ground. Vines swirled around it, as if beckoning us forward.

We had arrived at the tree conservatory, and our mission was about to begin.

Chapter Fifty-One

When we approached the door, Callan made a subtle motion with his hand, and I heard a soft whooshing to my right. Before I could look, Callan stepped forward and pressed an intricate knot in the wood—I assumed a doorbell of sorts.

I startled as a rounded piece of bark to the side of the door hinged open silently, and a woman's voice called through the curtain of green vines.

"Credentials?" she asked.

Callan turned his face toward the window, and I looked up at the thick tangle of vines with white flowers that seemed to be pointing directly at us, tucked into the canopy above the door. Smaller, yellowish leaves were swirling around the front of the flowers, as if a miniature tornado was taking place only there. I glanced at Callan, understanding dawning. The wrist flick and whooshing noise. He had sent the swirling leaves up there to cover the flowers.

"Patricia, is that you? I'm Callan Rhodes, and this is a friend, both lead tree affinities."

"Callan Rhodes? I didn't know you were coming," the woman's voice called.

There was a clicking sound, and the door swung inward. Callan stepped through first, and I was right on his heels. As soon as I crossed over the threshold, I felt access to my powers cut off, just like at Evergreen Academy.

"Good to see you, Patricia."

"Callan, this is quite the pleasant surprise." Patricia seemed a little flustered, despite her words. "Usually, someone calls ahead if a member of the family is visiting. We would have made arrangements for whatever you need."

"Don't worry about it. Last-minute decision. There is no need for anyone to accommodate us."

"Are you sure? I can call one of the research assistants to come—"

"I insist," Callan said, voice kind. He reached into his backpack. "And I brought something for you. Fresh cider from Evergreen Academy."

Patricia beamed, finally relaxing. "No one makes cider like they do. Thank you." She unstopped the cork of the glass bottle and took a sip. Her eyes briefly closed. "Delicious. Okay, let me get visitor badges for the two of you. Make sure your friend signs in there."

Patricia was reaching for a stack of green lanyards on the counter when her eyes suddenly went a little fuzzy.

"That's our cue," Callan whispered, and with a touch to the small of my back, he gently pushed me forward.

"Please tell me that wasn't what I think it was," I said, moving steadily through the narrow chamber of bark, Callan's hand still gently propelling me forward.

"Depends what you think it was."

"Something to erase her short-term memory, like you and Kaito planned to do with the rest of the Root and Vine Society if we didn't opt into the group?"

"Invoking my rights against self-incrimination," Callan said. "I feel kind of bad about it. Patricia is a sweet lady. She'll be fine, though. I mixed it to only block out about a minute of memory."

We were climbing a set of narrow stairs carved into the tiny tree entrance, as if going to another level. "And the swirling leaves outside... I take it those were blocking a scouting vine?"

"The entrance is riddled with them. I thought it was better if they didn't have anything to report except for a little wind."

We emerged out of the dark tree hallway, and I drew in a sharp breath. We were standing on a slatted trail, which swung softly as we stepped farther onto it. Thin handrails made of vines stretched from our tree to one about twenty feet away.

There were a series of slender wooden trails identical to this one running across the forest in every direction. Some were an even height to ours while others were above or below, giving the illusion that the forest was a skyscraper, with botanists working in tree-houses on every floor.

I reached out to a floating, glowing orb the size of a raindrop.

"Bioluminescent sap," Callan explained.

The orbs were sprinkled through the air, casting light throughout all levels of the forest. They resembled fireflies but in slow motion, floating with a carefree, silent magic.

"What happened to all the moisture?" I asked. While the humidity had been intense outside, it felt drier in here.

"There's a shield, kind of like the one at Evergreen Academy. Douglas Vitalis, my ancestor, was credited with the magical tech-nology that put the shield into place. He did something similar here so that the conservatory could be open to the sky but not susceptible to the quantity of rain that occurs in the surrounding forest."

"I feel like I'm in some kind of Amazon kingdom. The lost city of trees."

"That's not too far off." He pointed toward a collection of trees to our right. "That's the tree hall of fame. We have moon trees

—trees grown from seeds that went to space with an astronaut who was a magical botanist—"

I cut him off with a shocked look. "A magical botanist was an astronaut?"

"I told you, local. Friends in high places."

I rolled my eyes at his joke, and he continued to point out trees in the hall of fame. "There's a sycamore. An American chestnut, planted here before the blight wiped so many of them out. That one's a dragon's blood tree..." He continued to describe various unique trees, spinning little tales about them.

I became completely entranced in tour guide Callan, his love of these trees coming through brighter than he could possibly have imagined.

"You're amazing," I said when he finally came to a pause in the presentation.

"It is amazing," he said, referencing the enormous Australian banyan he'd just been telling me about.

I took his arm and turned him toward me. "Not it. Well, it *is* amazing. But I meant you."

His face rearranged itself through the strangest sequence of expressions, as if he couldn't figure out what I was talking about.

I let out a laugh. He was adorable.

And then our eyes met, and it was like everything I wanted to convey to him about how much he meant to me, how welcome he'd made me feel, how supported I had been by him throughout my journey as a magical botanist, was reflected in his eyes.

For that moment, I forgot what we were there to do. The whole forest revolved around the two of us in this magical place among the trees that was a supersized mirror of all the nights we'd spent getting to know each other in the treehouses at Evergreen Academy.

He slipped an arm around my waist, a wisp of air enveloping me with it, setting goose bumps across my skin.

I lifted a hand to his cheek.

His voice dropped an octave, and he dipped his forehead to mine. "Not a day has gone by this past year that I haven't thanked my lucky leaves I met you, Briar Whelan."

I sucked in a breath but couldn't help biting my lower lip into a smile. "Are you sure about that because I think there was this one time when we were working on math problems that I—"

I was cut off with a warm press of his lips to mine. Suddenly, I had no idea where I'd been going with that sentence. All that mattered was that the world smelled like sandalwood and peaches and Callan Rhodes was kissing me.

Every inch of my body warmed as I was aware of all the places we were connected. His hand on my waist and one delicately in my hair. The warmth of his cheek just before I dropped my hand and slid it around his back. And our lips, his warm and caressing, mine tender and eager.

There was a loud crash nearby, and we broke apart as I jumped, surprise ratcheting through me. Callan tugged me toward him and looked around, wind whipping around us, then I felt his body relax.

Holy leaves. I could feel Callan's abs through his T-shirt.

"It must be limb removal day," he said with a soft laugh. He turned back to me and took my face in both of his hands. "I'd love to stay up here and do *that*"—his gaze dropped to my lips then returned to my eyes—"all day with you but my number one goal is to get you through this mission safe and undetected. You ready to tap in?"

I nodded, smiling at the echo of the words he'd used in the pivotal moment of Capture the Roses last year. My head was fuzzy, brimming in a buzz of happy chemicals from the most heart-stopping moment of my life. I finally knew what it felt like to kiss Callan, and one kiss was definitely *not* going to be enough.

But Callan was right. We needed to stay focused. So I took a deep breath and nodded. "Lead on, captain."

Callan grinned and picked up my hand. He gave the back of it a soft kiss—eyes locked on mine—and walked backward a few paces before turning to lead the way.

My heart rate kicked into high gear again. *By the leaves*, I was in trouble.

<h1 style="text-align:center">Chapter Fifty-Two</h1>

"We need to head to the library. The archival area where the quill will be stored before going on display is in there."

I followed Callan down a swirling staircase that wound inside the tree we'd just reached. There were exits at different levels, leading to treehouses and platforms throughout the conservatory.

As much as my heart was racing from what had just happened between us, I hadn't forgotten what Yasmin had said about the conservatory libraries potentially having books on the Renaissance botanists. While I knew that wasn't a priority while we were here, if I had an opportunity to peek, I was sure as sunflowers going to take it.

When we reached the forest floor, there were wooden signs pointing toward a variety of research rooms including signs for Transgenic Breeding Lab, Bonsai Garden, and Agronomy. The one labeled *Library* was pointing north. Callan headed straight for it, never glancing at the sign.

Being on the ground floor of the tree conservatory was strange. There were layers of treehouses and trails above us, so in some ways it felt like there was a roof over our heads, but in many ways, it also felt like we were outside, with smooth dirt and moss making up the floor. Mushrooms were scattered across the ground like gumdrops, coalescing around the bases of the trees.

Callan came to a halt, and I looked around for the entrance to the library. It was like we were in any part of the forest, except the trees around us were massive and each was adorned with an antique-looking brass lantern about eight feet up their thick trunks.

Callan seemed to read my mind. "You're looking at it. Each tree is a different section of the library. They're hollowed inside like the tree at the Evergreen Academy library. The archival area is in a tree hollow toward the back."

We wended our way through the library, where botanists were flitting in and out of tree hollows. Thankfully, none of them gave Callan or me a second glance. While this place was enormous and there were likely hundreds of people here, Patricia being on a first name basis with him at the entrance hadn't boded well for us going incognito. But Callan had previously assured me that he knew very few of the workers here. His parents mostly hobnobbed with the higher-ups, who came in for special occasions or were locked away in high-level meetings.

"I wish I had more time to look around the library," I said wistfully.

"Actually, I think that may be in the cards for you today, local."

I raised an eyebrow. "What do you mean?"

"The quill isn't going to be sitting there defenseless. I need to test it and its container for any protective charms that are surrounding it and then unravel them before swapping it out. It shouldn't be too bad. It'll be basic tree defense mechanisms. Nothing as advanced as what you've been working with."

I suppressed a smile. While my field studies assignment was supposed to be top secret, it didn't surprise me that Callan had guessed at least part of what I was doing there.

"Okay, so you'll do that while I look around and then come and get me?"

"Yep, if I haven't found you in thirty minutes, come back here."

He made it sound so simple, and I nodded again, trusting his plan despite my anxiousness. We arrived in front of a tree that was engraved Archives.

"Here it is." He scanned the area around the tree. "No sign of scouting vines. Okay, I'm going in. See you in thirty minutes. Less, if my magic's any good."

"Your magic's always good. Callan"—I reached out and took his hand, giving it a little squeeze—"good luck."

His palm pressed warmth into mine in return, and I practically floated at the emotion that I somehow felt in it.

"Thanks, local. Try not to get too lost in the library hollows."

My heart gave a soft flutter as he flashed me a gorgeous, mischievous smile before pulling away. I touched a hand to my lips, still imagining the feeling of his there. *Stay focused, Briar.*

I watched as he stepped up to the opening of the archival tree, posture and steps casual and confident as always. Then I turned my attention to the nearest available library hollow. The word magically carved into the bark was Dendrology. I moved past it and scanned the titles on the other hollows until I saw one labeled *Historical Texts - Unsorted.* On an impulse, I pulled open the arched door and stepped inside.

The space was small, and rounded bookshelves formed a circle lining the entire interior, stopping only to break for the doorway. I let my hands run along the shelves. The old but well-preserved bindings were reminiscent of older texts I had seen and studied at Evergreen Academy.

When I reached a section of texts with worn brown bindings, I knelt to examine them. After skimming over a few of the faded titles, my fingers began to warm as if I were getting ready to perform magic. I frowned.

My magic was blocked in here, and I didn't see any plants in the room to connect with anyway, except for the tree I was in. My hands continued to tingle with warmth, increasing in strength until they landed on a book with a soft brown cover.

I slid the tome off the shelf, noting the yellowed edges and lack of anything on the fabric cover before I carefully flipped it open. I turned to the front interior page, looking for an author, but there wasn't one. The text on the first few pages was extremely faded, so it was possible any previous authorship denoted there was lost to time.

My hands tingled warmly again, and adrenaline flooded me. I had only felt this sensation once before, and it had been when I held the botanical journals of Leonardo da Vinci at Evergreen Academy.

I crouched there and skimmed the pages, trying to make out the faded drawings. There were many sections where the ink markings were impossible to discern.

While I was lost in exploring the book on the floor of the library hollow, half an hour slipped away in the blink of an eye. At the whooshing sound of someone opening the door, I sat up, expecting to see Callan. But another magical botanist entered the room and immediately went to work scanning one of the shelves, paying no attention to me.

With a prick of concern, I knew it was time that I go check on Callan. I looked around for some kind of system to borrow the book, but didn't see one. Besides, Callan had gone to some lengths to make it seem like we had never been here. I didn't need to go blowing our cover by putting my name to a library slip.

After a moment's ethical deliberation and a check over my shoulder that the other magical botanist was still occupied, I tucked the book into my backpack. I would return it eventually.

For a moment, I wondered if there might be enchantments on the library books, protecting them from unauthorized movements. But the warmth distributed by the book when I held it made me hopeful that *this* book, at least, wouldn't be subject to such enchantments.

I left the library hollow and headed straight toward the archival tree. There were a few botanists entering or exiting other tree hollows, with a short line queued outside one of them, but other than that, nothing had changed.

As I was about to turn the corner toward the archival tree, a strong breeze wrapped around me and whisked me between two nearby sequoias.

I let out a gasp as I tried to tug my arms free but found them trapped to my sides. Panic swelled in my chest until a comforting caress touched the back of my neck. My breathing relaxed. I'd felt that touch before.

Callan.

Callan was doing this.

But why? Before I could formulate any theories, I heard a voice.

"Well, isn't this a surprise. Long time no see, brother."

Chapter Fifty-Three

Brother? Shock coursed through me. I was suddenly desperate to peek my head out between the trees, but the air that had swept me behind them was still firmly in place.

It was as if invisible ropes were tied around my arms and legs. There was no sensation across my mouth, though, so Callan must have trusted me to keep quiet on my own.

"Didn't think to tell me you were making a visit to the tree conservatory?" The unfamiliar voice—Callan's brother?—asked.

"Didn't think you'd be here," Callan responded evenly. I still couldn't see either of them, but I imagined Callan forming the tense posture he often held around his parents. Was his relationship with his brother strained too?

"Needing something from the library?" his brother asked.

"Came for a book." I heard a soft rustle, as if Callan had waved a book in the air for proof.

"You traveled all the way to Washington for a book?"

"I'm visiting the moss conservatory with Meadow. Picking up a book I needed for field studies was a bonus."

There was a pause, as if the brothers were in some kind of

silent standoff. Callan was the one to break it. "I don't mean to keep you from your important duties. I have to get back to the moss conservatory."

"Were you here all alone?" The way his brother said it, I had a feeling he knew the answer.

Callan handled it masterfully. "Do you see anyone else around? I'm on my way out. See you later, Wyatt."

"I'll walk you out," his brother—Wyatt—offered. I heard the sound of feet moving away, and a few moments later, my magical bonds were released.

I poked my head infinitesimally out from the trees, confirming that the coast was clear. My eyes darted to the archival tree. On instinct, I dashed to it and stepped inside. Callan's backpack was sitting on the floor, almost blending in beside a messy stack of books. I unzipped the backpack and checked the contents. The case we'd brought the fake quill in was inside. I opened it and examined the quill.

"Spores," I murmured, realizing that it was the quill I had created. Callan must not have had time to swap it out. I began to search the archival area, and my eyes fell on a thick box that was propped open. I folded down one of the flaps and saw a label that read "Quill to the rumored *Vanished Compendium* – historical legends section." I pushed down the flap and peered inside. There, underneath a phytoglass display, was the real quill.

Well, I had wanted to help, and now was my chance. I might be powerless here, but I had gotten along in the world for eighteen years without any powers. I could do this... as long as nobody else unexpectedly showed up.

I took a deep breath and reached into the box, praying that Callan had finished removing all the defenses before his brother interrupted. When I was able to touch the phytoglass without getting zapped—or whatever would happen with tree defenses—I assumed Callan had done his part.

After a quick glance to the entrance of the hollow, I unlatched the phytoglass door and gently lifted out the quill. I remembered the protective bag we'd brought along and reached into Callan's backpack again, heart pounding as my fingers felt for the bag. Once they landed on the smooth silky fabric, I yanked the bag out of the backpack and slid the quill inside.

I couldn't tell if I was breathing as I reached for the dummy quill I had created and set it in the phytoglass container then closed the clear door.

I glanced around. The archival tree was still empty, but I heard voices, and they were getting louder. Someone was approaching.

Without Callan, I wasn't going to be able to put the defenses back on the phytoglass. That would leave more of a trail than we'd been hoping for, but I saw no other option.

Doing one quick check to see that the angle of the quill and the rest of the box were exactly as I'd found them, I returned the box's top, picked up Callan's backpack, hurriedly exited the tree, and rushed away from the library hollows.

When I saw a sign pointing toward the exit, I followed it, keeping an eye out for Callan and his brother. I hoped they were far enough ahead of me that I wouldn't run into them until Callan had managed to shake his brother.

My legs were on autopilot as I climbed a spiral tree path to the second level then headed for the exit. My heart raced like I was a thief sneaking a priceless painting out of an art museum, and I tried to keep my pace steady as I passed magical botanists at work. I hoped my expression wasn't giving away how nervous I felt.

Act natural, Briar. No one has any reason to suspect you.

I clenched the straps of Callan's backpack so I had something to do with my hands. A cool sweat formed at the back of my neck, and I had to force myself to breathe normally as I approached the entrance. I imagined walking along this path with Callan instead of alone, and instantly, my breathing relaxed. The bioluminescent sap was still floating like near-motionless fireflies in the air, but I barely noticed it.

I was nearing the exit when a head of bright blond hair caught my eye, and I slowed to turn, the way our brains automatically gravitate toward faces and body shapes that are familiar. My brain knew I shouldn't be slowing or stopping now, but the odd tug of familiarity didn't allow me to keep going.

Was that—

No. It couldn't be.

The man's head turned slightly to the left, and he let out a laugh at something the person next to him was saying.

I suppressed a gasp.

Alex?

What was Alex doing at the tree conservatory?

Thoughts struggled to connect in my brain.

But that meant... Was *Alex* a magical botanist?

The man Alex was talking to began to turn in my direction, and I ripped my eyes away from them, quickly hastening my pace toward the exit.

My heart felt like it was beating a million beats per second. Too much had happened in the last few minutes for me to do anything but surge forward, hoping to find Callan, who was still nowhere in sight.

We had more than one problem on our hands now, and I desperately needed to get out of the tree conservatory before I blew our whole mission.

Chapter Fifty-Four

Patricia didn't pay me any attention as I exited the tree conservatory, my steps too quick. I continued down the path toward the forest where we had entered, trusting Callan would find me there eventually. We hadn't planned for what to do if we were separated, but his words to his brother indicated he had headed for the exit and that I should follow when I could.

My power came back in a rush as I left the conservatory's boundary, my connection to the abundance of plants in the lush forest around me restored. Instantly, my fear began to ebb, as if having access to my powers had become a source of security without my realizing it.

When I reached the little path in the forest, I swiveled to see that the tree conservatory was completely out of sight behind me, as if it had been swallowed up by the woods. I climbed down to the ground level, wanting to put as much space between me and the conservatory as possible.

"You made it. Thank the leaves."

I jumped at the sound of Callan's voice as he dropped out of the trees above. I took in the sight of him, hair disheveled and eyes full of a wild concern, and I instantly relaxed.

"Are you okay?" He stepped forward and put his hands on my arms, scanning me.

"Yes, I'm fine. How about you?"

Callan cast a glance over his shoulder. "Better now that you're safe. I see you got the backpack. I was hoping you'd see it." Callan began to walk, and I matched his pace. "Were you able to get the quill? I had just undone all the defenses when I heard voices outside. I didn't have time to make the swap. I tried to give you as much of an opening as I could, but if you didn't have a clear shot at it—"

"Callan." I cut him off. "Relax. I got the quill."

He came to an abrupt halt and turned toward me, a smile splitting across his face. "You did?"

"Yep, and replaced it with the fake. I couldn't redo the defenses, though..."

Callan nodded, following my line of thought. "I knew that's a risk we were taking. I thought we might be interrupted. I just didn't anticipate who was going to interrupt us. You got away clean?"

"Define 'clean.' I was sweating like a criminal. But I don't think anyone noticed anything."

"It was worth it, then," Callan said definitively.

"There's something else." I hesitated, still in shock about what I'd seen and the adrenaline of the escape crashing all around me. My legs were beginning to shake.

"What is it?" Callan raked his eyes over me, as if looking for an injury.

"Back there in the conservatory, I thought I saw... No, I *know* I saw... Alex."

"Alex?" Callan's face screwed up in confusion.

"From SCC."

I saw the awareness dawn, and Callan went deathly still. "You're sure?"

"It was him."

"Holy pine needles."

"Exactly."

"But that means... Wait. The shield..." His brain was going to the same place mine had only moments before.

"We know it was done by someone with a tree affinity, which we can assume Alex has since he was at the tree conservatory. You don't... know him, do you?" I wasn't sure where the question came from, but it felt like Callan was connected to everyone in the magical botanist world. That this could catch him off guard made me even more uneasy.

Callan shook his head. "There are thousands of people with tree affinities, and I've mostly been part of the circle of founders' descendants and their allies." His tone was terse.

"Alex never let on that he was a magical botanist or knew about... any of this. That can't be a coincidence." I tried to search my brain for every conversation I'd ever had with him, wondering if I had given anything away about the academy.

"No, not a coincidence," Callan agreed.

My mind ran through my interactions with Alex as we hurried along the forested path. "Was that why he befriended me, or was that just chance? And why is he attending SCC and not Evergreen Academy? Wait. Do you think he is even college-aged? And what about..." My hand flew to my mouth.

"What is it?" Callan asked, a hint of alarm in his voice.

"Maci! She and Alex are dating, remember? What if..." I could barely stomach the thought. "What if he has an agenda for being with her?"

Callan winced, but when he spoke his voice was calm, steady. "I think we need to assume that's the case. I don't see any reason a magical botanist who knows about their powers would be attending SCC and not Evergreen Academy. Since Alex was at the tree conservatory, he is obviously plugged into the community."

I blew out a breath. "This is bad, Callan."

"We will talk to Professor East as soon as we get back. He may be able to get access to information about Alex—or whatever his name is."

My face twisted as my stomach dropped even further. "You don't think Alex is even his real name?"

"I don't know," Callan said, voice still too calm. "But we'll make sure to keep Maci safe."

"How? It's not like I can tell her any of this."

Callan scratched the side of his jaw, and I had a feeling he was as concerned about this new development as I was, but he was keeping a brave face for me. "Let's not rush into anything until we talk to Professor East, okay?"

I nodded and simply said, "Okay."

"Now, we need to get back to Meadow's house. Hollis should be around here somewhere. Our visit here was more dangerous than I realized."

"Can we agree not to say anything about Alex to them? I don't know what's going on here yet, and I think we should keep that piece of information close."

Callan nodded. "It's your discovery to share. I won't say anything."

Just then, Hollis sped toward us on the golf cart, mossy strands splaying from the front frame like bangs. He pulled to a stop. "How'd it go?"

"We've got good news and bad news," Callan said. "But we need to get out of here—and quickly."

Chapter Fifty-Five

Once back at Meadow's house, we filled her and Hollis in on *almost* everything that had happened at the tree conservatory. As I had requested, neither of us mentioned Alex. That was something we were going to have to parse out more extensively when we were alone.

"You saw Wyatt?" Meadow raised an eyebrow. "How was that?"

"About like you'd expect. You can always count on Wyatt to be in the wrong place at the right time," Callan said.

He passed me a bowl of flour he had magically enhanced with his trailing harvester ability, and I began to whisk it together with the baking soda. I needed to let off some steam, and since I had somehow forgotten to pack any art supplies, I was resorting to my aunt's favorite way to de-stress: baking. We had a little time before we needed to leave for the moss annual meeting, so here we were.

I listened intently, glad to let Meadow ask the questions for once. I was eager to know more about Callan's brother and why the encounter had set him on edge.

"He still on his high horse?" Meadow asked.

Callan grunted. "You could say that."

"Weird that he ran into you right when you were at the archival tree. Do you think he was there for the quill?" Meadow kicked her boots casually as she sat on the barstool near the counter. I could hear the faint thud of them each time they hit the wood.

"There are lots of reasons he could have been there," Callan said cautiously. "Hard to know what his motivations are. His loyalties are tied up." He watched me as I mixed the dry and wet ingredients, and he held out the cake pan when I was ready to pour the batter inside.

"What do you mean?" I asked. Alex had been foremost on my mind when we were fleeing the tree conservatory, but my curiosity about Callan's brother was intense.

Callan sighed. "My brother works for an... organization. He's beholden to their directives, not his own moral compass."

"Way to be cryptic," Meadow said with a snort.

"Seriously," I murmured, smoothing the batter then sticking the cake into the oven.

"Throw us a bone," Meadow said. "Wyatt used to be fun growing up. Then he just disappeared."

Callan's gaze dashed to Hollis, who was building a pine needle castle at the dining room table but listening to our conversation. "My brother is... an interesting person. He's hyper intelligent but not always emotionally so. He made it into a position he's always wanted, and now, he is jockeying to climb the ladder further. He'll use anyone—and any scrap of information—to make that happen."

"What kind of position?" I asked. The previous year, Callan had said he didn't have the clearance to talk about his brother's job —or something along those lines. Was that still true? Had anything changed in what we could talk about now that I was part of the Root and Vine Society?

Callan studied me, seeming to consider his next words.

I beat the butter and sugar for the frosting, holding my breath in anticipation of whatever he was going to say next.

"My brother works for the Department of Botanical Intelligence, the DBI."

Meadow whistled, and the kicking against the counter ceased. "Didn't see that coming."

I considered the name and whipped the frosting more quickly. "Intelligence... What? You mean like the botanist's version of the CIA?"

A ghost of a smile touched Callan's lips. "Kind of. Without the life-or-death stakes, usually."

"What kind of work does the DBI do?"

"They keep tabs on the greatest threats to the plant community. My brother is on the team that combats smuggling of rare species."

"That's a thing? I've heard of animals being smuggled but... plants?"

"Oh yeah," Hollis pitched in. "Succulents, orchids, cycads. There are massive underground operations for these things."

I mulled it over as I finished whipping the frosting. Each time I thought I was understanding this world, new information would knock me down several pegs.

"All right, now that we all know Wyatt's a big shot, are we ready to check out this quill?" Hollis asked, effectively halting our conversation. But I tucked all the information about Callan's brother away, hoping to discuss it with Callan at a less intense time.

"Thought you'd never ask." Meadow jumped from the stool and went to Callan's backpack. She removed the quill from the protective bag and set it on the table. "How do we activate it?"

"A connecting Floracantus. That's what the old botanists used to tie their quills to the books. Saying it again should refresh it and get the quill to respond," I said, pulling all the information from what I had researched.

Callan nodded in agreement. "Go ahead, Briar."

I readied myself, drew on all of my affinities, then said, "*Simul sumus*," and the quill shivered.

We each stood completely still as the quill spun slowly on the table. For one moment, it seemed to bobble toward the southeast, but then it began to spin again, occasionally switching directions erratically. My hopes deflated so quickly that I could practically feel them leaving me, like oxygen from a plant's stomata.

"I take it that didn't work?" Hollis asked, his question directed at me.

Callan shook his head. His eyebrows were deeply furrowed.

I gathered myself and leaned closer to the quill, reaching out to the oak gall that made up the ancient, preserved ink inside it. There was a snag on my power, and I stilled. Something wasn't right.

"What is it?" Callan asked, picking up on my use of magic.

"It's strange. The magic... it's constricted. It's like it's being blocked somehow."

I glanced between the three of them. Meadow was biting her lip, but Callan's eyes were locked on me, and he nodded encouragingly.

"How do you know?" Hollis asked.

"I can feel it." The sensation was familiar from when I worked on detecting the defensive aspects of plants in my field research with Petra. I could feel that something with a purpose other than life and growth was in the ink.

I reached out with my powers again, prodding more deeply. But unlike in my lessons with Petra, when I could undo the defense, this one was locked away, as if there was something contributing to it that I couldn't feel.

"A blocking spell," Callan murmured, a hint of surprised awe in his voice. "Complicated magic."

At his words, I reached out again, concentrating with every cell in my being. Finally, I let out a breath. The cells of the plant felt like they were fighting to work for me, but they were bound by miniscule ropes.

"And how do we unblock it?" Meadow asked, more to the group than to me.

"I'm not sure. Blocking spells were banned some time ago and are very uncommon now. I'll do some research on how they work as soon as we get back to the academy," Callan said.

I nodded. "Me too." If there was a chance I had been right about the quill working for me and that all we needed to do was remove this blocking spell, I would scour every piece of research I could find.

"Okay, let's put it away. We need to get ready for the gala," Meadow said, reluctance in her voice.

I ran my hands along the feather of the quill before placing it into its protective bag and returning it to the backpack. It felt like we were toting around a stolen copy of the Declaration of Independence.

And given the structure of the society of magical botanists, perhaps in some ways, we were.

Chapter Fifty-Six

About ten minutes into our hike to the moss conservatory, I understood why Meadow had provided me a pair of trekking poles.

Shortly after leaving her house, we had stepped off the main trail into a section of the forest with a sign on the ground that read "No walking in this area. Sensitive ground plants."

Now, the path began to increase in incline, and soon we were climbing a set of natural stairs, made of earth and moss and tree roots. Meadow extended her trekking poles, and I followed her lead.

The soft sounds of the forest and the birds and critters within were soon replaced by the rushing of water. We had to be approaching a waterfall. We rounded a bend on the steep, narrow trail, and I paused to admire the streaming expanse of water trailing off the rocks to our left.

Heavy mist sprayed my face as we climbed, so close to the waterfall that it felt like it was raining. Rainbows danced inches above the moist ground below us.

Finally, Meadow stopped her ascent. She waited for the three of us to reach her then stepped between two trees in the thickest part of the forest. When I got closer, I saw that one tree was growing to the right, the other to the left, forming an intertwining of branches that created an arch. Moss covered nearly every inch of the bark.

"Here we go," Meadow said before disappearing through the arched thicket.

I glanced back at Callan, and he nodded. "Go ahead."

With one last glance at the waterfall to my left, I turned and stepped through the arching trees. We were at a moss-riddled entrance to a green building, the entire area camouflaged to the outside, perfectly protected by trees and draping moss.

"Has anyone ever stumbled across this who wasn't supposed to?" I asked. I assumed that any person who came through here without knowing what they were looking for would stroll right past—that was how well hidden it was.

Callan nodded toward the emerald ring on my finger. "Everyone needs a charged gemstone to pass through and see what's really there, just like at the academy. If someone did get close, a botanist dressed as a park ranger would quickly arrive to escort them away from the *sensitive plants*."

"Ready to go in?" Meadow asked, and we nodded. "Okay, then. Time to meet my mom." Meadow pushed open a door concealed with a curtain of moss, and we followed her inside.

Just like when we entered the tree conservatory, I felt access to my power leave me, but I couldn't dwell on it for long as I took in the area.

My eyes traveled everywhere as I examined the spacious room. Everything about it felt alive. There were bright, warm lamps of various shapes and sizes littering the floor, and a domed glass ceiling let in natural light. There was a modern reception counter to the right for visitors to the conservatory to check in, a large open area with tables and displays of various plants and equipment, and then four hallways that I assumed led to other rooms off of this central, rounded glass pod. The entire floor was a carpet of moss.

We walked to the reception counter, and Meadow waved at the man behind it.

"Meadow! Your mom said we could expect you and some friends today. I'll page her."

I tilted my head upward, taking in a few slashes of light from outside. The light in the room had a soft green cast, due to the moss that was creeping over the dome above.

"This is spectacular," I said, imagining what it would be like to grow up with this as your playground and study area.

"Meadow, there you are!" Meadow's mom pulled her into a hug, and I watched with amusement as Meadow tried to escape the full force of it.

I recognized her mom from the brief glimpse I'd had on the summer solstice at Evergreen Academy. Meadow's mom had the same heart-shaped face and espresso eyes as Meadow, but instead of the black hair touched with a few faded pops of purple, her hair was a more natural black, her skin a warm brown, and she stood with much better posture.

Her outfit indicated she was already dressed for the gala, and she looked regal in an evening gown of deep-green. Still, there was a hint of working scientist remaining in her formal dress. She wore a badge hooked to a lanyard hanging from her neck, showcasing her credentials.

Meadow's mom finally released her from the hug. "Callan, Hollis, hello again. And you must be Briar. I'm Marisol. It's a pleasure to have you here. Now, I wish I could chat longer, but you all need to get changed for the gala. Meadow tells me you have some observations you need to make for a school project? Help yourself to any equipment. Enjoy yourselves tonight."

"Let's get this over with," Meadow murmured and led us to a multipurpose room that was reminiscent of a swanky spa. The walls were wood-paneled, the air a touch humid. Callan and Hollis peeled off to the rooms on the right, and Meadow and I stepped behind separate curtains to get dressed.

When I emerged in a business-casual outfit I had prepared for the annual strategic meeting, Meadow shook her head. "Sorry, that's not going to cut it. Luckily for you, I keep a few outfits here."

Meadow riffled through a closet that was camouflaged to the room behind a wood-paneled door and then held up a silky basil-green dress. "You're a little taller than me, so it might be a bit short, but this is more on dress code. Now, you know *I* don't care about those sorts of things, but if you stick out like a sore thumb, it's not going to do us any favors."

I took the dress from Meadow and changed, and then we both tackled styling our hair. Other magical botanists began to enter the room, entering in hiking clothes and leaving runway ready.

"I'm not in a hurry to get out there. It's going to be a social nightmare for me," Meadow said. Both of us were fully ready, but we plopped down on some cushioned benches and snacked on nuts and hummus.

"Everyone wants to talk to the daughter of the moss conservatory caretaker, I'm guessing?" I asked.

"Not only that, but they want to know about school, what I'm planning to do afterward, etcetera, etcetera. Sometimes, I try out different outrageous responses just to see how they react. We can hide out in here for a bit and pretend we're working on the 'research project' you all supposedly traveled here for."

I laughed. It felt good to unwind with Meadow like this after the intensity of the morning and before we put on our party faces and joined the others.

"How long will your mom be the caretaker here? Is it an elected position?"

"It's application-based. Or, at least, it was."

"What do you mean? Is something changing?"

Meadow's expression tightened. "There's a proposal out to shift the position to a founder's descendant appointment only. My mom might be safe, but she's in an interesting position. She's not a founder's descendant, but my dad was before he passed away, and I'm obviously a founder's descendant. It's hard to say what will happen if this proposal goes through. My mom has put on a brave face, but I think she's privately nervous."

Something clicked into place then. "Is that why you were eager to join the Root and Vine Society?" I whispered even though the lounge was now empty. "Are you against that proposal?"

Meadow sighed but nodded. "Callan, Hollis, and I are a new wave of founders' descendants. Or maybe an old wave. We want things to remain fair across the society of magical botanists, like it was for our grandparents. But there are a few powerful people in the current generation of control who are trying to move power back into the hands of founders' descendants as the fracturing between the affinities is brewing. They seem to think that will make us stronger."

It tracked with everything Callan had ever told me. "And that's why we need the book."

"There are groups trying to resist these changes in other ways, but the book would be a major point of leverage, for sure. If this proposal passes tonight... a lot is going to change for the mosses who aren't founders' descendants."

"It's being voted on tonight?"

"Yep, and word is that some of the other affinities have similar proposals up for discussion at their annual meetings this week as well."

My stomach dropped. No wonder Callan had been so eager to get the search for the book underway. While I didn't fully understand the structure of the society, it was clear from the reaction of these three that things were changing. And if they—founders' descendants who stood to benefit from these changes—were actively resisting it, what did that mean for people with less power, like my friends back at Evergreen Academy?

"Well, I guess we've left Hollis and Rhodes on their own for long enough. Ready to do this?"

I took a deep breath and smoothed the skirt of my borrowed dress. "Lead the way."

Chapter Fifty-Seven

When we returned to the main room, the atmosphere was transformed, with the lights lower and the place already beginning to fill up. Meadow had been right—the moss conservatory's annual strategic meeting more closely resembled a swanky early New Year's Eve party than the board meeting I had been picturing.

Each attendee was dressed in varying shades of green, and moss boutonnieres were pinned to our chests as we entered the main room. I smiled when I realized Meadow had bucked the green dress code as much as possible, wearing a silky black pantsuit with only the moss boutonniere adding a splash of green. I spotted Callan and Hollis, who were both in deep-green suits.

"I'm going to try to spy on the meeting," Meadow whispered. "You all have fun *mingling*." She put a heavy emphasis on the last word, as if that were exactly what we had been invited here to do.

Callan picked up three agendas, and I scanned the one he handed to me. The paper was obviously recycled and had a grayish tinge. According to the inked text, different portions of the annual strategic meeting took place every thirty minutes out in the sphagnum bog, with only the relevant parties invited.

"Bryology research highlights... moss ecosystem recovery... genomic advancements... leadership changes..." I listed off some of the topics on the agenda and paused on that one. It must have been what Meadow was referring to. "Meadow told me about the vote," I said, raising my eyebrows at Callan and Hollis.

"My dad let slip that something similar is on the agenda for the fern meeting," Hollis said.

"Do you think it's going to pass?" I asked.

Hollis shrugged, though his face was hard. "I think there's been some pushback from the less powerful fern families. But whether they'll prevail... we'll have to wait and see."

"I take it you don't support these changes?" I asked, wanting to confirm what Meadow had said.

"Look who's on the list for that agenda item. Four people. *Four.*" Hollis pointed to the paper. "Should so few individuals be in charge of making decisions for everyone?"

I raised my eyebrows, startled at his boldness. I should have known his sentiments would match Callan's—they were best friends.

"It's the Board of Regents driving it all," Callan murmured, voice low as his eyes coolly slid over the moss botanists in the room. His facial expression was pleasantly bored despite the heat I sensed in his words. "They've obviously been lobbying to set all of this up. I never imagined it would come to a vote so quickly."

Of course. We were back to his parents.

"I'm getting some food. Want anything?" Hollis asked.

Callan shook his head, and I declined as well.

I was about to ask him more about the proposals when we were approached by a woman with long dark hair adorned with gemstone clips who was wearing a moss-green sari.

"Mr. Rhodes, I didn't know you were going to be here this evening. Are your parents in attendance?"

Callan gave her the most disarming smile I had ever seen and shook his head reluctantly. "I came here with Meadow for a school project."

"Ah! Evergreen Academy never sleeps, does it?" She turned to me. "And who is your friend here?"

Callan tensed, but it was washed away so quickly that I thought I might have imagined it.

"Of course, let me introduce you. Lira, this is Briar, one of my classmates at Evergreen Academy. Briar, Lira is a member of the Board of Regents. She represents the mosses."

I tried to cover up my surprise at being introduced to one of the members of the board that we'd just been discussing. We shook hands, and I said, "Nice to meet you."

She eyed me more carefully. "The pleasure is mine. You wouldn't be Briar Whelan, would you?"

"Guilty," I said, letting out a forced lighthearted laugh. We had not prepared for this level of attention, and if the quill was discovered to be missing, our presence here this weekend wasn't likely to go unnoticed.

"Well, you made quite the splash with the board. I was told you have a strong affinity for *every* plant group." Her eyes were assessing as they scanned me, as if she might get a glimpse of my powers through my skin.

"You heard correctly. Though I'm still developing my affinity powers. I'm afraid my skills might be a little bit of a letdown."

"There was some debate over what field study options would best suit you this year. I know more than one affinity was hoping to get you on a topic of interest to them. Judging by how cozy you two look, I'd say the trees had an advantage. It seems plans were changed at the last minute. You are quite the hot commodity."

I swallowed, startled by this revelation, but kept my voice steady and my expression neutral. "How flattering."

"Alas, the board didn't get the final say on your assignment. I'm told it is classified. I hope you are finding it beneficial?"

"I am," I said, keeping a mask of composure on my face. Questions were flooding my brain like seedlings after a rainstorm.

"Lira, you look lovely as always," Callan interjected smoothly, putting a steadying hand on the small of my back. "I was just getting ready to give Briar the full tour. It was great seeing you again."

Lira turned her attention back to Callan, seemingly unable to resist his charm. "Thank you, Callan. I must attend a session out in the bog in a few minutes. But I'll see you at the midsummer gathering, if not sooner. I heard conditions are looking good for a super bloom."

She turned to me. "I'm sure we'll meet again, Briar." She nodded to each of us then turned and walked away, leaving me dizzy with questions.

Chapter Fifty-Eight

My hands were shaking from the interaction with Lira, and Callan gently but swiftly guided me through the crowded central room of the gala.

We spotted Hollis engaged in conversation around the food table, a moss-tini in hand. He raised it to me in a mock toast. His eyes flicked to Callan for a moment, then he returned to his conversation. A moment later, Callan and I stepped through a curtain of moss.

I only glanced at the room enough to see that it was empty of other people before saying, "What was she talking about?"

Callan looked as if he was selecting his words carefully. "You knew finding you a field studies assignment would be... complicated, given your complex powers."

"She made it sound like people were bidding over me." My chest squeezed in dissent, and I realized I was getting a little taste of how Callan must feel all the time. "Sorry, I'm sounding selfish. It's just... What did she mean that the board didn't get the final say on my assignment? I thought they selected all of the assignments this year."

Callan shook his head. "You are many things, local, but selfish is not one of them. My understanding is that Professor East was allowed to choose your field studies assignment."

"Really?" I asked, calming slightly. "Did he get to choose anyone else's?"

Callan averted his eyes. "Not that I'm aware of."

Something about that didn't sit right with me, but I had gotten an amazing assignment that was possibly going to help me undo the poisoning of my powers. I was the last person who should be questioning how the field studies had shaken out.

Callan spoke again. "Listen, I think we need to talk."

My heart rate kicked up. "What about?"

"Not here," Callan said, and I finally stopped to look around. We appeared to be in the moss conservatory's library. The stacks filled the entire room, moss coating the sides of the shelves. Rounded couches made of green velvet scattered the area, perfect for settling in to read.

Callan snagged a moss blanket from one of the couches, but he didn't sit. "This way." He put his hand gently on the small of my back and ushered me through a curtain of moss I hadn't noticed.

"Where are we going?" I asked as we walked down a narrow corridor lit on either side by moss-covered sconces.

"You'll see."

The sound of rushing water began to form around us, and my eyes widened as we stepped onto a thin bridge. One side of the bridge led to the back of a cave, and the other had a thin see-through wall that showed the most mesmerizing display I had ever seen.

"Are we... Are we inside the waterfall?"

Crinkles formed at the corner of Callan's eyes as I dragged my gaze away from the shimmering stream to look at him. "We're right behind it, yeah. This bridge connects to another part of the moss conservatory, but this is also a great place to come and think. Or talk without being overheard."

I shivered as a whisper of water sprayed over the protective glass wall.

"Here." Callan lifted the moss blanket and settled it around my shoulders.

I shivered again but this time at his proximity.

Now that we were standing here alone, inside a *waterfall*, the kiss that somehow felt like it had happened both moments ago and days ago was instantly crowding my thoughts. I cleared my throat and tucked it away, wanting him to take the lead on that conversation.

"So, what's this about? Usually 'we need to talk' never ends well," I said, trying to keep my voice playful despite the anxiety his words had sparked.

Callan took my hand. "A lot has happened today. And it has reminded me how much is at stake here."

"Okay," I said slowly, trying to anticipate what he might say next. I met his eyes then, which were dark, the muscles of his face tense. "What is it?" I asked, though I was beginning to feel that I already knew. It was written all over his face.

He skimmed a finger down my hair, which was loose and wavy around my shoulders, the moisture from the waterfall making it curl beyond its typical waves. He swallowed. "We need to talk about the kiss. It was... amazing. But..."

My heart fell. It was the word I had been expecting but was still dreading.

"As much as I tried to keep things... friendly between us all year, things have shifted. For me, at least, there's no going back after... that. But"—he cleared his throat, as if taking a moment to gather his thought—"events of today reminded me why we agreed to keep things the way they were in the first place." He said it softly, almost reluctantly.

"Circumstances being all the influences hanging over our heads?" I tried to make light of it, putting a little laugh into my voice, but it came out shaky at the end.

"Alex is an unknown threat, my brother is a known one, and between my parents and the board all vying to get their hands on you... this afternoon was a stark reminder that us being together... it's just another target on your back." His voice was low.

I pulled back slightly, forcing him to meet my eyes.

His long, dark lashes swept side to side as he studied my face.

I knew he was right, but I hated the thought of going back to just friends, in public *or* in private. "What if being with you makes the target smaller?" I reached for his hands and was relieved when he took mine. "What if we're stronger together?"

Callan looked pained, and I wanted to pull him into a hug. "I wish it worked like that, but that's not how my family operates. They have enough of a reason to scrutinize you with your powers already. Seeing my brother there... it reminded me how connected they are to *everything* in this world. Lira and her comment about us looking 'cozy' is further evidence that the other affinity groups think the trees might be trying to get to you first. If they found out we were..." He paused and ran a hand through his hair. "Please, just trust me on this, okay?"

I nodded but couldn't speak.

He sighed and glanced toward the waterfall. Its mist was settling in his hair like flecks of diamonds. "It's not because I don't want to... be with you. Staying away has been harder than you can imagine. But I'm trying to protect you from being a part of all of this until you're ready to make your own choices. Until you have full access to your power."

"Okay," I said tentatively then stopped to chew on my lip. "You make good points, but here's my counter."

Callan raised an eyebrow.

"Life is too short for us to make decisions rooted in fear."

Callan nodded, and I waited to see whether he would agree. "There's a difference between being brave and being reckless, local. Not taking precautions now, as more trouble is brewing, is bordering on reckless. And after seeing Lira tonight, I won't be surprised if word of our presence here reaches my parents. It was stupid of me not to consider that she would be here. The Board of Regents had their own meeting, but of course she left early to attend the moss strategic meeting."

I sighed, but I wasn't ready to give up. There was more than one way to be brave. "Okay, let's say we do it your way. How do you see this all playing out?"

Callan smiled softly. "You're powerful, Briar. More than any of them know. One day, you *will* outmaneuver them. But right now, if it's between me having you and you being free of them"—he swallowed, and I watched his Adam's apple rise and fall—"I choose your freedom."

My stomach swooped at the intensity of his words. I understood where Callan was coming from. A large part of me admired it even if I believed in a different approach. He had a desire to protect me. Was it because he had never been protected by the people who should have been there for him the most? That thought nearly broke my heart.

I slipped my arms around his waist, and he returned the hug, pulling me close until my head rested on his chest. I wanted to pour so much love and admiration into him that he would never feel powerless again.

But words weren't enough for Callan. He needed to see it in action, so that's what I would do.

I was gaining power.

I couldn't tell him about what I was working on with Petra in my field studies. Not yet anyway. But my skills were growing, and I was doing everything within my control to wrest back full access to my powers. It was the thing Callan was fighting for, too, in a different way, and I was flooded with affection for him every time I was reminded of it.

I pulled back to lean on the see-through wall and looked up at Callan's clear brown eyes, which were drinking me in like I was the first bloom of spring. My heart was racing, the memory of our kiss almost palpable on my lips. I whispered, "There aren't any scouting vines out here, are there?"

Callan shook his head, his forehead brushing mine. And before I could second-guess it, I went on my tiptoes and gently pressed my lips to his.

As if on instinct, his hands nestled into the hair behind my neck and he drew the kiss deeper, as if he knew it was the last one we would share until this battle with the elites was over and someone emerged victorious.

When we broke apart, I took a deep, fortifying breath then slipped the blanket from my shoulders.

"We'll do it your way, for now." I said the words slowly, deliberately, then offered the blanket to him, dangling it on the tip of my finger. When he took it, I gave a little twirl in my slightly-too-short dress. "But I won't always be a damsel in distress. And you won't always need to save me."

His eyes tracked me as I moved backward along the narrow bridge. "Maybe I like saving you," he whispered.

And I walked away from the waterfall and out of the library with a flush of heat in my face and a touch of wind to the back of my neck.

Chapter Fifty-Nine

"You two must have had quite the night." Hollis nodded toward where Callan was loading the plane with a vigor that was more appropriate for chopping wood than loading luggage. "He went tree walking before sunrise. It's kind of one of his stress signals."

"Did he?" I asked evasively.

"Something tells me it's related to you," Hollis said, voice dripping with implication.

I sighed. "The stress of everything that's going on is leading him to put... parameters on our relationship."

Hollis nodded again, as if he wasn't surprised. "Aww. Yeah, I kind of saw that one coming, especially after his brother showed up."

"I take it those two don't have the best relationship?"

"Things are changing right now. It has us all on edge. And with you having the power that you do, Rhodes doesn't want to see you taken advantage of."

"Yeah, it seems like yesterday spooked him. We spoke with Lira —the mosses representative on the Board of Regents—last night, and she brought up how 'cozy' the two of us looked." I put the word in quotes. "And she made a strange comment about my field studies, but it seems like the board relinquished their control of my field studies assignment. So shouldn't that make Callan less worried?" I had been thinking about it overnight, and more questions had arisen.

Hollis glanced toward the plane again, making sure Callan was still preoccupied and out of earshot. "What did she say about your field studies?"

"That the board didn't get to have the final say on it. Callan said Professor East was allowed to select my study."

Hollis hesitated before his next words. "Did Callan ever tell you why he started the school year so late?"

"He was helping set up the field studies assignments." I said it slowly, wondering where Hollis was going with this.

"Yes, but do you know why he agreed to do that?"

"I kind of assumed his parents made him."

"Listen, he's going to be pissed at me for telling you this, but I think you should know. He wasn't forced into it. Callan made a deal. He agreed to serve as a student ambassador and take on the field studies assignment his mom wanted for him. In exchange, the board agreed to allow Professor East to have control over one field study of his choice."

"What?" Something was twisting uncomfortably inside me even as the words confirmed what Lira had hinted at. "And Professor East chose me?"

"Either he did, or someone"—his eyes darted to Callan— "helped him arrange the whole thing all along."

My stomach dropped. "So he agreed to do his parents' bidding and work on a project he has no passion for... for me?"

"That pretty much sums it up. I wasn't privy to all the details, but based on what I know, it's not a hard leap to make."

"No... Oh no." My stomach was twisted into knots. All this time, I had been enjoying a field studies assignment with Petra that was exactly what I needed and free of any kind of pressure from the board, all because Callan had elected to forgo *his* dreams on my behalf. "I feel awful."

"You shouldn't. That was Callan being Callan. He's a born protector. But I'm not sure that he's ever had anyone he cares about as much as you. He's going to make decisions that keep you out of harm's way even if it costs him something."

Startled by the unexpected insight from Hollis, I cast my eyes toward Callan. He seemed to be double-checking every inch of the exterior of the plane.

"I wish he would have told me. Maybe we could have made some other arrangement. Not that I want to be under the board's thumb, but I hate that he had to take all that on."

Hollis shook his head. "I know him better than almost anyone, and even if he had told you what was going on, I don't think it would have changed how things shook out. There's a battle of wills in that family, and Callan's is as strong as the rest of them."

A door slammed behind us, and Meadow emerged from her house, hair wild and backpack hanging off one shoulder. "Is it time to load up?"

"Someone stayed up too late dyeing all the party favor moss soaps purple." Hollis smirked.

Meadow scowled. "Hey, you helped. It was satisfying to break up some of the green in the room. Especially after the outcome of the meeting."

"The outcome?" I asked.

"I'll fill you in on the flight. But it's not the one we were hoping for."

As I followed her to the tiny plane, I took one last look around the towering forest that surrounded her home. Our trip had been bittersweet.

Callan had taken me into his arms, and we had both finally poured everything we felt about each other into that kiss. We'd gotten the quill. Our main mission was accomplished. But Alex and Wyatt had set Callan even more on edge than he already was, and things were shifting within the society that could have implications far beyond the four of us. Our focus had to be on combating those changes, on fighting to preserve the world that had become my second home.

The magic that had overtaken us in the tree conservatory and caused Callan to let his guard down long enough to give me two kisses I would never forget was being left behind in Washington.

It was time to go home, where real life, including an Alex-sized problem, was waiting.

Chapter Sixty

"It's official, then?" Hollis asked. "The mosses will be putting founders' descendants or their designated appointees in charge of all major operations?"

Meadow nodded. She had brought a chunk of moss with her, and she was now growing it up and down her arms.

"What does that mean for your mom's job?" I asked.

"She gets to keep it, for now. They're considering her a 'designated appointee' based on her relationship to me. If only they knew how little I sided with them," Meadow said. "But this probably means changes at the academy."

"What do you mean?" I asked, invested as always in anything to do with our beloved school.

"The teachers aren't founders' descendants. Those positions have historically gone to people who have achieved top research achievements in their fields. The school has had a good balance of power between the instructors and the founders' descendants who charge the shield. If these changes go that far, they could be pushed out in favor of members of founders' families," Callan explained.

A shiver passed over me as I thought of all my teachers. Each of their faces flashed through my mind, ending on Professor East. I couldn't imagine the school without them. A cold resolve solidified in my chest. This threat might not come to fruition, but if it did, I wouldn't let my instructors be pushed out without a fight.

"Woah. You okay there?" Meadow's voice broke me out of deep contemplation.

"What do you mean?"

"You're stealing my moss."

I glanced down and saw that the fluffy green clump that had been on her arms was slowly inching across the seat in my direction. I unclenched my hands, and the moss ceased its movement.

Meadow scooped the fuzzy material back onto her arms. "Hold onto that feeling," she whispered. "It might come in handy."

I was startled at whatever had just happened, but I forced myself to relax. My aunt had always taught me that there was no point in stewing about something that might happen. Instead, focus on what I could control now. And currently, we had the quill, and I had my field studies where I could continue to work on un-poisoning my powers. I pulled up a mental image of a field of wildflowers and took a few calming breaths.

The rest of the flight back to California was uneventful, except for the quill seemingly burning a hole in my backpack as we went. The group had decided I should be the one to hang on to it for now since I was the only one who could use it. I had now officially smuggled stolen goods across state lines. Did that make me a felon? Did the magical botanist community have felonies?

Shortly after we landed in Weed, it began pouring rain. Water slammed the windshield of Callan's truck as his wipers worked incessantly in a futile effort to keep the glass clear. In the woods before we reached the academy grounds, Meadow yawned and asked, "Should we try the quill here just to see if it still behaves like it did in Washington? Then I'm calling it an early night."

I glanced through the windows of Callan's truck. While it was hard to see beyond the pounding rain, the forest around us appeared empty of other humans. The bit of frost that had been on the ground when we'd left had been washed away, replaced by mud.

"Good idea," Callan said. He nodded to me.

I removed the quill from my backpack and its protective bag and unraveled the defensive charms I had placed on it at Meadow's house in Washington.

"Do it, B," Hollis said.

I turned my attention back to the quill and said, *"Simul sumus."*

We all watched in rapt attention. Even Meadow, despite her proclaimed exhaustion, was leaning over the front seat to have a clear view.

The quill began to spin just as it had in Washington, though this time, it was spinning even faster and more erratically.

I reached out and sensed for the blocking spell. "The block seems to be even stronger here than it was in Washington."

"Maybe we're closer to whatever is blocking it?" Meadow suggested.

"That's a good hypothesis," Callan said. "Something to investigate when we do our research. I'll start tonight." He didn't have to say what we were all thinking—with a stolen quill in our possession, the clock was ticking to get it to work.

Callan drove us onto the academy grounds, and Hollis and Meadow collected their bags and headed straight to the glass building, Hollis shielding them from the rain with two large fern fronds.

"I'm impressed that you sensed the increased strength of the blocking spell," Callan said.

"Well, I have been working on my defensive plant powers in my field studies. In case you thought I was just messing around and burning time once a week," I said, adding a little teasing to my voice to break the tension I felt building.

We were alone in the truck now, and my mind was, annoyingly, reminding me of another time we'd been alone together. And I could still smell that darned cologne. The one he had created just for me.

I jumped at a sound behind us and turned to see Hollis opening the back door. He put his hands up. "Sorry, forgot my wallet."

When I swiveled back around, Callan had opened his door. "We better head back too," he said softly.

I wanted to protest, but I didn't. Callan wasn't the type of person you could push.

"I'll see you in the morning?"

"Of course. We'll talk to Professor East about Alex first thing."

As I lay in bed that night, all the revelations of the weekend preventing me from sleeping, I had one calming thought.

Callan had told me he had the patience of trees, and he'd proven it to be true over and over again. He was protective of me, but I was getting stronger and better at using my powers by the day. We had the quill, even if we couldn't use it to lead us to the book yet.

If I could get full access to my powers or if we could figure out how to undo the blocking spell, maybe, just maybe, he would forget about protecting me and give into the connection between us for good.

Chapter Sixty-One

The next morning, I left the campus early, before sunrise. I had formulated more protective plans for the quill as I fought sleep the night before, trying not to think about the conversation Callan and I would soon have with Professor East about Alex. The rain had ceased sometime during the night, leaving the plants in the forest a bright, vibrant green.

When I walked through the gate to leave the academy grounds, I immediately felt access to my affinity powers return and tried to draw on the strength and reassurance I felt from that as I crafted my plan.

Taking inspiration from some of the plants in the Perilous Grove, I grafted a few defense mechanisms to repel water and light, for basic protection, then imitated the mechanism of the lithops pebble plants, which appear like stones to the untrained eye.

"Instead of a quill, I'm going to make you appear as a bald eagle feather," I whispered before murmuring a camouflaging Floracantus I had practiced with Petra. I watched in delight as the quill metamorphosed before my eyes, its grayish feather shifting to the distinctive white and black of a bald eagle. The quill tip sealed and shrunk, emerging as nothing more than a normal feather shaft.

Satisfied with the work, I slipped the feather into my bag. As I prepared to return to campus, my phone rang. I was surprised by the caller.

"Hey, Bryce," I answered. "Everything okay?"

"Hey, B. Sorry to bother you. Your aunt says you're busy with studies and all of that. I just wanted to get your opinion on something."

"It's no problem. What's up? How are you both?"

"It's Vera. She's fine—there's nothing you need to worry about —but she is acting a little... strange."

I chewed my lip, wondering where this was going. "Strange, how?"

"She won't stop talking about flowers. She wanted to stop at every florist on the way to visit my brother's family, and she's been preparing flower arrangements and covering every spare surface in the house with bouquets." He hesitated. "I guess I'm just wondering... do you think this might be some sort of weird post-wedding blues?"

I frowned, processing what he had said. I wasn't sure if Bryce was prone to hyperbole, but my aunt's actions did sound a *little* unusual. "On Christmas Eve, she mentioned that I had inspired her with the flowers I did for your wedding. Has she said anything about that to you?" I asked.

"She did say she was thinking about it as a new business venture. I didn't think it was serious, but now I'm not so sure. Have you ever seen her get obsessed with something like this before?"

"I mean, sure. She can get on little kicks. She was obsessive when she first started the bakery. There were days our kitchen was completely overrun with scraps of numerous in-the-works recipes. And she's always maintained her patio garden. Maybe she's just getting antsy for spring. You have a whole yard for her to landscape this year."

"Yeah, you're probably right. I'll indulge her. It's not like my brother and his wife are complaining about too many flowers in the house."

I laughed. "Yeah, I'm sure it's nothing. But if she starts to take over their house completely, maybe no more trips to the florist?"

Now Bryce laughed, audibly more relaxed than when we had first started talking. "Thanks, B. I think it's just nervous newlywed stuff on my end. This is the first time we've visited my family together. It's a big step."

"Look at you two, doing cutesy married stuff," I teased.

"All right, all right, I'll let you go. Happy New Year. We'll see you soon?"

"Of course. You two owe me dinner for getting straight A's this fall, remember?"

We hung up, and I walked toward the academy gates. The sun was creeping over the horizon, and I stopped to watch it as the sky split orange and pink around the backdrop of Mount Shasta.

Professor East drove by on my way in, and I flagged him down after he parked. "Good morning. I know it's early, but Callan and I were hoping to talk to you about something important. Do you have time today?"

"Sure," Professor East said. "Just let me get inside and set up a little. I'm returning from a trip. Say, thirty minutes?"

"Sounds great. Thank you." I hurried off to find Callan.

When I entered the teahouse, Callan was pouring himself a cup of coffee the size of a quart of milk.

"Woah there. Rough night?" I asked.

Callan's smile pulled at the corners of his mouth. "The thought of the contraband in your room did have me a little anxious, yes."

At his words, I gripped the strap of my bag, and he noticed. "We'll have to find somewhere safe to stash it until we can figure out the blocking spell." He twisted around and looked over the empty tearoom. Most students were still on winter break. As far as

I knew, the two of us, Hollis, and Meadow were the only students around. "You were up early," Callan said, changing the subject.

"I wanted to be ready when Professor East arrived, and I had a few things to do off campus. He said we can meet him in thirty minutes."

Callan nodded. "Everything okay? The reason you went off campus, I mean."

"Oh, yeah. I mainly needed to check my phone." As we stood there, I was hyperaware of what Hollis had told me about how Callan had made concessions in his field studies all so that I could get the training I needed.

I turned so that we were facing each other again. "Before we go talk to Professor East, I just want to say that it means a lot that you're always looking out for me." There. I hadn't spilled the beans on what Hollis had shared, but hopefully he got the message that I knew he had my back, even at his own expense.

"What kind of tutor would I be if I threw you to the thorns?" He asked it jokingly, but there was a note in his voice that told me my heartfelt message had gotten through.

"Hurry up and get that coffee kicking in. I'm about ready to get this conversation over with. How are we going to tell him about Alex without mentioning our trip to the tree conservatory?"

"I think we're going to have to tell him about that. I'm not worried about it. Do you want to take the lead, or do you want me to?"

"You," I said, relieved that he'd offered. "I think I'm still in shock about the whole thing."

Callan nodded and took a large swig of his coffee. Then he set the enormous carafe on the table and said, "All right, then, local. Let's see if Professor East can help us smoke out a weed."

Chapter Sixty-Two

Callan lifted a hand and knocked on the door to Professor East's office. It slid open with the tug of a vine.

"Good morning." Professor East looked slightly more perky now, and I attributed it to the mug of tea resting on his desk.

"We have some news we'd like to discuss with you," Callan said.

Professor East nodded toward the chairs across from his desk. "Of course. Ms. Whelan said as much. Have a seat."

I slid into the chair closest to the door, sitting forward and angled toward Callan.

He gave me one last look then turned to Professor East. "Briar and I visited the tree conservatory this weekend. We were invited to the moss conservatory by Meadow and decided to stop in while we were there."

My heart felt like it was going to hammer out of my chest. We had tried so hard to ensure that no one knew about our visit to the tree conservatory, and now we had to tell Professor East. Well, with Wyatt having seen Callan, perhaps the seeds were already out of the packet. At least Callan wouldn't have to full-on lie.

"I'm sure that was an educational experience for you, Ms. Whelan," Professor East said, looking between us.

I swallowed, hoping the sudden warmth on my skin wasn't visibly betraying me. My mind went straight to our kiss, and that was *not* what I needed to be focusing on in this moment. "Very," I said, thankful it didn't come out as a squeak.

"While we were there," Callan continued, "we ran into someone we weren't expecting. I'm afraid it may pose a security concern for the academy or for Briar."

Professor East leaned back, fingers steepled and forehead furrowed. "Who did you see?"

Callan turned to me, and I spoke up. "A student I know from SCC. Alex."

Professor East's eyebrows rose, but it was so subtle I almost didn't notice it. "You saw an SCC student at the tree conservatory? Someone who does not attend here?"

I nodded.

"I didn't recognize him," Callan said. "Though that doesn't mean anything. There are plenty of tree affinities I don't know. But based on the information Briar gathered earlier this term..."

Professor East quickly filled in the gap. "Whoever poisoned the soil last year had a tree affinity."

"That can't be a coincidence," I said.

"I'm inclined to agree." Professor East rolled his chair forward, closer to his desk. He took a deep breath.

"Thank you for bringing this to me. I can get some basic information from Alex's student records at SCC. Full name, address."

"There's something else you should know," Callan said. He cast a wary glance in my direction. "Alex befriended Briar at SCC last year, and he's currently dating her best friend, Maci."

"I see. That is... concerning," Professor East said.

I turned to where Callan sat in the chair next to me, taking comfort in the fact that he was here. I was reminded of the evening a year ago when my powers had first been activated on the winter solstice. Things had turned out all right then, so maybe they would now too. But with Maci involved, the stakes felt so much higher.

"I'll do some subtle inquiring and get back to you both when I have information to share. It doesn't seem as if your friend is in any immediate danger, Ms. Whelan, but you will need to decide if you'd like to warn her or not."

"Warn her…" The words floated out of me as I struggled to process them. Of course I needed to warn her. But how? She didn't know about magical botanists, tree affinities, or verdant shield poisonings. What could I tell her that wouldn't sound like me coming off as a jealous friend?

"You'll think of something." Callan's voice was reassuring, and I nodded.

"He—Alex—told Maci he was going home for the holidays, so she's not expecting to hear from him for a while. I'll try to figure out how to approach her about this before he returns," I said, hoping I sounded more confident than I felt.

"Very good. I'm sorry this has happened, but I'm glad you both brought it to my attention. Is there anything else either of you would like to speak with me about?"

Oh, just the stolen quill—a precious magical botanical artifact—that's currently in my bag. No big deal.

"Not a thing," I said, perhaps too quickly.

Callan's mouth tugged into a smile that he effortlessly straightened as he rose. "Thanks, Professor East. Let me know if there's anything I can do to help."

"I will. In the meantime, why don't you two try to enjoy the remainder of your break."

We left Professor East's office and descended the stairs. I wasn't sure exactly where we were going, but fresh air seemed like a good idea. A hysterical laugh bubbled out of me when we reached the entry atrium.

"Briar," Callan said, pausing in the atrium and gently taking my hand in his, "we're going to figure this out. Okay?"

I nodded, focusing on the warmth of his hand as he rubbed a thumb on the inside of my palm. "I know. This is all just... a lot. It was exhilarating seeing the tree conservatory." I quickly cleared my throat. I couldn't think about that too hard while I had the sensation of Callan's fingers so near my hand. "And getting the quill, but then there was the thing with Alex, and now the quill doesn't seem to be working. After the decision at the moss conservatory and what you all think that might mean for our professors... It feels like things are spiraling out of control."

Callan took my other hand in his. "We have the quill now. And it's all because of you. We'll figure the next steps out together. And, actually, I thought of something while we were sitting in Professor East's office. There was a painting of a—"

Callan abruptly cut off whatever he was about to say.

"Briar," Callan's voice was sharp. He dropped my hands and spun around, facing the exit to the grounds. His body was tense, and I followed his gaze out of the atrium and to the flower gardens. All I saw were the bright blooms.

"What is it?"

"Do you have the quill on you?" Callan whispered.

I nodded. "It's in my bag. What's—"

"Take it and go off campus. Use the petal portal. Hurry."

"Cal—"

The door to the entrance atrium blew inward, as if it had been pushed open by a vacuum of wind from the other side.

Callan's face fell for a moment then turned to a mask of stony nonchalance as he crossed his arms and faced the door.

"Two times in a week. Mom and Dad might start to think we're leaving them out on purpose."

"Hello again, Wyatt."

Chapter Sixty-Three

"Hello to you," Wyatt said, a tense smile forming on his face. He shifted his gaze to me, and I saw his eyes take note of my auburn hair. "And this must be the famous Briar. This is a pleasant surprise. I thought I might have to track her down." The words were delivered with a note of humor that I thought should probably unnerve me.

But as much as I was in shock at Wyatt's appearance at the academy, I couldn't help studying him, not having gotten a glimpse of him at the tree conservatory. Both brothers had the olive skin tone and rich chestnut hair of their mother, but Wyatt was a tad stockier and had a thick beard that was speckled with a few flecks of red, obviously from their father.

"What brings you to Evergreen Academy, Wyatt?" Callan asked, his voice pleasantly neutral.

Wyatt stepped closer, lowering his voice. "I think you know what," he said to Callan then sliced his eyes to me, a slight smile still lingering on his face.

I shifted my weight on my feet.

"You're going to have to elaborate," Callan said, voice still unnervingly calm.

"Someone stole a little"—he moved two fingers in the air, as if using a writing utensil—"artifact."

My stomach sank. Our fake quill at the tree conservatory had worked for a whole day or two, but now we were busted.

"I'm here to retrieve it," Wyatt continued.

"I wish you good luck," Callan said, his eyes never leaving his brother's. There was a soft rustling sound, and vines from trees on both sides of the atrium began snaking casually across the ground.

Wyatt eyed the vines that were heading for his ankles. "I thought we could handle this more casually—family to family, you know," Wyatt said.

"Callan," I said slowly, hoping to cool the situation. The vines receded, just slightly.

"Yes, family to family," Callan agreed. "Briar, can you give us some space? My brother and I have some business to sort out." He shot me a look, and his eyes were filled with a depth of expression I knew well. He was buying me time.

"Sure, take all the time you need," I said, trying to convey that I understood.

"Not so fast," Wyatt said. "Something tells me this concerns you too."

"It doesn't," Callan said firmly, and to my surprise, Wyatt relented with a casual shrug.

As I headed toward the central vein, movement along the floor caught my eye, and I noticed a vine pull back, snaking into a small vacancy near the door. I didn't have time to dwell on whether Callan was going to threaten his brother with vines again, and I hustled into the hallway. There, I had to make a decision. I could either run for the exit door and go to the petal portal, like Callan wanted, or I could pursue the plan that was rapidly forming in my mind.

Callan's plan for me to hide the quill somewhere was the logical choice on such short notice, but how long would that work? Wyatt obviously knew that the quill had been taken. If the quill—and, subsequently, the *Vanished Compendium*—were as important to the magical botanical community as the Root and Vine Society suggested, we needed to throw them off the trail.

And I needed a way to make sure this didn't come back to Callan. He had sacrificed enough for me.

I squared my shoulders and ran up the stairs to the second level instead. I nearly tripped on the last step but steadied myself and headed straight for my room. My heart was beating faster than an unfurling fern coil as I dropped to my knees and sifted through my trinkets shelf, suddenly very grateful that Yasmin hadn't returned from winter break yet.

If Wyatt wanted a quill, I would give him one. *"Family to family,"* I murmured. Well, when your family was as sketchy as Callan's, you made your own. And today, that was me.

Callan thought he needed to protect me. That was all well and good. But this time, I was going to be the one to look out for him. I just needed to buy us a little time. I found what I needed then carefully settled the silk pouch into my satchel.

I was heading to the entrance atrium when the door to Professor East's office swung open. He ushered me inside. "The elder Mr. Rhodes is here for the quill, isn't he?"

My eyes widened as shock coursed through me. Professor East knew about the quill?

"Do you have it on you?" Professor East asked, obviously realizing that I was too startled to answer his first question.

"How…"

"Do you trust me, Ms. Whelan?"

I nodded without hesitation. "Of course."

"Give me the quill. I'll take care of it."

"But I was going to—"

"Your plan is a good one, but you will get in serious trouble. We don't need the DBI or the board having any reason to target you right now, Briar. Give me the quill."

I opened the flap of my satchel and passed the goose feather to my instructor.

He took the quill and twirled it slowly. "Clever, Ms. Whelan."

My stomach clenched. Did he know?

Before I could respond, he said, "Thank you. And Briar..."

I met his eyes, which were kind but shadowed with sadness.

"I hope I can buy you some time," he said. "Make good use of it, all right?"

"Professor East, what are you—"

"I'll take it from here. Go on back into the entrance atrium, and I'll join you in a minute."

Adrenaline was still pumping through my veins, but I nodded and had to keep myself from running back to where I had left Callan.

I didn't know what was going on, but I didn't have time to process the hollow feeling that Professor East's words left in my stomach.

Chapter Sixty-Four

"She doesn't answer to you." That was Callan's voice, and the strength in it made me smile and steeled my nerve.

The two brothers had moved out of the entrance atrium and were now at the bottom of the stairs. Callan and Wyatt were standing in tense positions across from one another, both falling quiet when I arrived. I couldn't help wondering if they'd stood that way as little boys, arguing over a toy.

"Have you two had enough time to chat?" I asked, moving to Callan's side.

Wyatt's eyes shot to me.

"More than enough," Callan said. "Wyatt thinks he'll be searching my room. You may want to stick around for the show." The muscles of Callan's forearms were flexed, but his outward appearance suggested utter calm.

Wyatt followed as Callan turned swiftly and began to climb the stairs. "It's fun that you think I won't be able to get past your wards."

The three of us climbed the stairs and stopped in front of Callan's room.

Callan lifted a hand, and vines snaked across the door from

bottom to top, forming an impenetrable wall of thick plant material.

There was movement down the hall, and I glanced in that direction to see Meadow's head appear from her room. She kept her body behind the door, seemingly assessing the situation.

Wyatt sighed. "Play nice, Cal. I'm afraid I'm short on time, and I'm not leaving here without the quill."

Callan's face was stony. "I've already told you; I don't have what you're looking for."

"Are you sure about that? Because I have evidence to the contrary." Wyatt tsked. "Is Professor East aware of your excursion to the tree conservatory this weekend?"

I winced.

"He is, in fact. Though I'm sure *you're* aware that visiting a conservatory is not against any school rule," Callan said.

"It wouldn't be if all you did was visit. I need the artifact, Callan." Wyatt's voice was losing patience now.

"And I already told you, I don't have it."

Well, he wasn't lying.

I glanced at Callan's door, which now had moss creeping along the cracks, as if sealing it closed. I glanced to Meadow, who flashed me a quick smirk.

Wyatt's lip twitched. "Dealing in semantics now? Fine. I'll lay out the evidence. I find you by the display at the tree conservatory where said quill has recently arrived. A bit odd since no one had expected you at the conservatory, but as a tree founder's descendant, you have every right to stop by. As part of—we'll call it a routine check—we scanned the exhibit that night. Imagine our surprise when we realized the defenses were down."

I winced again. That one was on me. If only I'd been able to put the defenses back up. The block on my powers was really starting to tick me off. My hands twitched at my sides.

"We take a look at the quill—just to be safe—and something's a little off about it," Wyatt continued. "Don't get me wrong, it was masterfully done. It was unfortunate for you that someone I was traveling with has a specialty in these things. It didn't take long to put two and two together."

"Doesn't sound like evidence," Callan said. "Sounds more like conjecture."

"I've been given leave to search your room," Wyatt said, a note of finality in his voice. He turned to the door once more.

"Good luck." Callan returned his attention to the door again, too, and gave a leisurely wave in its direction, but I noticed him frown when I assumed he spotted the moss. He glanced over his shoulder, but Meadow had already closed her door and disappeared.

Wyatt sighed, as if he was getting bored of the resistance. "Look, I was hoping to avoid turning this into a spectacle, but if you insist. I'm getting the quill. Now." He raised a hand.

But before he could say anything else, Professor East stepped onto the landing.

"Quill?" our instructor asked, voice calm and slightly inquisitive. "You wouldn't be talking about the artifact from the tree conservatory, would you? By the way, it's nice to have you visit again, Mr. Rhodes. Your visit wasn't announced."

Wyatt's gaze shifted to our instructor in surprise, and I saw Callan's eyebrows lift slightly as well.

"Hello, Professor East. My visit is time sensitive, I'm afraid. You know about the quill I'm here to collect?"

I waited with bated breath as Professor East spoke. Callan, though his expression remained stoic as always, was rubbing the side of his neck.

"That's what this is about? If so, I apologize for the confusion, Mr. Rhodes. I requested to have the quill on a temporary display here for students to research this spring, with the agreement that it would be returned to the tree conservatory at the end of the year. It arrived this weekend. Were you under the impression that it had been misplaced?"

I cast my eyes to Callan as time seemed to slow down. Was Professor East... covering for us?

Wyatt hesitated. "You have the quill from the new tree conservatory display?"

"It's secured in the library, ready for students when they return from the break," Professor East said, and I nearly balked at his smooth-as-silk delivery.

"Well, then let's take a look," Wyatt said.

Wyatt and Professor East headed to the library first, and I let out a slow, deep exhale as Callan and I followed them.

"What is going on?" Callan whispered.

"I think we're getting bailed out," I murmured. We followed the two men into the library, and my stomach did a flip that I couldn't decide was from tension or relief when Professor East led the way to a collection of magical botanical trinkets that was always on display in the library.

The quill I'd handed him was settled among a few other trinkets, resting underneath a clear phytoglass cover.

Wyatt stepped up to Professor East's side, appraising the display.

Callan turned and caught my eye, giving a slight disbelieving shake of his head.

"Is this what you were looking for?" Professor East asked, hands clasped behind his back and posture straight. This man was getting my vote for teacher of the year, hands down.

"Let me see." Wyatt removed the phytoglass then tested a few Floracantus on the quill, which resulted in several shivers of the feather.

I tried not to let on how nervous I was as we all waited for the verdict.

"Yes, this seems to be it. I'm not sure why it was released to the academy, but I'll need to take it back." Wyatt reached into his jacket pocket and flashed something at Professor East, who nodded.

I assumed it was a DBI badge or whatever kind of identifier they used.

"Of course," Professor East said. "Perhaps we'll be able to host it on display here another time."

"Glad you got what you came for. See you around," Callan said, turning to go.

Wyatt looked at his brother, and I thought I caught a flash of tenderness there, but then his business face was back on. "See you around." He nodded to me. "I'm glad we finally met, Briar Whelan."

Wyatt nodded at Callan then marched out of the library, Professor East shadowing him. As they passed us, I thought I heard Wyatt murmur, "I won't be able to keep this under wraps."

But before I could be sure, Wyatt and Professor East disappeared down the stairs. My heart was still beating so wildly that I wondered if I should have my health checked.

Before I could gather my thoughts to process what had happened, Callan surprised me by taking my hand and tugging me aside instead of heading down the stairs.

"What—" I began.

He reached toward a lantern on the wall that had metal flames shaped like leaves creating its sconces and pressed his peridot stone against a recess at its base. The light flickered, then a hidden door swung backward into the wall.

Chapter Sixty-Five

I let out a soft gasp.

Callan ushered me through the slender entrance he had just revealed, and we began to climb the narrow, curving stairs inside the wall. The door slid closed behind us.

"What is this?" I asked, the words barely more than a whisper.

"An old hideaway of the founders." We climbed a dozen more steps and emerged in a small wooden room with leaf-shaped stained glass windows the size of my hand running along the top of the wall. Sunlight streamed through, casting rainbows all around us.

"We're in the roof of the academy?"

"Basically. A small corner of it." Callan pushed open a large, oval window, and I saw that thick tree branches reached right to the window.

"Wait. Do you get to the treehouses this way sometimes?"

Callan nodded. "It's a shortcut."

I turned my attention back to the room, which had a few wooden seats with deep-green cushions, three or four small, rounded tables, elegant gold lamps, and a few dusty bookshelves filled with thick books. A large skylight porthole window above provided all the light the room needed at this time of day.

"Are there more of these?" I asked, but when I twirled around toward Callan, he was watching me intently.

"What happened back there?"

"I was hoping you could tell me. Do you know why Professor East helped us?"

Callan's jaw flexed. "I believe I do. Let's just say that his goals align with ours. Unfortunately, I think he just fell on his sword for us. And now that Wyatt has the quill... our plans are going to have to change." He ran a hand through his hair, his brain already roving through the options.

I didn't let him rove for long before I took his hands in mine. His words about Professor East chilled me, but I had one sliver of hope to offer. "Wyatt doesn't have the quill," I said softly.

"What do you mean? Professor East let him take it."

"Professor East let him take *a* quill. The quill I gave him."

Callan's eyes narrowed then widened. "What did you do, local?"

"I did what any member of the Root and Vine Society worth their salt would do. What are the tenets? Detect, distract, decoy..." My lips twisted into a smile.

Callan tilted his head. "Decoy?"

"Oh, Mr. Rhodes, you didn't think I let your brother walk off with the *real* quill, did you?" I could barely contain my mirth now.

"But he tested it out. He said it was real."

I pulled the eagle feather out of my bag and gently ran a finger along its edge. "Is he sure about that?"

Callan eyed the eagle feather, cocking his head. "That's not the quill from the tree conservatory."

"It doesn't *look* like it is," I conceded.

A smile spread across his face so slowly that it was like watching the sun rise over Mount Shasta. Glorious.

"You didn't," he said.

"I did."

"Then what quill does my brother have?"

"I made more than one fake quill in prop class. When you warned me to run off with the real one, I snagged the second fake instead. It was sitting in a box in my room, waiting for its time to shine. I wasn't sure if it would fool Wyatt indefinitely, but it buys us a little time to try to get the block off of this one."

"I should know better than to underestimate you by now, local."

"You really should." I pursed my lips.

"I had no idea your defensive skills had grown to this level. You managed to push the properties of the camouflage beyond the plant-based ink and into the rest of the feather." He twisted the base of the feather in a slow circle. "Your power... it's astounding."

"So you don't think I'm in need of protection anymore?" I asked, pushing my luck. Our conversation at the moss conservatory's gala was still fresh in my mind.

Callan hesitated. "My concerns have nothing to do with what I think of your abilities and everything to do with not trusting others. It comes from experience. And I think things are about to get a whole lot worse."

My stomach clenched at his predictions, but I wanted to hold on to this moment between us a little longer. "Well, you've never experienced my full power, have you?"

"No," he said slowly, a touch of delight in his voice. "I don't think I have."

We stood there, locked in eye contact that was as intense as the rays of sun on the hottest day of summer until I finally broke the spell.

"I know one thing I want to do with my power," I said, stepping back and reaching out to try to catch one of the rainbow beams that had cast itself in my direction.

Callan raised an eyebrow and cocked a half smile. "What's that?"

"Find the *Vanished Compendium*."

Callan's grin widened. "Well, then local, you and I have that in common."

I met his eyes. "And if we can figure out how to unblock the quill and it leads us to the book?"

His eyes were locked on mine, and they crinkled at the corners. "If we find it, then the power balance shifts."

"Exactly." We had a brief moment of staring blissfully at each other until Callan cleared his throat.

"About that," he said. "I think I know what's blocking the quill from working as a compass. I was getting ready to tell you my theory when Wyatt showed up."

There was a reluctant note in his voice, and I tried not to sound wary as I asked, "What is it?"

Callan swallowed. "I'm not sure you're going to like the solution."

"Just lay it out there, Callan."

"I think we're going to have to kill Frank."

"Frank?" Confusion roiled through me. Why was Callan talking about killing someone?

"Weed, California's oldest tree."

I sucked in a breath. "By the *leaves*. Tell me everything."

Official correspondence

Your request to serve as director of Evergreen
Academy has been approved, effective immediately.

Wendy Rhodes
Magical Botanical Board of Regents

The end

The end... for now
The story of Evergreen Academy will continue in book three.

Want more magic?

Want to know what your plant affinity power would be?

Want to join the Society of Magical Botanists reader group on Facebook?

Go to Heather Schneider's Bonus Content page on her website (heatherschneiderauthor.com) for access to all of the above!

Do you want to follow other writing projects Heather is working on?

Sign up for Heather's newsletter to stay up on the latest new releases and reader opportunities.

If you enjoyed the story, please leave a review. Reviews help indie authors find new readers, and help readers find new books to love.

Thank you for reading and being part of Heather Schneider's reader community!

Acknowledgments

I want to start with a heartfelt thank you to everyone who has shown love to Evergreen Academy. Your enthusiasm for the story propelled me through writing Evergreen Conservatory and has me dreaming big for the world of the Society of Magical Botanists. So, thank you for each review, email, and social media message or post telling me you loved the book. Please keep them coming!

For the whole crew at Nellis Air Force Base who has been so supportive of me as an author—thank you! Special thanks to Julia Couch for helping me host my launch parties. You definitely have a harvester affinity mixed in there with those florals.

Thank you to my beta readers for your invaluable feedback. Rachelle Foley, for reading the book first and providing such helpful, detailed, and kind feedback. Danielle McCloskey, Nicole Fuscaldo, Jen Winters, Kass Bruinier, and Rebecca Shirley, thank you for reading when the book was close to the end and helping me get it over the finish line (and for hyping me up about the story).

Bethanie Finger, thank you for our writing sessions, author talks, and coffee dates! Here is to many more years of writing and growing as authors together.

Thank you to my fabulous ARC team for Evergreen Academy and now for Evergreen Conservatory. This indie author could not get her books out into the world without you!

As always, thank you to my amazing, supportive family. Zach, Mom, Dad, Becky, Chelsea, Brian, Shirley, and the Yoakums. Love you all!

To my cover designer, Krafigs Design, thank you for creating such an enchanting cover (again). It is a delight to work with you!

To the editors and proofreaders at Red Adept Publishing, thank you for all your care with my work.

About the Author

Heather Schneider is an author of young adult and adult contemporary and cozy fantasy novels, always with a love story.

Heather lives with her husband and their two dogs. When she's not writing, you can find her reading, listening to podcasts, traveling, or spending time with family.

As an indie author, Heather loves to engage with readers!

Please connect with her on Instagram or Facebook @heatherschneiderauthor and leave a review wherever you review books.

You can visit her website and subscribe to her newsletter at heatherschneiderauthor.com.

www.ingramcontent.com/pod-product-compliance
Lightning Source LLC
Chambersburg PA
CBHW020242010826
48973CB00006B/1623